Readers love Z. ALLORA

The Great Wall

"I am very excited to check out the next books when they come out and definitely recommend this book and author."

—Rainbow Gold Reviews

"The growing love is sweet and strong despite all the difficulties."

—Diverse Reader

The Librarian's Rake

"If you are looking for a quick, relaxing read I would recommend picking this up."

—Just Love: Queer Book Reviews

"*The Librarian's Rake* by Z. Allora was an extremely sweet and cute book."

—Love Bytes

Secured and Free

"This is a great story full of well-rounded characters who are full of emotions. I loved each and every character in it."

—Long and Short Reviews

By Z. ALLORA

Bent Not Broken
The Craving
Illusions & Dreams
The Librarian's Rake
The Longest Night
Rocking Thin Ice

ENTWINED DREAMS
Lock and Key
Secured and Free

MADE IN CHINA
The Great Wall
The Temple of Heaven

Published by DREAMSPINNER PRESS
www.dreamspinnerpress.com

BENT
NOT
BROKEN

Z. ALLORA

DREAMSPINNER
PRESS

Published by
DREAMSPINNER PRESS

5032 Capital Circle SW, Suite 2, PMB# 279, Tallahassee, FL 32305-7886 USA
www.dreamspinnerpress.com

Bent Not Broken
© 2020 Z. Allora

Cover Art
© 2020 Tiferet Design
http://www.tiferetdesign.com/
Cover content is for illustrative purposes only and any person depicted on the cover is a model.

ISBN: 978-1-64405-577-9
Digital ISBN: 978-1-64405-576-2
Library of Congress Control Number: 2020930912
Paperback published June 2020
v. 1.0

Printed in the United States of America

This paper meets the requirements of
ANSI/NISO Z39.48-1992 (Permanence of Paper).

To Everyone who has struggled to survive violation
And to those who help us thrive and live

To MY therapist: Molly, without your assistance I'd never have been able to write this book. I still hate those EMDR buzzers from Hell, but I appreciate your guidance through my nightmares. Took me four years, but we got here. (And now the real work begins.)

To my love: You are my everything. I know we help each other through the ups and downs of life, but you supporting me as I wrestle with demons decades old so I may not only find but begin to use my voice is going above and beyond. Although I appreciate that you think it's part of your job description.

To my Pretties on Facebook and my Z-bies in my Yaoified Love Group: Your support both publicly and the private messages makes me glad I've TMI-ed about this topic.

Thank you for untangling my words and giving me information: Eden Winters, MT, Andrew Marks, Derrick McClain, Danny Bruggeman, Katie Obbink, Kirk Waite, the fabulous Desi, the ever-sweet Andrea, and all of Dreamspinner's editing staff.

Sending much appreciation and love to Dreamspinner Press and all their staff. Thank you for publishing the stories that need to be told and getting them into the hands of people who need the hope and validation our books hold.

CHAPTER 1

IN THE shadow of the old Victorian house turned BDSM club, a figure leaned against the back wall. Stefano Rossi slid off his custom motorcycle and tried not to see the other man kneeling in front of the silhouetted figure—his head bobbing.

"I've got to go, Mama. I'll see you next Sunday for church. Love you. Bye." Stefano ended the call. He adored his mother, but talking to her at a BDSM club, even in the parking lot, was a no-go.

Stefano unzipped his leather jacket and dragged his ass into the Edge, the local BDSM club on the outskirts of New Hope. The club didn't have a ton of rules or high fees, just a cover charge, which put it within his price range and closer to his comfort level.

"Didn't expect to see you here tonight," sniped the man who worked the door.

Jesus! How could the guy wear only a pink tutu and black combat boots? Wasn't he cold or embarrassed or—

"Stop wishing upon my nipple rings. You don't even know my name, so fork over ten dollars, sexy, or hit the road."

Grimacing at him, Stefano set a ten on the table. God, let this night go quickly.

"It's Ember, by the way."

"What?" Stefano hated feeling lost.

"My name. It's Ember, because all you've got to do is blow and I'll spark into flames."

What the fuck? Stefano had to escape—the nervous excitement that ripped through him was fueling his confusion.

"And don't forget to sign the book, honey." The doorman blocked his entrance and tapped a black-polished nail on the book.

He signed *Stefano R.*

"Do you want me to hold on to your biker jacket?"

Pushing his hands into the pockets, Stefano tugged his jacket closer around himself. "No, thanks. It's usually cold in there."

Ember fanned himself. "I wouldn't know—I'm always hot."

Stefano stumbled through the foyer of the old Victorian house. The reasonable cover meant the club was more dump than charm. As he stepped into the main room, his eyes adjusted to the dim lighting of the few working sconces. The Edge really was a hole, with a ton of scuffs on the black walls and furniture donated by the members—most of which should probably have been put on the curb.

Some mismatched tables were pushed against the wall, creating a space for the folding chairs and couches that all faced the stage.

The Edge was close enough to Jamison, where Stefano lived with his workaholic brother, yet far enough away from Philly that he didn't worry about any of the boys from the neighborhood crawling this far north.

Long dark hair swirled. *Was that...?* God, there he was... Riku Tao.

Stefano didn't know whether Riku was hot or cold... no, he was definitely scorchingly aloof.

Master Riku—the Dominant who did amazing bondage demos. Goddamn, that guy, the demo he did two months ago... though it was probably the woman he tied up who made Stefano feel—

"Excuse me, Sir, would you do the honors?" A sub in a loincloth, which was tucked in a way that exposed his red ass, tried to hand Stefano a paddle as he bent over.

"Um... no, thanks." Stefano fled to the bar, abandoning the frowning sub in his wake. He wished he could stop worrying about where Master Riku was and what... or who he was doing. Not that it mattered to him.

"Hey, Joe." He gripped the copper rail running the length of the black lacquer bar and nodded to the bartender. The guy was a laid-back sort who always gave Stefano a bit of calm in this overstimulating and, at times, overwhelming BDSM den.

"Stefano, what are you doing here on men's night?" Joe made it sound like Stefano had been abducted by aliens.

Stefano tried not to look for... anyone. His gaze landed on the two guys sitting at the bar, a couple of stools away. They wore tangled nipple chains and were making out. The tenderness of their kisses—

A weird disconnectedness swept through Stefano. That slow, crawling need wormed its way to his cock whenever he saw two men—

No.

He turned back and stared at Joe, who was waiting on him. "I'm going to require a drink to get through this evening."

Joe grinned. "What can I get for you?"

"A beer. Whatever's on tap." Stefano adjusted his dick and kept his gaze off the loving couple. Desire and curiosity mixed and mingled, but he tried to ignore the confused feelings. His eyes followed a deep chuckle, leading him back to Master Riku—head thrown back in laughter.

Joe slid a cold glass in front of Stefano. "You don't usually come in on Sundays."

At the Edge, Sunday night was men's night and usually called male Doms and subs out to play, with free rein of the club. Not Stefano's thing. "Just doing my Mistress's bidding. I'm hoping she comes later and meets me somewhere."

"I bet you hope to come too." Joe chuckled as he wiped the bar top with a loving caress.

"You've got that right." The whole orgasm-denial thing had lost its luster a while ago, so why his current Mistress demanded he not come for three days before he watched this silly denial play put on by some members made no sense. But it wasn't for him to understand.

Mistress Drama and her adorable sub, Serina, tried to bust his chops whenever they could. Not that he didn't enjoy the challenge of following her orders, but being here tonight....

He raised his glass to Joe and took a big gulp of beer.

"Enjoy the show." Joe moved to serve another customer.

Turning on his barstool, Stefano looked around the room. Lots of men milled about, laughing, talking, cruising. A Dom in the corner was getting sucked off by a sub... a really pretty male sub. Master Riku was nowhere to be seen.

Stefano shivered as want wound its way through him, forcing him to turn back and take another swig of his beer. Pushing away the odd wishes slashing through him, he counted the Philadelphia Eagles' wins and losses from last season.

Yes, there was a reason he stuck to Mistress-dominated nights on Tuesdays. He didn't deal well with the baffling questions men's night raised. Not that he had any issue with male Dominants or gay people. They just weren't his thing. He gulped some more beer.

Hell, he had a hard enough time trying to figure out the Mistresses of the moment willing to take him on. Most wanted more permanence than he'd ever cared to give.

Maybe someday....

However, sitting through a denial play put on by all men did nothing for him. He hadn't safeworded, so he should put his ass in a chair to complete his assigned task. Hopefully his Mistress would see what a good sub he was, and dare he hope for a reward?

He chugged the beer and threw a five on the bar. Joe was involved with another customer, so he gave him a wave.

God must be pissed that Stefano was in a club on Sunday night, because his search for an empty chair showed only one seat available. Why did it have to be in the first row and dead center in front of the stage? Though calling it a stage might be an exaggeration. It was little more than a homemade raised-plywood platform where BDSM demos took place.

Meandering over to the front while trying to be invisible proved impossible. He tried not to make eye contact with the men he passed because most gave him come-hither and wanna-go-play looks.

Fuck it. He hurried to the empty seat and asked the guys on either side, "Is this chair taken?"

The one twirling a riding crop gave him the once-over, making him feel more like meat than a person. He tapped the chair with his crop. "It is now. Sit your sweet ass down. I've not seen you—"

"'Cause I'm usually here with my Mistress." Not quite a lie, but hopefully a successful misdirection. He'd gotten skilled at those as a teen in an attempt to avoid trouble.

The man sagged in his seat with a frown and looked genuinely disappointed. "Well, at least allow me to keep the wolves, bears, cubs, otters, and daddies at bay."

Stefano had heard those terms but had no clue what all the definitions were, so he responded, "Sounds like a zoo in here."

"You don't know the half of it." The expression on the handsome man with salt-and-pepper hair morphed into a grin.

He might be surprised at just how much Stefano knew....

The African American man on his right held out his hand. "Ignore Sir Charles."

Stefano shook his hand. "Hey, I'm Stefano."

The man looked a lot like the actor from *Barbershop*—what was his name? Ah, Michael Ealy. The Michael Ealy look-alike smiled at Stefano. "I'm Devon Williams, but everyone calls me Doc. If you need help—"

Sir Charles's riding crop hit the floor.

Stefano dropped to his knees and offered the instrument to the Dom with two hands.

Charles arched an eyebrow. "Well done. I guess certain things translate beyond orientation and gender."

Stefano didn't quite know what Charles meant, but he shrugged and muttered, "Yeah," as his ass found his seat again.

Doc leaned toward him and mumbled, "He's harmless, but beware of his charms. He could talk a monk into sex."

"Oh, I'm not... you know." Stefano felt the need to clarify.

Doc nodded. "Whatever you say, man. And, Sir Charles, I think you might want to attend my class on BDSM as an orientation to help you define the point you were trying to make."

"So, if you're not a member of the *boys' club*, why are you here tonight? Just into orgasm denial?" Charles asked.

"Oh, um, my Mistress sent me."

"You're a very good sub for coming. I mean, doing what she said." Sir Charles's words and smirk teased something deep within Stefano.

He opened his mouth to give a response, but Doc elbowed him and pointed to the stage.

The man in the loincloth who had asked Stefano to smack him with the paddle took the stage. Even with the loincloth untucked, the material barely covered his hips. The length showed off the man's long legs, a wide expanse of chest, and a beautiful face.

Stop!

At least there would be no more conversations to trip him up.

The man in the loincloth strutted to the center of the stage.

Everyone cheered or wolf-whistled. Stefano clapped a few times because he didn't want to be a total dick. But he wasn't here to see men perform. His Mistress sent him. This wasn't for enjoyment but fulfilling his task.

"Greetings, and happy Sunday to everyone." The man squinted into the overly bright spotlight. He blocked the glare with his hand and called out, "Hey, Murray. Can you fix the lights?"

After a couple of seconds, the lights dimmed to less blinding, and the man continued, "Thanks, Mur. Now back to the show. Tonight, the men's play group is putting on *Total Virgin*. The writer and actor who would be playing the Master in search of a sub contract is down with the flu."

A mumur worked its way through the crowd.

The man put his two hands out in front of him. "Not to worry. Dom Harley's subs, Fred and Maurice, are taking *very* good care of him."

Stefano pushed aside the images of how Fred and Maurice might be helping their Master feel better. He was sure none of their methods would have been approved by the medical community. Sucking dick didn't cure the flu.

Sucking cock would—no!

Mr. Loincloth gestured to one of the men standing in the shadows. "Oh, and a big thank-you to Riku Tao for reluctantly stepping in as the role of Master."

Sir Charles nudged him. "Wow, we're in for quite a show. Riku's so sexy and hot I'd consider bottoming for him. And I don't say that lightly."

Stefano bit his lower lip, his attention glued to Riku. In truth, he would have problems refusing the Dominant on the stage anything.

Anything? Where had that come from?

Doc leaned over Stefano and told Sir Charles, "No worries. I'll make sure I tell him you'd bend over for him."

"Please spare the Ice King my confession," Sir Charles sniped back. He shook his head. "The guy never takes on a sub and only does demos."

Doc sighed and glanced at Stefano. "He's always been the epitome of control, even as a kid."

Stefano sat on his hands and rocked. He tried not to imagine Riku in leather; instead he focused directly on him.

The stage light caught Master Riku's long hair and made the strands shimmer like a raven's wing. He was tall and had striking features, but the way he moved his long, lean body with the liquid motion of a dancer fascinated Stefano.

And his Dominant control—Stefano swallowed hard—that was another thing.

CHAPTER 2

WHY DID I agree to do this play?

Riku pulled at his ill-fitting, too-short toga. He was going to kill Devon. There had to be a way to murder his best friend slowly and not get caught. Why had he let Devon convince him to do this idiotic play?

He joined Master Max and sub Daniel on stage. They all wore togas because for no understandable reason the play was set in ancient Rome, and the only other reference to the setting was a bowl of olives sitting on the floor.

Riku didn't mind participating in demonstrations. He did those to teach newbies and to help this club establish safer habits. But this play was simply salacious hotness catering to orgasm-denial fantasies and didn't intersect with reality all that much. Not that there was anything wrong with fantasies per se, but without moving beyond the wishes and dreams to a purpose, BDSM would evolve into chaos.

And he had no plan of getting the scripted blowjob onstage, so his fellow actors better stick to their agreement of cutting that nonsense.

He tugged at his sheet again and glared at Devon.

Wait, who was that man in the leather biker jacket sitting with Devon? The guy looked familiar… perhaps a sub? He wore a needy yet skeptical expression that made Riku want to show him what it meant to be a sub.

Riku had the urge to run his hands through the stranger's dark shoulder-length curls. Too easily, he could imagine those big dark eyes staring up at him and the man's full red lips doing delicious things. He was pretty and would have looked feminine, but his five-o'clock shadow wouldn't allow it. The guy might have stepped out of a copy of an Italian GQ with his—

"Greetings. I'm Master Max, the proprietor of this establishment, and we have only the finest subs in Rome."

A bright spotlight caught him dreaming. "I'm Master Riku."

"It's a fine day to contract with a submissive, and mine are trained to meet your every need." Max was a decent guy, but an actor he was not.

The spotlights had dimmed and regular lighting came on. It looked like the lighting guy gave up.

"Every day is a good day to get a submissive," someone from the audience called out.

Riku pressed his lips together. *Pandemonium. Unruliness. Anarchy.* But what could be expected? He glared in the general direction of the heckler. "It is always a good day to enter into a consensual contract as long as all parties are willing."

Master Max smirked and said under his breath for Riku's ears, "You can never let go of a teachable moment." Riku's slight shrug encouraged Max to go on. He gestured to Daniel. "Sir, allow me to tell you about our subs."

"Please do." Riku enunciated the actual line as he glided around the sub, trying to act as if he were sizing him up.

He had played with Daniel in the past. As a sub, Daniel was unfortunately untamed, careless, and had no desire to refine his skills of submission. Riku should've never wasted his time with someone who was so stubborn, yet Biker Jacket wore a similar "prove it to me" expression, and Riku craved to do just that. Though first Riku needed to do this play.

"All our subs are here voluntarily and are aching for a Master such as yourself to care for them. Tell me, are you looking for a virgin sub or a total virgin sub?"

Riku Tao ran his fingers through his hair. *Yes, audience, here's where you suspend your disbelief or you'll never sit through the end of this drivel.* "Can you explain the difference to me?"

"Ah, yes. In our humble town, *virgin* means never been fucked but sucks continually." Master Max spoke to the audience, who clapped and hooted enthusiastically.

"I see." Riku wanted points from Devon for not rolling his eyes.

Master Max pointed to the loincloth-covered sub. "But he is a total virgin. Daniel, come over here and tell this fine Master what that means."

Daniel sashayed in front of Riku and seemed altogether too filled with rebellion. He put his head down, almost as an afterthought. "Master, being a total virgin means I've never fucked. I suck constantly, but I've never orgasmed."

"Never?" Riku bit back a chuckle. Daniel had been, and always would be, a "spank me and make me come" sub, if he ever met one.

Daniel shook his head with a mournful frown and peeked up at him like he hung the moon. "Never, Sir."

"Oh, I see." Riku gasped and widened his eyes in an attempt at acting surprised yet titillated.

The audience chuckled.

Riku turned to Master Max and gave him the line: "How have you kept them so pure?"

"Answer him, sub." Master Max smirked, seeming to take perverse pleasure in hearing the words.

Daniel leaned forward. "Master constantly watches us."

"What else?" Master Max asked, tilting his head to the right and leaning in, overacting more than a little.

Pushing his blond hair off his face, Daniel appeared more tormented angel than sub. "All the submissives here are taught to beg for spankings when we want to come."

Riku tried to look astounded and lustful but was positive he failed.

Master Max twirled his index finger in the air, indicating he wanted Daniel to turn around. "Show us your backside."

Daniel spun around with a flourish and flipped his loincloth away from his ass. He glanced over his shoulder with his bottom lip caught by his teeth and gave a little wiggle.

The audience whooped.

Riku wasn't sure if Daniel was asking for more or just showing off.

Chuckling, Master Max gestured to Daniel's well-rounded backside. "As you can see, he's been pretty horny today and begged nonstop. Please see for yourself."

Riku ran his hands over Daniel's reddened but quite firm rump. Looked like some of the people the sub asked for spankings before the play hadn't held back. "You're still warm."

Daniel whimpered. "I'm so hot, Sir."

Master Max pulled Daniel front and center, waved a finger at him, and then pointed at his loincloth. "Looks like you're pitching a tent, my sweet little virgin."

Regardless of the play's dialogue, the audience hollered with glee when the sub pouted and nodded.

Riku had to admit Daniel was a decent actor, and of course, no one could say he wasn't handsome, but Riku's gaze drifted to Mr. Sexy Biker Jacket. The guy had leaned forward and licked his lush lips.

Master Max turned Daniel toward the audience and flipped the front part of his loincloth up over Daniel's erection. He teased his fingers over the shiny crown.

Shifting positions on the stage put Riku right in front of where Devon sat. Who was Biker Jacket? His hungry expression undid Riku's good intentions of focusing and drew him in.

Daniel gasped, making Riku turn back to the stage.

Riku stepped over to them and rested a hand on Daniel's shoulder. The stage direction was to adopt a condescending tone, so he tried. "Oh, you poor thing. Your dick is wet!"

Master Max grinned at Riku but waved him off. "Oh, this is nothing. I have my subs masturbate to the edge of orgasm a couple times a day but always make them stop short of climax. Don't I, sub?"

Daniel whimpered. "Yes, Master Max."

"You should see him when he gets close to shooting off. He pants and begs so prettily for me to spank him, right?"

Daniel shivered. "Yes, Sir."

Master Max teased Daniel's erection with a few gentle strokes. The slit of his angry dick frothed with precum.

Daniel opened his eyes and stared out into the audience with an unfocused gaze.

The script stated Riku should enjoy the side view, so he tilted his head to get a good look, but he couldn't stop himself from using the opportunity to glance over at Biker Jacket.

Their eyes met.

Everything in Riku froze. Their gazes locked, and a dare seemed to be issued. He had been challenged to give in to every Dominant whim he had, and Biker Jacket would handle it.

The guy licked his gorgeous cock-sucking lips and let out a soft gasp that seemed to carry directly to Riku's ear.

Or maybe that was Daniel. It was impossible not to imagine Daniel's next line dropping from Biker Jacket's lips. "Ohhhhh, I might have to be spanked again soon so I don't come."

Riku begrudgingly admitted there might have been some appeal to this fantasy, but only if the right guy was acting it out with him. Though he'd never confess it out loud, swapping out Daniel for GQ Biker Jacket nearly gave him an unruly erection.

Geez, how old was he—twelve? Where was his focus and control?

Master Max reached down and cupped Daniel's nuts in his hand. "Whatever you need."

Daniel groaned, all pretense of acting gone.

Riku got his head in the play and gave Master Max a nod of appreciation. The man knew his way around a frustrated submissive and what ad-libbed words were needed to stoke the flames.

Looking around, Daniel quickly bent over. He thrust his ass in the air, giving a perfect target. "Please, Master Max, I need a spanking so I don't come."

Riku's experience with Daniel told him that was a bold-faced lie.

Master Max warmed his hand on Daniel's ass. "This one loves a good rump roasting and really drains a cock afterwards."

Riku didn't roll his eyes at the crass scripted words because a number of subs and Doms out there were gagging for them… including Biker Jacket, who was on the edge of his seat.

Master Max's erection tented his toga as he started smacking the sub's wiggling ass again. "Talking about denial always excites me. Tell me, Master Riku, do you want to see the sub's mouth in action while you give him his punishment?"

Riku stared out at the audience for the answer like the script directed, but he used the opportunity to stare at the guy next to Devon.

Everyone predictably shouted, "Yes."

He couldn't be sure, but he thought he read Biker Jacket's lips mouthing, "Yes, please, Sir."

Riku tried not to melt and turned back to Master Max. "I'd enjoy that."

Master Max gestured to his cock.

Daniel whimpered. "Yes, Sir. I'm here to satisfy you." Then he turned to Riku, presenting an even better target. "If it pleases you, Sir."

"Oh, it does. It truly does." Riku tried to sound enthusiastic and then punished Daniel with his hand.

Wiggling against the palm of his hand every time it connected, Daniel moaned.

"That's right. You deserve your ass spanked for being horny," Riku ad-libbed and added from his experiences with Daniel. The right amount of humiliation turned Daniel's embarrassment into erotic teasing.

"Yes, Sir. Thank you for my deserved punishment." He pushed out his butt, which was a nice shade of dusky pink, making his ass an appealing target.

Master Max looked around the stage. Someone had forgotten to put the chair out. He clapped. "A chair."

One of the audience members pushed a chair to Max.

Master Max sat and parted his toga. He teased the tip of his arousal over Daniel's parted lips. "Ahhh, too bad. There's no pleasure for you, only me. You only get a sore ass and a mouthful of my satisfaction."

Daniel, along with most of the audience, groaned as Master Max licked his hand. Max shifted Daniel and reached forward. He polished his palm over the sub's wet tip.

When Daniel was fairly shaking with the need to orgasm, Max pulled Daniel's lips to his cock. "Lick me."

Riku rubbed the sub's ass while Daniel put his tongue to work on Master Max's cock. He gave Daniel what he remembered he enjoyed most, which were soft caresses mixed with medium slaps of his open palm.

Daniel's mouth hovered over Master Max's erection. "May I?"

"Oh, Daniel, don't you wish you were going to get your dick sucked?" Master Max asked with a sadistic bent that Riku never quite understood.

Daniel thrust back into Riku's palm and wiggled with the rubbing. "Of course, Master Max. But only Masters deserve to come, not me."

The audience hooted their agreement.

Biker Jacket squirmed in his seat.

"You like being put in your place and used, don't you?" Sadism continued to run high in Master Max's taunts.

"Yes, Sir. I was born to be used for a Master's pleasure. I'm here for your satisfaction." Daniel seemed to be loving all the attention, especially when Master Max shifted him upright and made him edge an orgasm by rubbing one finger along the underside of his cock.

Daniel shivered and whimpered.

When Max was done teasing him, he demanded, "Good, then suck me off."

Daniel kissed the tip of Master Max's erection. He slid his mouth over Max and swallowed the length. Without delay, he began bobbing his head.

Riku had to admit as he smacked the sub's red ass, the scene was hot, but having Biker Jacket in this position....

Daniel whimpered and pushed back against Riku's palm, surrendering to his will.

Trying to focus, Riku ghosted his hands over Daniel's ass and slid up his back.

The crowd went silent.

Daniel's struggle of sucking and not coming was a sight.

Master Max breathed harder. "You want to come badly, but you won't, and like a bastard, I'm making your suffering worse. Do you appreciate my teasing?"

Daniel pulled off Max's shaft. "Oh yes, Master Max. I love it."

Riku rubbed Daniel's arms, trying to ease him. Master Max's throat clearing got Riku to remember his line. "Are you close to climax, sub?"

"Yes, sir… very close. Don't worry, I won't come. I serve better this way." Daniel licked his full lips, and even Riku couldn't miss their promise of delivering any man to heaven.

The crowd seemed to moan with him as Daniel returned to his task of dragging his lips up and down on Master Max's cock.

Master Max gestured toward Daniel. "See, Riku, I've learned horny subs suck better."

Riku grunted and didn't say, *No, kidding, genius.*

"How's that ass?" Master Max asked the sub who tended to his erection.

Daniel wagged his butt. He pulled off and answered, "Very sore, Sir. Master Riku gave me a very thorough spanking, Sir."

"Even with a red bottom and no further attention to your cock, you want to give me the climax you don't get to have? You want to satisfy me by sucking me off?"

Every Dom in the club seemed to lean forward, needing those words of surrender. They wanted Daniel to crave Master Max's dominance.

Daniel dragged his mouth off Master Max's cock and pleaded with a trembling voice, "Yes, Sir. It is my honor and pleasure. I beg to swallow your orgasm even though I'll have no climax."

"You may." Master Max gasped as Daniel slid his plush lips across Max's erection.

Master Max threw back his head and groaned as the sub sucked him all the way to the root without pause, again and again, with no gagging. Daniel always did have a talent for providing oral pleasure.

Riku felt like an idiot, standing on the stage with nothing to do but watch. His gaze slid to the audience.

Want and need was written all over Mr. Biker Jacket, along with… fear.

Wait, where was he going?

CHAPTER 3

FUCK IT! Stefano couldn't handle any more of this freaking play. Muttering his safeword to no one in particular, he slipped out the back exit of the club to the smoking area—a patchy square of grass dedicated to smokers in need of a fix. It had a rusty bench and a metal cigarette receptacle standing in judgment of his addiction.

He really should quit because the habit wasted money.

A shiny coil captured his attention. Someone had tried to throw the scrap of metal away but missed the receptacle. Good thing, because it was exactly what he needed. He pocketed the newfound treasure.

The voice snapped, *What, you think you're an artist? Make a few sculptures with trash and now you're Donatello. You should still be working for Marco at the shop. But no, you think you're a big man, going to be a mechanic and an artist. You're nothing.*

Staring out at the parking lot, he silenced the abusive commentary on his life coming to him in his father's voice. Quiet came, and then the snippets of the play started to run through his mind on an endless loop. Somehow the sub in the play disappeared and he was the one onstage being denied and spanked. Tantalized and made to suck until a deep familiar voice told him to come—

No, dammit! Riku Tao should not be in his head. *Focus!* He tried to hear his current Mistress, but only Riku's rich, warmed cocoa tones infused with iron echoed through his brain.

That is just wrong!

Stefano paced, trying to ignore his hard-on chafing against his jeans as he tried to catch his breath. What he'd witnessed—

Blessed Mary, but he craved the type of attention Riku gave that sub. The soft petting in between the smacks—which had nothing to do with correction—especially enthralled Stefano.

The taunting voice of his deepest truth echoed, *You want someone like Riku to give it to you.*

No! How could he want that?

Those caresses were about touch and connection, making Stefano's heart ache for a bond he'd never experience. No Mistress had ever bothered to gentle him during correction.

Heaven help him, but Stefano couldn't stop yearning for that kind of interaction.

His father's voice sneered, scorching his brain, *You don't deserve good things. Just take what you can get and be satisfied. You barely deserve that.*

Fuck! Stefano kicked at the brown grass and wished he could appreciate what he did get.

But no way in hell he would sit there and watch the sub in the play receive everything he craved but would never get. There were many reasons he'd never have that kind of attention from a Master, but being unworthy of it should not be number one.

The biggest reason should be he wasn't gay. Why was that like an afterthought? Shouldn't that be top on his list as to why he'd never have Riku doing those things to him?

I safeworded. How could I safeword a goddamned play?

He could take a lot of pain. Hurt was easy to withstand. Once you figured out you couldn't stop or prevent the suffering, you simply survived and endured. His mind escaped into a place of acceptance, a place where he allowed the suffering to happen, so he must deserve the punishment.

But he fucking safeworded over this stupid denial play. What the hell was that about? Wait, this flip-out was probably because his Mistress hadn't been there to receive his safeword and that ate at him.

That's what this crazy uncertainty had to be... right?

Goddammit, watching the actors had set off fireworks in him. All these needs and cravings broke through from where he kept unspeakable longings hidden.

It had always been, if you didn't think about what you wanted, you didn't really want it.

Riku... Stefano wasn't turned on by *him*. He didn't find Riku—men—attractive in that way. He couldn't.

Maybe he was overthinking, the way his sister accused him of doing. Perhaps the play had simply been arousing, with lots of fantasy triggers, and any sub would get heated. Yeah, the idea of struggling not to come, asking to be spanked because you want to orgasm, and the vast number of deliberately aborted climaxes—that was all kinds of hot.

Lava ran over Stefano as he tried not to ponder his mouth giving pleasure while he couldn't have any. The unrealistic fantasy of a sub never having had an orgasm didn't make the idea any less mind-melting.

How the fuck could anyone watch such tantalizing pleasure and not feel overwhelmed? But why couldn't he see himself worshipping between a Mistress's knees... only Riku's?

Who the fuck was Riku Tao anyway? Stefano enjoyed his educational demonstrations, which were given on nights the club was open to all; they were always *interesting*. He appreciated how Riku always put safety before the mystique some Mistresses and Masters felt the need to front at all costs.

Riku as a Master....

Maybe a smoke would calm him the fuck down.

His hands fumbled, and he dropped the cigarette.

Dammit!

Trying to still his hands, he pulled out another from the pack. The second made the journey all the way to his mouth without incident. He flicked the lighter his father had given him at sixteen, then repocketed it. Inhaling the bitterness, he attempted to settle into the familiar ritual.

He blew out a puff of smoke and snagged the suicidal cigarette from the dirt. What a waste, especially at ten bucks a pack. He pushed the cigarette that had kissed the ground into the receptacle.

After sitting down, he inhaled and then exhaled the smoke again and again.

Why was he drawn to Riku? If he were honest, this wasn't the first time either. The last bondage demo Riku taught flashed through his brain. Stefano's wants never made sense, because he wasn't gay.

He wasn't a homophobic asshole like his middle brother, Marco, who used to smack him around while calling him a fag. The homophobic and transphobic slurs, along with overall bigoted comments were one of the reasons his little sister and older brother rarely wanted to be in the same place as Marco.

Stefano stared at the burning end of the cigarette. He couldn't be gay or even bi.

He let the index finger of his other hand get close to the burning ash. Closer. No, he couldn't be what his father hated, what the Catholic Church said was wrong. And how could he be what caused him—

The heat from the cigarette made him hurt, but he pressed his finger against the burning ash. Intense pain shot through him.

"Ow. Son of a bitch." He pushed his singed finger into his mouth. That was going to blister.

His crazy couldn't be about Riku. Nope. This denial play had thrown his head into such chaos that he wanted to know what a truly hard spanking from a man's hand felt like? A quieter and much stranger wish whispered through him: What was Riku like?

No, that was ungrateful to his Mistress.

Stefano jumped up and paced back and forth in front of the rusted bench. Then finally, with nowhere to go, he sat again. He took another drag on his bad habit.

The play kept dancing through his mind. He couldn't stop the unreasonable jealousy, especially when the acting evolved into hints of subspace. That unlocked a desperation in Stefano, making him long for silence in his head. How incredible would it feel to only be concerned with his Master's… um, Mistress's pleasure?

No matter how many scenes he'd done, he never fully got there. Sometimes the edges of subspace taunted him with a place where serving was better than receiving. Subspace teased him with promises of a contented calm but always remained out of reach.

God, if only, even once, he could find that dreamy place where he might recharge his heart for a little while. A part of him believed he could live the rest of his life with only one moment of it.

Stefano tried to snap himself out of the lust coursing through him, because it kept circling back to wishing he had been the one receiving Riku's attention, which was odd. Wasn't it?

How could he ever be with a guy after all that had happened to him? There was no way, but Riku was stunning, with his dark eyes, past-the-shoulder-length dark hair, strong build, and an inner strength that could stabilize any sub. Plus his way of teaching simply worked for Stefano a bit too well. The guy was a perfect picture of dominance.

Maybe Stefano longed for the protection and balance Riku could give him.

May God save him.

No, God had forsaken and abandoned him years ago. And what the fuck had Stefano done to redeem himself in the eyes of God? Nothing. Absolutely fucking nothing.

Bang!

Stefano leaped to his feet. He would never be the victim ever again.

Damn, it was only the club's back door that slammed open. The mechanism of the screen door had busted years ago, but loud noises never failed to send fear shooting through him.

"Riku, I still don't see why you didn't go upstairs with Daniel. The way he begged to give you a hot, wet blowjob, how could you refuse a sub in need?" A guy walking with a slight limp and a cane burst through the door.

It was Doc… and *him*.

"Not my thing, and you know that." Riku sounded like the haughty Ice King that Sir Charles had complained about, in complete control of the world around him.

An Ice King who Stefano would never be able to serve….

Shit!

Why couldn't he see Riku Tao as anything other than enticing? The moonlight did Stefano no favors as the beams highlighted Riku's high cheekbones, determined jaw, clean-shaven face, his "too straight, never been broken" nose, and lips that—the man was a work of art.

Damn the icicles of desire that ripped ragged tears through Stefano. Instead of freezing or melting under Riku's gaze, Stefano stiffened his spine. Sub or not, Stefano wasn't anyone's doormat.

"Blowjobs are—oh, hello, Stefano. Riku, this is the man I sat next to during your spectacular stage debut." Doc remembered him.

"I should have never been a part of that." Riku glared at Doc, but his gaze shifted to Stefano, and fuck if it didn't make Stefano's hand holding his cigarette tremble.

Doc rolled his eyes and waved Riku off. "Stefano, allow me to introduce my best friend, who is a rather stubborn ass, Riku Tao."

Riku's eyes spoke volumes as he narrowed his gaze onto Stefano's cigarette like he held a weapon of mass destruction. "You shouldn't be smoking."

Not *hey* or *hi* or *hello* or any other normal greeting. No, not Riku Tao. Who the fuck did he think he was?

He wasn't Stefano's Master, nor would he ever be. Who was he to judge anything Stefano did?

Stefano longed to tell him off, though experience told him nothing would be forced out of his mouth. Not even the word *no*....

When in doubt, go big or go home, so he used his only weapon. He inhaled and then exhaled a rather perfect smoke ring in Riku's general direction.

"Well, at least you know he's good with his mouth," Doc stage-whispered with a smirk.

Stefano's phone buzzed. He grabbed the cell out of his pocket and looked at the screen, which displayed a new text.

Sorry, S. Can't join you. Night. Mistress Drama.

Dammit, he'd hoped to get her and her sub off with his tongue to earn his own orgasm. Even a ruined one caused by a riding crop in her presence would have been something.

He needed to clear his head. Fuck it, he had an early morning tomorrow, with nothing to show for this evening but confusion and a boner from hell.

Hey, now! Maybe that was his problem. Stefano hadn't done anything since he'd seen her and her full-time sub earlier in the week, so naturally anything remotely sexual would make him overwrought. He'd come to the club horny and without release, so no wonder he was turned-on and needed to safeword.

There. Mystery solved.

"Problem, Stefano?" Doc asked like his answer mattered.

"Nah, just that my Mistress won't be coming here tonight." He pushed his smoked cigarette into the receptacle.

Riku gave him a nod of approval like he had something to do with Stefano not finishing the cigarette.

Stefano ignored the blessing from Riku and how Riku's acknowledgment of doing something good lit him with peace and rightness.

Right now, another part of him wanted to light another cigarette in defiance, but at fifty cents a pop, the rebellion wasn't worth the money.

"So, you really do have a Mistress?" Doc asked.

"That's what I told you and Sir Charles in there." Stefano made it clear he wasn't a liar.

Doc shrugged. "I thought you were simply letting Charles down lightly. Have you been with your Mistress long?"

"No, just a few weeks. We have a temporary arrangement." Why did Stefano feel the need to get that piece of information out there like it was relevant to them—who kept studying him.

Riku's eyes narrowed, making Stefano's insides clench. "I see."

Stefano refused to make eye contact with the sexy—no, overbearing twit. He chomped down on the *"No, you don't either!"* and kept his mouth closed.

"Why did you leave before the play was over?" Riku asked, like he had the right to know the answer.

What the fuck could Stefano say other than "Have a good night"?

"Leaving so soon?" Doc asked, frowning at him and then at Riku.

"I've got to be up early tomorrow." He trudged to his bike, and like Orpheus, he had to look back.

Mistake!

Riku stood glued to the spot, dark gaze following his every move.

Stefano didn't turn into a pillar of salt like Lot's wife in the Old Testament for turning around, but he was sure he'd be wandering through life like Orpheus. Though his loss would be of something he never had.

Stefano threw a leg over the seat, pulled on his helmet, and rode off. He hoped like hell the crisp wind would blow away his confusion.

It didn't.

CHAPTER 4

BEEP! BEEP! Beep!

Fucking alarm clock! Riku buried the urge to throw the noisy nightmare across the room as he turned it off. His eyes adjusted to the dim light filtering through the space between his drapes.

How did he sleep through the alarm for thirty-five minutes?

He stumbled to the bathroom, used the toilet, washed his hands, and brushed his teeth, dropping the toothpaste twice and his brush once.

Not a good start to the day, but sleep hadn't come until early this morning.

Maybe he should ask Devon to open the office, or should he just skip his exercise routine? Or do a speed workout or….

Lack of sleep led to indecision and disturbed him.

He grabbed his phone and texted Devon. *Can you open today? I'm running 35 mins behind.*

An immediate text came back. *Are you OK? Hurt? Do you need me to do something?*

Sometimes Devon could be an alarmist. *No, not hurt. Yes, do open the office.*

What happened?

I apologize. I overslept. Sighing, Riku hated how irresponsible he had been.

You oversleep?

Why was this a foreign concept?

Yes. Embarrassment and humiliation did not taste good to Riku. This was why he never had such lapses in control.

Now that you're an actor, I guess it's understandable.

Riku reread Devon's dickish response twice. At the risk of being brusque, he texted, *Thank you.*

He pulled on his sweats and jogged down into his black-carpeted basement. Half of the space had a bike, an elliptical, and a treadmill, with weights along the wall. On the other side of the hand-painted shōji screen was where Devon had convinced him to make a movie theater.

The area had six black overstuffed leather recliners with cup holders and theater lights underneath. Devon had even given him a popcorn maker that he insisted they use during their monthly movie fest.

Riku started warming up on his elliptical. Why hadn't he fallen asleep until almost dawn?

He grimaced as the answer he didn't want surfaced yet again. The ill-mannered sub from last night who blew a smoke ring at him.

Never had he felt such an overwhelming draw to correct someone the way he had with Stefano. Even his name was sexy: Stefano. The man desperately needed someone to help straighten him out.

Riku hated how alluring Stefano's five-o'clock shadow appeared in the moonlight and how much he wanted beard burn. Waxing poetic about how good Stefano's pretty pink lips would look around Riku forced him to dirty two towels with his overactive dick last night. Normally, Riku prided himself on being in total control of his body, but the image of those O-ed lips as Stefano released a plume of smoke tormented him.

He increased the intensity of his workout by pressing a button, making each stride more difficult to take. Then he focused on running while pumping his arms at a steady pace.

Ill-mannered subs had no place in his world. During his twenties, teaching someone the ropes, *literally*, held appeal. When he hit his thirties, the work outweighed the pleasure. Now thirty-four, he'd do demonstrations, but taking on a sub—he didn't see that happening again.

A sense of loss seeped in. He ran faster, trying to outrun the nagging pull.

Besides, he no longer had the determination to fix anyone. Of course, this was countered by his best friend's voice in his head, lecturing about how you can't fix anyone but yourself.

True, but there were ways to assist a sub. Stefano's dark hair and tanned skin against his sheets had appeal. Taming the man's wildness into something more manageable without taking away Stefano's heat and passion… Riku could—

No. He would finish his workout and get to work. There might not be many appointments on his schedule today, but there were always walk-ins and plenty of other things to do.

Riku reached for his water, which wasn't there. *Argh.*

Inhale, exhale, calm down. Lack of sleep causes forgetfulness.

He needed to keep his attention on the office, which he and Devon opened less than six months ago on the edge of New Hope. His parents were proud of him, but they would have preferred him closer, in a Philly office space instead of the tiny borough in Bucks County, which they referred to as the "new age hippy town."

Though that's exactly where a practice that combined Western medicine and chiropractic services, along with holistic treatments, would be accepted. The community welcomed Devon and Riku into their fold, which helped business.

He jumped off the elliptical, grabbed a sparkling water out of the fridge on the other side of the screen, and sat down on the bike. Not in the mood for anyone's chatter, he didn't join a session but adjusted the screen so he appeared to be biking through mountain roads.

His mind drifted. *Stefano.* How ridiculous for him to be so affected by someone who hadn't even directly spoken to him. Besides, Stefano had a Mistress, and Riku didn't go down dead-end paths.

Slowing his pace to cool down, he finished the bottle of water.

He jogged back to his bedroom, and then he took a shower, hoping the warm water would clear away his confused frustration, but it didn't. Gazing out of the floor-to-ceiling window—which had a bamboo privacy fence six feet away, ensuring he didn't give his neighbors a show—he tried to clear his mind.

As he showered, he stared at the space between the window and the bamboo to ground himself in the present moment. Riku and his dad had laid out gray river rocks. A couple of stone-carved Chinese lanterns his father had gifted him, which he lit at night, and a large bell that rarely rang and was held by an ornate scrolled iron hook took up some of the space.

The view didn't give him the sense of peace it usually did.

Standing in front of the dark gray stone sink, he dried his hair, and then he trudged into the walk-in closet he had ruthlessly organized. After he straightened a tie on his automated tie rack in his suit section, he glanced over at his leather club wear collecting dust. In the past couple of years, his leather hadn't gotten much use, not even for demos. There didn't seem any point.

Riku missed the ritual of donning leather to do a scene, but demonstrations were about teaching, not a true exchange. He buried the sense of loss along with the other things he'd given up on and dressed in his navy scrubs.

In the kitchen, Riku sent a thank-you to the world for his pushy best friend strong-arming him into a fancy pod tea and coffee maker. He usually had green tea, but today his body demanded black tea, so he located an English Breakfast pod in his tea drawer and started the machine brewing.

Once he sat down to his high-fiber cereal and tea, he tried to focus on something positive so he could face the rest of the day. The townhouse. His townhouse.

Buying this had been a good decision. He made sure the decor reflected him. Everything echoed tranquility and serenity, with a mix of woods, and the rooms were decorated in creams, whites, and beiges, except for the kitchen.

His red backsplash and matching kitchen countertops over black cabinets had horrified his mom while making his dad smile every time he walked in.

Riku had rarely gone against the grain.

Now Stefano, he was the true rebel. Riku could feel defiance coming off him in waves. But why? Where did it come from? Sighing, he reminded himself he had to stop thinking about the guy.

Trying to stay in the present moment, he forced his thoughts to dwell on other things.

He looked around the kitchen as he ate. Ah, the big stainless-steel Viking stove made him feel guilty. He rarely used anything beyond the front burners, though he did burn some cookies once.

Did Stefano cook?

He groaned and turned his attention to the island bar, where he sat. Running his hand over the smooth surface of the island, the insane notion occurred to him: it could serve as a platform. The handles were at the perfect height in each corner to tie off a length of rope—

He jumped off the stool and hurried to the sink. After rinsing his dishes, he set them into the dishwasher, then finished his hot tea, burning his tongue.

As much as he liked a taste of excitement, he didn't need chaos in his life. He was over welcoming drama.

He set the townhouse alarm system, then walked the five blocks to work, trying to appreciate the decorations of hay, pumpkins, and makeshift porch graveyards.

Why hadn't he grabbed his jacket? He could almost see his breath in the morning air.

Wait… where was his to-go cup of tea?

When he opened the front door of the office, Janie Peters, the only receptionist both Devon and he agreed on, grinned at him from behind her desk. "Good morning, Dr. Tao. Um…."

"What?" Riku stared as her grin turned into a frown.

"I guess you forgot it's not Friday." She pointed at his navy scrubs.

"Ah… no. It's Monday. Oh, right. Turquoise scrub day, huh?" How could he forget? When they first moved into the office, he'd come up with the great idea to coordinate their scrubs with the various blues the office was decorated in.

She closed her mouth and dropped her hand. "We've got a walk-in coming. A garage in Jamison had a mishap. The patient is reluctant, but the owner doesn't want to get sued. The patient may've had a previous injury that was reaggravated."

And so it began. "Okay, how soon?"

"About twenty minutes."

"Thanks. Let Devon know, 'cause he'll want to evaluate first." Riku could go home and change, but that would be a silly waste of time. Besides, he needed some more tea.

He burned his hand on the hot water as he made his tea, then stumbled over the threshold to his office. When he finally sat at his desk, he was almost afraid to move.

Fifteen minutes later, Devon knocked on his open door. "You okay, man?"

Riku couldn't stop the nerve under his eye from twitching. "Yeah. I just didn't sleep well."

Devon dropped into one of the teal office chairs in front of Riku's desk. "You don't seem right."

"I know. I'll get a good night's sleep and be fine tomorrow. Janie tell you we have someone to evaluate?"

"Yup, I'm on it." The buzzer went off. "Can you grab that? I sent Janie out for office supplies, and I'm still prepping room one."

"Sure." Riku nabbed his tea and hurried out front. He tapped the button behind the desk and buzzed the person in, gathered the papers the new patient needed to fill out, and took a sip of his tea.

"Um, my employer called. I'm fine, but he's making me get checked out." The man limped in, using the wall to support his weight.

Fuck. Couldn't be.

Riku pulled the cup away from his mouth and spilled tea on his uniform top.

It was.

Stefano.

He was even more mouthwateringly beautiful than Riku remembered. He had on the same type of clothing—snug-fitting jeans, a faded black T-shirt—and that black leather biker jacket he'd worn last night.

Riku kept his voice even. "Dr. Williams will be with you soon. May I help you to a seat?"

Stefano stared, recognition written all over his face and in his widened eyes until his face became a mask of indifference. "Um, nah, I got it."

In that moment, Riku saw Stefano clearly. His defiance was rooted in his lack of trust, and all that knowledge did was make Riku want to protect him from whatever caused his wariness. He aspired to help guide Stefano to a place where he could feel—

"Okay, I'll bring these forms to you." Riku forgot how the clipboard worked and all the papers slid to the floor.

Stefano hopped to the closest chair and sat.

The papers kept slipping through Riku's fingers like he wore mittens, but finally he clipped them down and held out the items. "Here's the papers and a pen."

"Thanks." Stefano's fingers brushed his when he accepted the items. Stefano's brown eyes and blown pupils widened, but all too soon a frown replaced any interest Riku had read.

Chaos filled Riku's mind, but finally his professional side kicked in. "Are you in a lot of pain?"

"Define 'a lot.'" Stefano's voice was husky, probably from cigarettes, not enthusiasm.

The defiance lurked, calling to Riku's Dominant parts to surface and help Stefano find boundaries.

Inappropriate at work! He flipped the pages over the clipboard to display the pain measurement happy-and-sad faces under the plastic coating.

Stefano pointed to a 7.5, which meant severe pain.

"Let me see if Dr. Williams is ready for you." He escaped to exam room one, poked his head in, and said, "The patient's here."

"Great." Devon tugged him in and shut the door. "But what's wrong?"

Sometimes having someone know you so well was an annoyance. "The patient is in the severe range of pain." Riku tried to tell himself it was no big deal. People came in here all the time… but this was Stefano. He needed to keep his emotional distance professional, though this situation did feel like fate was trying to force his hand.

"And?"

"It's the guy from last night."

Devon tilted his head, staring until his mouth dropped open. "Oh, the hot straight boy who eye-fucked you in the parking lot."

What? "He did not eye-fuck me—" Shoving aside his small tendril of hope that Stefano showed him interest, he stated, "Let's see if he's comfortable staying with this office."

Devon shrugged. "If he's not, I'll take him to the place run by Melanie and her partner in Jersey."

"That will work." Riku hurried back to the waiting room. He made sure to enunciate each word with calm control. "Dr. Williams can see you now."

Stefano grimaced as he moved to stand.

"Let me help you." Riku wasn't taking no for an answer.

"I can do it," Stefano insisted.

Riku admired the independent streak, but he didn't want Stefano to hurt himself. "I know, but lean on me to take some weight off your ankle. I don't want you injuring yourself further."

"How did you know—"

"Your limp, and how you're favoring your other side." Riku put an arm under Stefano's and around his torso to give him support.

"Thanks," Stefano muttered, but he still didn't utilize Riku to stabilize his movements.

At least he was polite.

Stefano gasped when they entered the exam room, and then started to chuckle. "You too, Doc? Isn't this inappropriate?"

"No, we see a lot of people from the club. But if you're uncomfortable, we know a place in Jersey. We can get you there, no problem."

"Nah, it's fine." Stefano moaned as he tried to pull himself onto the table.

When Stefano almost slipped, Riku stepped over and steadied him, whether he wanted assistance or not. "Don't hurt yourself. Let me help you onto—"

"I got it," Stefano sniped.

Riku frowned and withheld comment as Stefano struggled.

"Argh! I hate feeling helpless," Stefano growled.

Wanting to reassure him, Riku stated, "You're not helpless. But when we're injured, we occasionally need some assistance, right?"

Stefano frowned but gave him a conceding shrug.

"May I?" Riku gestured to the table.

"Fine. Yes." Stefano huffed out a breath laced with impatience.

Riku lifted a fidgeting Stefano onto the table.

"Thank you," Stefano mumbled.

"Anytime."

Devon glanced from the blank pages he studied and gave Riku a questioning stare. "Since the paperwork is incomplete, let's have a look and I'll ask you the questions as we go."

Riku felt foolish for not ensuring the documentation was filled out. He needed to pull himself together.

Stefano stared at his feet. "Look, maybe you shouldn't waste your time, 'cause I can't pay. It's my fault for not watching out better. I'm only a temp at the garage, and my guess is this mishap won't work in my favor to get a full-time slot when the garage has an opening."

"Temp or not, your employer has worker's comp insurance. Besides, we don't turn away people who need us."

"I don't need nothing," Stefano snapped as he struggled to take off his boot.

"Let us be the ones to assess that," Devon stated. "Here, let me help you get this boot off so we can do an X-ray."

Stefano glared at Devon, then gave a quick nod.

"I've got him." Riku put himself between Devon and Stefano. After he untied his boot, he slid it off the injured ankle with as much care as possible.

"Thanks." Stefano grimaced and squirmed, but he probably wouldn't find a more comfortable spot on the table.

"When was your last physical?" Devon asked.

Stefano shrugged. "I don't know. High school."

"Why don't we do that as well?"

"I'm not a charity case." Stefano folded his arms over his chest.

"You're not, but I want to ensure this injury is the only thing we should be treating. If I recommend physical therapy, Dr. Tao needs to know some basic information. When someone brings in a car, don't you look under the hood to make sure you're fixing everything?"

Stefano blew out a breath, raising a curl from his forehead, and groaned, "Fine."

Riku left the room feeling better, knowing Stefano would get checked out properly.

He tried to sit down but bounced to his feet and paced a track in his office. Once he found his center, he breathed mindfully for a minute, then went into the physical therapy room.

Everything was perfectly sanitized, but for something to do, he pulled down clean paper to cover the table.

Devon knocked and walked into the room. "The X-ray shows no fractures or breaks. It's just a sprain. Janie scheduled him to come in tomorrow for a follow-up, and the results of his bloodwork will be in on Thursday. He's in good general health but experiencing some back pain, probably from favoring his foot. I recommend he come back to see you and you'd do the basics."

Instead of leaving, Devon stared at the painting behind Riku's head. "And?"

"He signed the confidentiality form that allows me to disclose information to you that would help you treat him."

Riku straightened his spine and waited.

Devon looked him in the eye. "I saw his back."

"His back?"

"Marked with scars. I'd say they explain why he's quick to get irritated and anxious, doesn't sleep well, and is stressed." Devon pressed his lips together, so Riku would bet he wasn't done.

"PTSD... from abuse?" He hated pulling out information from Devon piece by piece.

Devon frowned. "Sounds like it. And, um, Stefano also shared he *infrequently* visits Thirteenth and Walnut."

Riku schooled his body language. Thirteenth and Walnut was a crossroads in Philly to pick up men for anonymous sex. Maybe the straight vibe wasn't so narrowly defined, but the danger of—

"You said his blood test results come back on Thursday?"

"Yeah. I pulled some strings."

"Thanks. You're a good doctor." Riku knew how thorough Devon was as a doctor, but in this case....

"Well, there's that paper on my office wall. Says I'm board certified or some such nonsense," Devon teased, as usual trying to make Riku smile.

Riku, in need of a chuckle, replied, "Oh, I thought you were talking about the other framed picture, of you on the cover of the *Top 100 Doctors of Philly*."

"Shut up. You're the one who had that framed and insisted I display it." Devon chuckled.

"Stefano doesn't have insurance. I'll take care of any out-of-pocket expenses," Riku reassured him.

"And he drives a motorcycle? Damn, you know how to pick 'em."

"I didn't pick him. I was there on Sunday, and he sat next to you during the play. I didn't pick anything." Riku succeeded in curtailing his snappish tone. Though the problem was, he most certainly would have chosen Stefano if given the option.

Devon shook his head but wore a big grin. "Bro, you're in trouble."

Riku gave him a withering look, then got serious again. "Thank you."

CHAPTER 5

THE DOOR to the clinic closed behind Stefano. How could the world be so small he got the one guy who confused all of Stefano's carefully set boundaries as his new physical therapist?

Not to mention the irony of his injury happening because he'd been lost in a fantasy starring Riku Tao. Maybe God decided sending him to Hell after he died wasn't enough, so God was going to put him through more agony while he lived.

Stefano crutched his way unsteadily over to Bobby Mazza's truck, biting back the whimper of pain as he tugged himself into the king cab.

Bobby had been friends with his dad for years and owned the garage, so was now his boss. "They gave you an Aircast, so it's not broken?"

"Right, but they want me back tomorrow. I don't have to—"

Smacking the wheel, Bobby growled, "Hey, none of that stupid talk. They want to see you tomorrow, you go back tomorrow."

"Here, it's all in the paperwork," Stefano grumbled and set the pile on the seat between them.

Bobby skimmed the papers and pulled out Stefano's prescription. "I'll stop at the pharmacy so you can get this filled on the way home. You do exactly what they say. I know you're a good worker. You're a Rossi. All of you are hard workers, but don't be a bullhead like your dad. Do what the doc says."

Left unsaid was if his father had listened to the doctors, he might still be alive. Stefano shivered at the thought of his father still being able to throw things at him and call him names.

In between yelling at the talk radio show, Bobby asked, "After I stop at the pharmacy, you want me to get you a burger before I drop you home?"

"No, thanks. I'm good." Stefano rubbed his stomach to quiet the rumbles. Frank would have some leftovers he could eat. He lived on the third floor of his brother's townhouse.

"Am I dropping you off at your mama's in South Philly or at your brother's?"

"I've moved in with Frank to be closer to work."

"Frank's a good boy. Smart. Surprised he didn't go into the family business, but I guess Marco's got that under control the same way your dad did, huh?"

"Yup." If screaming at customers and making scenes with vendors could be considered being in control, Marco Jr. was on top of the family butcher shop.

Bobby ignored him about the food, and after they finished at the pharmacy, he pulled into the drive-through and ordered them each a burger, fries, and huge soda.

Once they had the medication and food in hand, Bobby drove to the townhouse complex. Stefano's brother Frank was getting out of his car, and his gaze narrowed onto Stefano as he opened the door. "Why are you...? What happened?"

"Nothing. I was stupid." Stefano slid out of the car, making sure to land on his good foot. Wasn't not-yet thirty too young to have a good foot versus a bad one?

"That says something went down." Frank pointed to Stefano's air-booted foot.

Bobby climbed out of the truck with Stefano's half of the fried deliciousness and another bag with meds. "One of the racks came unhinged, and your brother saved a car from a rolling truck tire. He twisted and went down with the damned thing. Just bringing him back from that new doc in New Hope."

Frank scrunched his face at Stefano. "Why didn't you go to Doylestown Hospital?"

"He didn't want to go to the hospital. Your little brother is as stubborn as your dad was." Bobby threw up his arms. "I only got him to agree to this office, which came highly recommended, when I threatened to call your ma."

Putting his hands on his hips, Frank frowned at Bobby.

Bobby rushed to hand Frank the doctor's instructions, medications, and bag of food. "They took X-rays, gave him instructions and some pain meds. He's seeing them again tomorrow."

Frank started asking lawyer questions, and Stefano tuned out. He'd had enough today, between not sleeping and being hurt. All he wanted was to lie down. He pulled his crutches out from the back of the truck.

Bobby reassured Frank again, "Look, you know I'll take care of Marco's boy like he was mine."

"Hey, Bob, I mean no disrespect, but I've got to watch out for my baby brother, you know?"

"I know. Family's got to do for family. But come on, me and your dad went way back. I'll do right by his kids." Bobby wiped a sleeve across his brow.

Frank nodded. "Please make sure all the worker's comp paperwork is turned in on time, and if you need help, let me know. I'll make sure everything goes smoothly for you. *Capisci?*"

Stefano bit the inside of his cheeks so he didn't laugh. When Frank tried to pull off an irate Italian, he came off more like he was auditioning for a remake of *The Godfather*.

"Of course. Give my best to your ma. And Stefano, listen to the doctors and follow their orders. We'll see you back only when you're ready, and oh, if you need anything, call." Bobby waved and headed to his truck.

"Come on, let's get you inside." Frank gestured for Stefano to use his crutches. He stayed behind him and spotted for him.

As Stefano moved down the sidewalk to his brother's townhouse, he focused on the bright orange-and-red leaves on the trees in the distance. "You home for lunch?"

"Yeah, though I think I'll work from home the rest of the day." Frank attempted to sound like he had planned that all along. He unlocked and then pushed open the front door.

"I'm fine." Stefano finally pulled himself up the three steps.

"I know, but let me big brother you a little."

Stefano was going to say something, but one of his crutches didn't clear the doorjamb.

If Frank hadn't caught him, he'd probably be at the dentist replacing his front teeth. "I got you."

"Thanks," Stefano grumbled, trying not to feel pathetic.

Frank righted him and patted him on the back. "Do you want to head straight up and eat in your room, or the dining room?"

"Mind if I go upstairs? We can have a picnic on the third floor." Hopefully, Frank would sit with him for a while.

"As soon as you get food in you, I'll give you your pain meds." Frank hadn't needed to ask if Stefano hurt. Just like always, Frank did his best to stop the pain any way he could.

After an eternity of hopping the stairs to the third floor, Stefano took a leak, 'cause once he lay down, he didn't want to get upright anytime soon. He washed his hands and hobbled out the door to find Frank straightening his unmade bed.

Frank gestured to his dresser. "I moved the spare parts from the bed over to the dresser."

"Thanks." Stefano wasn't sure how to work the scrap metal into the steampunk sculpture he was working on, but he had a feeling the gears would be perfect.

He used his crutches so Frank wouldn't get on his case, and made his way into his walk-in closet. After stripping off his work clothes, though he didn't even get them sweaty today, he tossed them into the hamper and tugged on sweatpants and a Philly jersey his sister got him for his birthday last year.

"Fuck, these crutches hurt." He took the few steps to bed and handed them off to Frank, who set them against the wall near his headboard.

"I remember. They suck. Here, eat." Frank set the tray with Stefano's burger, fries, ketchup, and soda on his bed. He'd added a cup of vegetable soup and a baggie filled with ice.

"Thanks, man." Stefano sighed when Frank elevated his foot on a pillow and applied the ice wrapped in a hand towel.

Frank sat on the other side of the bed and ate his soup.

"Want a bite?" Stefano offered his health-conscious brother a taste of burger.

Licking his lips, Frank shrugged. "Yeah, Just one bite."

Stefano bit back his laugher when Frank's one bite was a third of the burger. He'd happily share anything with his big brother.

After they were done eating, Frank handed him the pain pill. "Here you go. I won't bug you unless you text me. Let me know if you need anything. The remote control is next to your pillows. I'm going to pad your crutches so they hurt less."

"Thanks, Frank."

STEFANO COULD see himself as a teenager. He was about thirteen or fourteen.

No! Turn around. Move! Run! Go!

Instead a hand landed on his shoulder. Nausea and dread pushed down on him.

That's how it started. Little touches and back pats that turned into back rubs. Each time, he told himself it was no big deal. He must be overreacting.

Father Lucca was a priest, after all. Just because something was wrong with Stefano didn't mean the priest was doing anything perverted. The priest must be a touchy-feely kind of guy. Nothing weird was happening.

No, stop touching him!

He tried to protect the stupid kid, but he couldn't move and his screams were silent. Then his adult self morphed into him as a kid. His voice didn't work, so he tried to flag someone down, anyone, but no one saw him. Not one person could hear him. Didn't he exist?

He struggled to get away. Held tight, caught, trapped… he was stuck watching as he was shoved down over the table—

No!

Stefano sat upright in bed. The pain in his ankle brought him to full alert. The digital clock read 3:00 a.m.

Fuck. A dream. A motherfucking dream.

Again.

He sniffed and hobbled to the bathroom, took a piss, then splashed water on his face.

THE NEXT time he woke, bright morning sunshine streamed through the window.

Wow, those pills must have knocked Stefano out again. Usually, after a trip through the horror show in his mind, he never got back to sleep. But he must have, and now as he stretched, the pain returned.

His whole body hurt.

Searching the bed, he found no wet spots, and the baggie holding the ice had disappeared. Frank must have snuck in and rescued him from a watery mess.

He grabbed his cell. Nice! Frank had plugged it in.

Stefano checked his messages.

One from Frank: *Call me if you need anything.*

There was a second text from his current Mistress. He read the words twice to make sure he understood the full meaning.

You never wanted permanence. My sub does, so I release you back into the world. I wish you love and happiness. I hope you find what you need. No longer your Mistress but always your friend, Drama.

Not the first time a Mistress dumped him over text. He was pretty sure they cut ties this way because they were either afraid he'd be upset or they knew he wouldn't be.

While not upset, his loneliness clicked up a notch. He had always known she wasn't the one for him, though he couldn't help wondering if anyone would find him worthy enough to let him serve them.

Aw, well. What-the-fuck-ever.

Stefano swung out of bed, then immediately sat his ass back down. Damn, his ankle throbbed.

He hobbled to the bathroom on his swollen and bruised ankle, turned on the water, hopped over to the toilet, and took care of business.

After stepping into the shower, he let the hot water relax his muscles. Pain in his ankle or not, his cock woke up during the process.

Since there was no one to please with his denial, he sat on the marble shower bench and jerked off. As the hot water ran over him, his body crackled with sensations of greedy need.

He started stroking hard and fast, so desperate there wasn't time, so he didn't question why the image of Riku spanking from the play raced through his mind. What probably should have caused some worry was the spanked sub morphing into him, but he was too close to nutting to give a damn. This time after the punishment, Riku accepted the blowjob he deserved.

Stefano imagined dropping to his knees and sucking Riku off. Kneeling at Riku's feet, stroking himself off to the rhythm of his bobbing head, he made himself feel submissive and willing to serve.

His fantasy Riku wove long, slender fingers through Stefano's damp hair, urging him on. Oh yes. He pleased his Master. Every stroke, every grunt, every hip thrust said so.

In his head, Riku came down his throat and gave him permission to come.

Sheer joy flooded him that he'd been good enough and gained release. He stroked himself faster, making his dick hurt just a little by tugging too hard.

Close. Close…. He leaned against the shower wall.

Cupping his hand in front of his dick, he grunted and came. On and on his cock pulsated, emptying his balls. He caught his come with his palm.

Shivering, he licked his palm clean.

What the fuck?

Ignoring the chaos in his brain, he soaped up again, then rinsed off, and with a bit of difficulty, got dressed. After he put the Aircast back on, he hopped back into the bathroom.

Brushing out the snarls in his hair, he used the shit his sister said worked on her curly hair. Staring in the mirror, he left his five-o'clock shadow because then he couldn't be called pretty or girlie. Though Marco was always quick to point out his eyelashes were too long, and not even his twice-broken nose took away from his full lips.

Mama and his sister envied his looks, but he knew how he looked was one of the many reasons his father had beaten him way too often.

He grabbed his phone and texted Frank. *How early do you have to be in?*

A message came back as Stefano gathered his shit together. *I can give you a ride to your appointment. Where? When?*

Nine o'clock for PT. I can Uber.

His brother texted back: *I got you. I'll make your special latte.*

Thanks. He didn't deserve someone being so good to him.

Stefano checked his email. A bunch of spam and two more emails from Leo Ferraro.

Unease and guilt fought for the top position in Stefano's head. Denial beat both when he read the subject line: Sexual Abuse Survivors Support Group in Bucks County. He couldn't deal with this, so he hit Delete without opening them.

He wished out of sight really did mean out of mind.

AN HOUR later Frank dropped him off at the Wellness Center in New Hope. "I'll meet you at the Sunrise café for an early lunch, and then I can bring you home, okay?"

Stefano sipped the last drops of his favorite latte that Frank always made him and left the travel cup in the holder. "Not necessary, but I do want to take you out for lunch. You've gone well beyond—"

"*Sta 'zitto.* You know you'd do it for me." Frank's dismissal, given in Italian, somehow buffered the harshness.

But Stefano would never have to because Frank didn't do foolish things—ever. "I'll see you later. Text if you can't make it."

"I will, but I'll be here. Just listen to what they tell you." Frank was well aware of how little the Rossi family accepted medical advice, especially from doctors.

"I promise." He trusted the doctor… and Riku.

Frank, thankfully, didn't walk him inside and waved as he drove off.

Stefano would probably have to kill a couple of hours after therapy, but whether he sat at home or at a coffee shop, what difference did it make?

He tried to ignore the weird excitement that made him feel like someone juggled wrenches in his belly and the fucker kept missing the flying tools. The office door buzzed so he could enter.

A pretty woman about his age raced over to him to hold the door open and then guided him toward a seat. "Let me take those crutches from you. I'm Janie. You must be Mr. Rossi."

"Yeah, hi." He tried to catch his breath, but the strong masculine chuckle down the hallway refused to let him.

A few seconds later, the man who'd laughed stood before him. Goddamn his own rotting soul, but Riku Tao was stunning. The sun made his raven-colored hair shimmer. His expensive haircut highlighted the sharp cheekbones of his almost heart-shaped face. Fuck him, those lips were perfectly formed and the prettiest light pink he'd ever seen. The doctor wore teal scrubs that showed off his toned body. Him with ropes—

Shit, Stefano needed to stop. But how, when less than an hour and a half ago he'd jerked off, giving the man a fantasy blowie?

"How are you feeling today, Mr. Rossi?" Riku's manner was all business.

Dammit, Stefano needed to get with the program and stop acting like a desperate teen. *Mr. Rossi* made him bristle, especially with the distant tone, since he didn't like reminders of his father. "I told you and Doc to call me Stefano. Mr. Rossi was my father."

Riku pinned him with a perfectly groomed arched eyebrow that Stefano's cock took as a message to get hard. "Stefano, how are you feeling?"

Since it wasn't just a polite question, Stefano told him, "My body feels like I lost a street fight."

Riku frowned. "And the ankle?"

"Throbbing." No reason for Stefano to front. Maybe Riku could help him with at least one of the things aching.

"Here, sit down. Did you ice it this morning?" Riku asked.

Shit, he'd been too busy jerking off. "Um, no."

Riku tilted his head. "Did you take your pain medication?"

"Nope." Stefano felt like an idiot. He couldn't even follow basic instructions. Some sub he was. No wonder his Mistress dumped him.

Riku nodded. "Do you have your pain medication with you?"

"Yes." He searched his pocket. Ah, there the meds were.

"Janie, could I have—"

"Here you go, Dr. Tao." Janie handed him a small bottle of water. Stefano couldn't help but think Janie would make a way better sub than he ever thought about being, with her anticipatory fulfilling of Riku's needs.

"Since you were prescribed medication by Dr. Williams, don't you think it makes sense to take as prescribed? He did tell you pain management helps with healing, right?"

"Yeah. Frank, my brother, even reminded me after breakfast, but I completely forgot." Stefano hated feeling stupid, especially when the reason for being lost in daydreams was standing in front of him.

"It happens." Riku held out his water. He was so close Stefano could smell a hint of enticing cologne that seemed to enhance his manliness.

Shit, Stefano needed to get a grip. He pulled out the pill bottle fast, and the damned thing went flying.

Within an instant, Riku caught the bottle with almost catlike reflexes and held out the wayward container to him.

Stefano's toes curled without his permission, and he got a shock of pain that helped him stop swooning over Master—no, his physical therapist. The sub in him screamed Master Riku Tao was the best Master with ropes he'd ever seen and craved to be bound by his knots.

"Thanks. I don't know why I'm so clumsy." He popped a pill into his mouth.

Riku held out the water. "Take a nice big sip."

There was no avoiding the need to please. Stefano pocketed the pill bottle and drank all the water.

Riku gave Stefano a smile that made him perfect. In that one single moment, Stefano felt pure, good, and everything in the world was right because he pleased Master... no, Dr. Tao.

"May I help you stand?"

"Please." Stefano hated his need for assistance but clutched at Riku's strong forearm to get upright. Somehow the attention and care fed some odd longing Stefano couldn't put his finger on. He accepted the crutches and followed Riku down the hallway.

A door opened, and Doc popped his head out. "Hey, Stefano. How's the ankle?"

He pulled his gaze off the teal scrubs that clung to Riku's ass in all the right places and acknowledged, "Hi, Doc. Hurts."

"Dr. Tao will help you feel better."

Every dirty thought he wasn't supposed to have about men sprang to the surface. No! This could not be happening now. He thought about the Phillies' losing season and sobered.

"I'm sure he will." There, that sounded normal and not sexual, right?

Riku guided him into the room. "Allow me to help you onto the table."

"Of course." Stefano smiled at him. *Stop!* "I mean, thank you, Dr. Tao."

Setting down his chart, Riku pulled out the step, but Stefano's foot barely touched the stair as he just about lifted him onto the table. "I'm going to do a basic but thorough exam. I'll assess your reflexes, range of motion, muscle tone, and strength."

"Sure."

"Dr. Williams recommended I look into and work on your back pain." *Oh, God, no!* "It's not that bad."

Riku proceeded to move Stefano's limbs. "You don't want to throw off your posture and equilibrium. That simply compounds all aches and pain. Let me help you off the table."

Stefano sighed but allowed the help.

Riku assisted him into a chair and flicked some switches on the table.

The damn thing retracted the stair, stood upright, and another motorized step cranked out. Stefano grasped for something to say. "It's a transformer."

"Indeed. You stand here facing the table and put your hands on these pads." Riku got him onto the step and guided his hands to the cushioned pads. "Going down—I mean flat."

He ran a hand over Stefano's shirt.

Stefano wanted to curl into a ball. His scars where his father had beaten him with a belt buckle made his shame surface.

The voice in his head ripped through him: *Maybe if you'd been good, all the bad things wouldn't have happened.*

A gentle hand rested on his shoulder. "Stefano, is it all right if I lift your shirt for a moment?"

"Um…." *No!*

"Okay?"

"Yeah, but be warned, it's ugly." He pulled his T-shirt over his head and then dropped back into the padded head cradle.

It cut through his heart to hear the usual muted gasp, which happened every time anyone saw his back, reinforcing how unworthy he was of attention, let alone love. Each gasp rocketed him right to when he'd curled up, making himself as small as possible while his father beat him senseless for things that were both horrific, according to the Church, and out of his control.

"Did these happen at the Edge?" Doctor or not, the Master within Riku surfaced in his tone and broke over the question.

Ha, Stefano wished. "My father was strict."

"These scars have nothing to do with strict, Stefano. I'm sorry this happened to you." Then Riku muttered what sounded like "May karma visit him."

"Well, he's dead now, so…." As if that meant he could never hurt Stefano again, but that wasn't the case, nor did his death take away the scars.

"Do the scars bother you?"

"Other than being an eyesore, nah, not really. I mean, sometimes I guess they pull, and the skin always feels too tight." A couple of them had healed all fucked-up. No matter how much cream his sister put on him, they remained rigid and gnarled.

Riku remained quiet.

The silence made Stefano want to hide. "Um, should I cover up?"

"No, I'm going to relax the muscles here and here." He traced the major muscle groups and along the spine. "By adjusting the spine, we realign communication between your body and brain. Then I'll use a special mix of oils that will relax and ease the skin where the scarring is, even the older ones."

"Sounds expensive." He wasn't made of money.

"It's covered."

Stefano glared over his shoulder. *What?*

"What I'm talking about is part of the basic work I do," Riku assured him.

He hated sounding and looking foolish. "Oh, I didn't know. Sorry."

"No worries. First off, I'm going to use a machine along your spine that will give you taps. This opens your vertebrae. Let me know if it troubles you."

Stefano turned toward him with a smile. "Are you saying I need a safeword?"

Riku inhaled sharply, and his eyes went wide. He became the Master who saw everything Stefano was and hoped to be.

Staring into those kind, dark eyes made Stefano melt into the moment created between them.

"In this case, *ouch* will work." Riku crushed whatever nonsense Stefano had created.

Stefano jerked away and shook his head. "I mean…."

"Tell me if what I'm doing is painful." Riku dragged both them into professional and pulled a sheet over Stefano's back.

Nodding, Stefano turned around and dropped his head onto the cushion. He swallowed whatever inappropriate wishes roared to the surface of his mind.

The machine sounded like a mini jackhammer, and in places it felt like one too. Then the noisy tapper was set aside and the sheet slid down to cover his jeans.

"I'm going to continue with a massage." Riku touched him with care, running his hands over Stefano's back with such gentleness while applying the oil, releasing tension and stress Stefano hadn't realized he carried.

Riku's careful touch ripped Stefano open. Had he ever been touched so gently? Tears began to drip onto to the paper under Stefano's head.

What the fuck?

"Here's a tissue, Stefano. I want you to know that tears are a very typical and normal reaction to massage at times. Think of it as another release of stress."

Stefano sniffed and felt like an idiot, but nodded and didn't bother to speak because he didn't think he could. The attention overwhelmed him, and yet somehow, he felt—for maybe the first time—someone actually saw him.

Tension, worry, and fear started to flow from him like Riku had opened the oil drain valve on a car that was years overdue for a change.

All too soon, Riku cleared his throat. "I'm going to raise the table to stand. How do you feel?"

Boneless, delicious, ready. "Relaxed. Thank you."

Riku kept a hand on his back as he brought the table up into a standing position. "You're welcome. I'd like you to stay for another forty-five minutes so we can ice your ankle. Fifteen minutes on, fifteen off."

"I'll do whatever you say." And fuck him if he didn't mean just that. Riku could have suggested Stefano walk over broken glass and he would have done that.

This was a problem.

CHAPTER 6

ON THURSDAY morning Riku's appointments were in downtown Philly, and they concluded quicker than he expected. The doctors and office managers he met with were pleased to recommend patients who lived in Bucks County to him and Devon. He should be celebrating the huge win these connections were, but a restlessness ate at him.

A loop of the independent Stefano accepting his help to get onto the table, his trust in allowing Riku to work on his back, and those tears....

How did Stefano manage to get under his skin with such little interaction? A better question was how could he not?

Stefano was a sub in need, and any self-respecting Master would— *Lie!*

The worry about Stefano's test results, the abuse he'd suffered, and not getting the support he needed, carved open Riku's heart. Not to mention Stefano Rossi's defiance was based in a need to survive, but he was smart, and there was a kindness about him, a vulnerability. And as a sub, Riku hadn't a doubt Stefano would be his perfect match. Not a pushover, yet in need of guidance and stability, which made the Dominant side in Riku long to provide it.

So pity wasn't what Riku felt toward his new patient. No, he needed to admit he wanted to help enhance the quality of Stefano's life.

And you being in this guy's life does that how, exactly? Why did his inner voice always sound like Devon?

Stefano needed to be seen, appreciated, and to serve with a desperation Riku had rarely witnessed. The man's essence called out to everything, Dominant and otherwise, in Riku. He had a wicked craving to guide Stefano into a place where he could understand and believe in his own value.

Ridiculous projection! Once again, Riku attempted to place his wants and needs onto Stefano. When would he ever learn? The guy probably didn't spare him a thought.

He had to get a grip on himself before this afternoon. There was nothing scheduled for a few hours, so maybe he could stop at the

Philadelphia Museum of Art. Sitting in front of his favorite painting might help him think of something beyond Stefano Rossi.

Flashing the museum membership card his parents had gotten him for Christmas, he wandered through the main hall. He focused on his footsteps as they echoed over the marble floor of the uncrowded museum.

He made a left at the grand staircase and glanced up at the statue of Diana. She glittered in the sunlight as she guarded the museum with her bow drawn. Sparing a glance at the works lining the short hallway, he strolled into the Monet gallery. The round room had always been a place he could find his center, but today—*it can't be!*

"Stefano? I didn't expect to find you here."

Stefano and his crutches rested on the bench in Riku's favorite room. What were the odds? He wasn't a believer in fate, but….

Turning to glare at him, Stefano frowned. Gone was the pliable man who seemed to want to do whatever Riku requested. "Stereotype much?"

Riku hated the thrill of excitement that rushed through him at Stefano's deep, insolent voice. There was a piece of him that would take great pleasure in assisting Stefano in seeing the error of his rudeness, but it was impossible to miss the hints of uncertainty that bled through, making the stronger part of Riku want to protect this sometimes-surly man.

"I only meant I was surprised to see you here." That didn't seem to make it better.

Stefano scowled and mumbled, "Just because I'm a mechanic from South Philly doesn't mean I can't appreciate art."

"I know—"

Tell him you can't stop thinking about him!

No!

Riku changed gears and made a gesture toward the bench. "Mind if I join you?"

"I'm sure you'll do what you want." However true that statement, Stefano didn't have to point it out, though Stefano did pull his crutches closer, making room for Riku.

Riku took his wins where he could and slid next to Stefano. "You're sitting in front of my favorite painting in the entire museum."

Stefano's eyes widened, but he didn't look at Riku. "*The Japanese Footbridge and the Water Lily Pool*? It's my favorite too."

Maybe it wasn't fascinating that they both enjoyed the same painting, since who didn't love Impressionism? Though it was something he could build on. "I love the colors and the peacefulness of this version of the painting. Why is it your favorite?"

"Sometimes I imagine someone in the middle of that bridge." Stefano's voice grew quiet and a bit distant. "This person is trying to decide which side to cross over to, or do they simply not move at all."

He wasn't expecting such an honest and deep answer. "I can see that."

Was that someone at a crossroads Stefano?

Stefano continued in a soft voice, "Sometimes I wonder why they don't just drop into the water and float away among the lilies, abandoning everything."

"Abandonment seems freeing on the surface, but it means losing everything." Riku cringed. He despised sounding like a More You Know commercial, so he added, "Although that could be interpreted as simply following the path life has given you and not fighting who you are meant to be."

Stefano tilted his head, sparing Riku a quick glance. "Yeah, I can see that too. It's not about giving up a fight but not struggling against your destiny… or yourself."

Riku leaned toward him and inhaled the leather scent that seemed bonded to Stefano. "By the way, I wasn't stereotyping you. I was probably doing something much worse in your opinion."

Squinting his big brown eyes at Riku, he asked with suspicion, "What?"

"Worrying about you."

"Huh?"

"Wondering how you got here and hoping it wasn't by your motorcycle."

Stefano's lips turned up into almost, but not quite, a smile. "My brother dropped me off. He had an appointment in his downtown office. I really am trying to follow your—doctor's orders."

"Good." Riku exhaled.

The silence bled into tension as Stefano continued to stare at the picture.

Riku scrambled for something to say.

Stefano met his gaze. "You can tell me it's none of my business, but from what I've heard, you don't have a sub or subs of your own. Why?"

Trying not to show the shock at Stefano's direct question, Riku shrugged. "It never worked out."

"But how come?" Stefano sounded confused.

Part of Riku found the question pleasing that Stefano wanted to know him better, but the other part sighed at the sad truth of the matter. "I don't deal well with subs who aren't serious. I've played that game before, and it only equates to being with someone who isn't serious about BDSM or about building a life together. And frankly I'm tired of the disappointment."

Stefano nodded and looked away. "I understand disappointment, trust me on that."

That comment tickled awake the compulsion in Riku to help, and what Stefano needed right now was someone to hear him. "What do you mean?"

Without hesitation, Stefano explained, "I mean, other than here, I can't find much peace."

That was terrible, and possibly one of the results of his physical abuse. Without the security of a safe place to explore emotional relationships, it unfortunately made sense that those who had been abused would have a hard time trusting and sharing intimacy, and would more likely be anxious.

Riku had to clarify. "Not even in subspace?"

The question bounced around the empty circular gallery.

"Ha, subspace. That would be nice." Stefano combed his fingers through his hair, pulling the curls away from his face and securing the strands with an elastic, allowing Riku to see his lovely profile.

Stefano not only belonged in an Italian GQ magazine, as Riku thought when he first saw him—he belonged on the cover. His jeans, T-shirt, and leather jacket were elevated to casual elegance when you added his beautiful face. His dark wavy hair fought the elastic that tried to keep his hair back in a sloppy ponytail. Some strands escaped and framed his face, calling to mind Botticelli's angels. He had to have the longest eyelashes Riku had ever seen.

"Are you having trouble getting to subspace?" Concern mixed with Riku's words.

Stefano shook his head, making his dark curls bounce. "I should keep my trap shut, but apparently as a Dom, you have all the keys to a sub's lips. I guess it's hard for me to trust, and, well…. You don't want to hear this."

"Actually, I do. I want to hear what you have to say and to understand how you're feeling." Riku didn't mince words. This was important to him, and yeah, maybe he couldn't fight the overwhelming need he had to make Stefano's world just a bit better.

"I'm tired of Doms—Mistresses taking me on and never giving me what I want, let alone what I need." Stefano bit out his truth one word at a time.

"Your needs aren't being met."

"Nope. Not at all." Stefano crossed his arms but turned and almost dared him to do something about that.

Riku desperately wanted him to feel heard. "What aren't you being given?"

Stefano crinkled up his nose. "I should bail on this topic."

"But you won't." There was no question. Stefano, for whatever reason, reached out to him.

Stefano glared.

"What? You said I had all the keys, so I'm using them." Riku gave what he hoped was a tongue-loosening smile.

"How do you know I'm going to tell you?" Stefano's grimace attempted to put annoyance back into his deflection, but the words came out as exhausted.

"You like playing with fire. Tell me. What do you need?" Riku leaned closer to him, wanting to make it better.

Stefano ran his fingers through his curls. "I don't know. I guess to stop the fucking voice in my head."

"What does the voice say?" Riku let his sincere concern be heard in the question.

Stefano ducked his head but admitted, "I'm not good enough. I'm a terrible sub, and I don't deserve subspace."

"Why do you think the voice says that?" Riku hoped the gentle probing didn't feel like he was rubbing the juice of a ghost pepper in Stefano's eyes.

"Maybe I don't deserve subspace. Every time I trust someone to let me get close enough to subspace, they leave. So what's the point?" With every admission Stefano gave, he became less hesitant.

Riku hated that Stefano felt this way. Even though it wasn't the root cause of Stefano's anxiety, he pointed out the obvious. "People move on... leave for reasons other than you. You shouldn't blame yourself."

"I get that, but when there's a pattern that makes me the common fucking denominator, I've got to admit the problem must be me."

"Well, maybe if you—I'm sorry. We don't know each other well, and I shouldn't say something that could be perceived as judgey."

Stefano straightened his spine and stared at Riku, meeting his gaze for the first time. "You're right. And just because you're a Dom, don't think I'm a doormat."

"I don't… never mind." Riku backpedaled. He was too up in his head, and only chaos resided there since Sunday night.

Stefano glared at him. "As masochistic as I am, I need to know. Tell me. You've clearly got an opinion, so share."

Riku tried to find the proper wording. "Sometimes our past affects our current situation."

"You're talking about the shit that happened to me as a kid?"

"Yes." Riku hurried on before Stefano could shut him down. "Adults abused as children can have difficulty forming relationships. They might avoid them because of the stress and lack of control when in one."

"I've tried. I've had a ton of Mistresses."

"At the risk of sounding stalkerish, according to Devon, you pick unavailable Mistresses who are already in relationships. It's been said you start off making it clear you only want temporary, so maybe you're the one who leaves before—"

"Hey, why not cut to the chase, you know?" Stefano shrugged.

Stefano's mode of self-protection tried to save him pain. "I see."

"What?" Stefano folded his arms over his chest.

"You cut yourself before someone else can. Why?" As a Dominant there were responsibilities to a sub in need. How could these Mistresses abandon him? To Riku, abandoning Stefano was inconceivable, regardless that Stefano might get out of the relationship before he was in.

Just because you don't think you'd be able to walk away from him….

Stefano pulled out his cell and held up a text. "See? Another Mistress ending it with me."

"Through text?" Riku gasped as he read Mistress Drama releasing Stefano back into the wild. How terrible. "I'm sorry."

"Whatever. It happens a lot." Stefano shrugged like it didn't matter to him.

Riku worked to keep his voice even. "It shouldn't."

"Eh, what can I do? You know there's a whole lot of subs and not enough Dominatrixes to go around."

"What about Doms?" The question slipped out of Riku's mouth before he realized.

"I'm not gay. Why would you say that? Do I look gay?" Stefano's voice continued to rise the more agitated he got.

It shouldn't have surprised Riku, but the words ripped at him. "Hey, put your homophobia away and forget I said anything."

"I'm not homophobic, I'm straight."

Why did Stefano need to insist? The bigger issue was why his words sounded like a question.

Wishful thinking or....

Riku rested his hands on his knees and stared at the picture, wishing the pieces would fall into place. Something didn't make sense. "For the record, there are orientations other than gay and straight."

Stefano rolled his eyes. "Yes, bisexual."

Riku restrained a groan. They should teach orientation and gender identity in school along with a real version of sex education. "And demisexual, pansexual, BDSM-oriented—" Stefano's wide-eyed confused expression made Riku explain. "BDSM-oriented means the gender of the Dom and sub fades into the background. The need to be with someone who can dominate or submit matters more than the gender binary and—"

Stefano huffed out, "I get it."

Riku read only the chaos his words left in Stefano's head.

"Not caring about gender, just dominance and submission," Stefano muttered and shook his head. "But how is that possible?"

"Some people crave the dominance or submission, and like with pansexuals, it's all about the individual, not the gender. In this case, it's about the person and their BDSM relationship."

"But having sex with men makes you gay." Stefano spit out the words like they tasted bad in his mouth.

"Or you're BDSM-oriented, pansexual, bisexual, queer, or any number of other orientations." Based on what he knew about Stefano's trips to Thirteenth and Walnut, he added, "Or maybe there's not an attraction and it's simply the sexual activity that involves a same-sex partner."

Stefano opened his mouth, then shut it, but Riku could almost hear the thoughts churning.

Riku stood and wished he could think of something to say to erase Stefano's comments. His words dug at old wounds that were gifted to him by his first "boyfriend." The high school football star couldn't admit who he was either. Last Riku heard, the guy was on his third divorce.

He couldn't go down that path again, so he moved to the next painting, putting distance between himself and Stefano.

Stefano used his crutches to stand and trailed after him.

They meandered around the circular gallery in silence. Stefano crutched his way to each painting and seemed absorbed by them.

Halfway around the gallery, Stefano stopped and shook his head. "Look, I'm sorry. Sometimes when I open my mouth, old shit comes out that I don't even believe. But I've heard it so much, it's like an automatic response."

"I can't tolerate homophobia. I won't." Riku was clear on that point.

"I've taken a lot of shit from many different people about looking like a girl, and a lot of people assume I'm gay. Truth is, being gay wasn't an option where I came from."

Riku took in the sincerity of Stefano's frown. "What do you mean?"

"Italian Catholic. Gay isn't on the menu. Hell, I grew this just to stop my middle brother from calling me a sissy." Stefano touched his five-o'clock shadow. Ah, the light beard held more meaning, since his pretty face scaled the heights to sexy without even trying.

"Still—"

"You're right. Please forgive me, because I didn't mean to sound like a homophobic asshole. I'm sorry." His kind eyes seemed to plead with Riku.

Like it or not, Stefano's wariness and biting words drew out Riku's need to help. These were symptoms of being hurt on the deepest levels, and all Riku wanted to do was soothe Stefano and take away some of his pain.

"Apology accepted." He sighed and needed to remember everyone was not born with an understanding of LGBTQIA+ issues, and sometimes people said dumb stuff out of ignorance. As long as they did better when they knew better, it was all he would ask.

However, Riku was enamored with this beautiful enigma, baggage and all, so wanted to meet him halfway.

Buzz! Buzz! Buzz!

"What's that?" Stefano looked around the museum.

"It's my alarm. I need to head back to the office."

"Oh, okay. I should be going too. I have an appointment this afternoon with Dr. Williams." Stefano pulled his phone out of his pocket.

"Let me give you a ride." Riku used his Dom voice, hoping to help Stefano struggle less.

Stefano scrolled through his phone's screen. "Nah, that's okay. I'm going to Uber or call Frank."

"That seems silly. We're both going to the office. I even parked in the back, so it's not a long way."

Stefano opened his mouth but then sighed. "Thank you. I'll text Frank and let him know."

Riku guided Stefano out the door and down the ramp, glad he'd parked his car close.

"Good choice." Stefano ran a gentle hand along the body of the car.

When Riku slid into the driver's seat of his Lexus, he asked, "The car?"

"It's a work of art."

"I like it. Though I probably shouldn't tell a mechanic I'd really liked the silver color and Devon had been the one who did the research."

Stefano grinned and gave him a shrug. "I don't understand."

As he pulled out of the lot, Riku explained, "Cars are transportation. They need to be safe and reliable."

"Cars are so much more. They can be feats of modern engineering. The improvements from year to year can be astounding."

"I'll take your word on it." Riku decided to take the back roads to the office. Made for a prettier drive, and right now he wouldn't mind the extra time.

"Wow, look at the reds on that maple."

Riku never really paid attention, but the vivid fall colors were stunning. "The gold is lovely too."

"I believe that's a ginkgo tree. And that orange on the other side.... I don't know the name of that tree, but it's gorgeous." Stefano snapped some pictures with his cell phone.

"It's a rare gift to be able to appreciate things around you."

"How could you not? Just look." Stefano gestured out the car windows.

Heaven help him, but Riku was crushing hard. "Did you always want to be a mechanic?"

"No, but after I could no longer stand working with my brother Marco in the family butcher shop, I took a temporary job working for a neighborhood garage."

Riku stayed quiet and hoped for more.

"I enjoyed working on engines. They make sense to me. Each part working to allow another piece to do their job." He shrugged. "It pays the bills. So I went to school for it. I'm hoping the garage I'm working at will take me on full-time as soon as a position opens."

"Sounds like a good plan." Riku had a plan. Before he could think it through, he announced, "After you see Devon, I'd like to take you home."

"You don't have to." Stefano shook his head.

"It's no problem. Senseless for you to Uber."

Stefano gave him a small smile and relaxed into the passenger seat.

Something uncoiled in Riku.

CHAPTER 7

JANIE BROUGHT Stefano to Doc's office instead of an exam room. Stefano collapsed into a chair.

Dear God, please let me not have caught anything bad. I don't want to die. I'll never go to Thirteenth and Walnut again. Ever!

Shit! I should have stopped and had a cigarette before coming in. But no, I didn't want to earn a frown from Riku—Dr. Tao.

How weird was it that they had the same favorite painting? How many times did they miss meeting each other in that very room, and why did that feel like a loss?

This office was where they'd tell him he was dying. He wished he could pace, but no, he kept his ass in the chair and waited.

Retracing this past year, he hadn't had sex with a stranger since before Christmas of last year. The experience had been terrible, so he hadn't gone back.

Please, dear God, save me one last time. Even if I miss... doing it. No more. I'll be done with that.

He tried to wrestle his anxiety back down to its usual level, where he worried he would die a horrible death alone and that he deserved it.

What if today the doctor told him he had HIV? How many options did he actually have? Had his reckless behavior already chosen his path? Maybe he'd been floating down the river among the lilies in a coffin.

It would be so much easier to ignore everything that held him on this bridge and simply let go and be—

The door opened and Doc ambled in, carrying a clipboard. "How are you, Stefano?"

Stefano couldn't wait another second. "Give it to me straight, Doc. What do I have?"

Doc sat behind the desk. "Currently, none of your tests have come back positive."

He wasn't surprised. "I knew it. I have HIV. How long do I have?"

The doctor set his clipboard on the desk and waved his hands. "First, HIV is no longer a death sentence. Many people live long, full lives. These new drugs being developed can take the viral load down to undetectable, but by the look on your face, let me clarify. All your results came back with the best possible outcome."

Stefano gasped. Right… negative medical tests were good news. "I'm okay?"

Doc leaned toward him. "Currently. I want to retake the HIV test in three months. When was the last time you were down at Thirteenth and Walnut or had unprotected sex?"

Stefano sniffed. Shit, this was too good to be true. *Thank you, dear God. I know I don't deserve it, but thank you.*

He answered, "Not since before last Christmas, and I've only provided oral to my Mistresses, and all of them insist on female condoms."

"If that's true, you're already past the testing window, although I'd like to retest anyway, just in case you've forgotten an experience." The doctor shrugged.

"I haven't." Each event was etched into his brain with guilt and regret.

"Good. But I'd still like to retest, and I'd like to get you on Descovy; it has fewer side effects than Truvada. Though we'll have to watch your kidney functions and bone density."

"What's Descovy?" Stefano had never heard of the medication.

Doc pulled out a pamphlet. "Maybe you know it by PrEP. When you take Descovy every day, along with safer sex practices, this medicine actually helps reduce the risk of getting HIV-1 through sex."

"I'm not gay." What was it about him that made everyone think he was gay? He liked women… and, well, he never really counted his experiences with the occasional man.

"You don't have to be gay to participate in risky sexual behavior."

Stefano folded his arms. Taking the medicine felt like an admission of sorts, one he didn't think he could make. "No. I can't."

Doc took off his glasses and tossed them onto his desk. He pinched the bridge of his nose for a moment and then stared at Stefano for far too long, making him squirm.

Sighing, Doc continued to study him. "Look, my older brother died because he couldn't accept he was bisexual. He didn't use protection when he had sex. Somehow, having a damned condom in his pocket when he went down to Thirteenth and Walnut was something he wouldn't do. Even though he knew he'd be finding strangers who wouldn't judge him for what he wanted. Maybe he couldn't admit what he looked for there, or maybe he wanted to be punished. I'll never know."

Stefano pressed his lips together. His head throbbed worse than his ankle.

Doc bunched his hands into fists. "I can't stress enough the importance of preventive medication. Condoms with Descovy might save your life."

Stefano folded his arms over his chest. Everything crashed down on him. Stuff he'd always avoided knocked him on his ass yet again. "But I'm never going down there again. Ever."

"Stefano, I don't care if you're gay, bi, a straight guy who likes it up the ass, or a straight man who only has sex with lots of women. Everyone needs protection unless you're in a perfectly monogamous relationship or are abstinent." The doc's voice broke in pieces, and those shards drove themselves into Stefano's heart.

All the things Stefano tried to avoid his entire life were laid out in front of him. But he didn't want to die. He'd been given a second chance of sorts. "Okay."

Doc let out a puff of air like he'd been holding his breath. "Good. Good."

"Any side effects?" That was a reasonable question.

"Most are very mild and only last a few days, but you can have diarrhea, headaches, nausea or vomiting and possibly fatigue. Like I said, we'll need to follow your kidney functions, and I want you to take calcium to strengthen your bones. Descovy becomes effective within seven to twenty days, so keep that in mind. Any questions?"

"How am I going to pay for it?" Medicine was expensive.

Doc smiled big and waved him off like money shouldn't be a concern. "I've got samples to give you. So let's get you on the table so I can check your ankle."

Stefano followed the doctor into the connecting exam room and hopped onto the table with no assistance. "I've been doing everything you advised. I've stayed off of it until today, used crutches, and I've iced it until I felt like my foot lived in the Artic."

Doc moved his ankle around, compared the injured one with his other ankle, and then said, "It's probably still tender, but you can use the Aircast to walk. We don't want you to lose muscle, but don't overdo it.

You can wear the Aircast for the next two weeks as you feel you need it, and then I want to see you in here again."

"Can I work? Ride my motorcycle?"

"Yes, you can return to work and use your motorcycle unless it's causing you pain. I've added a note to your employer that you can do light duty and need to ice it every three hours when you're standing, especially the first couple of days back."

"Jesus, they'll put me on inventory." But nonetheless, he shook hands with Doc. "Thanks."

Doc strapped the Aircast back on and handed him a premade bag. "Your medicine. Take it every day as directed. Call if you have any questions."

"I will." Stefano slid off the table and onto both feet. The strained one hurt but felt stable and much better. And he wasn't going to die *just yet*.

Riku was in the hallway, and when his gaze landed on the bag of medicine, he smiled wider.

"What?" Stefano asked as he let himself be led into a dimly lit room with a chair and a TV monitor.

"One, you got meds, so your results were good and you agreed to take them. I'm happy for you." Riku guided him into the massage chair.

Stefano raised the bag. "All that from a bag?"

Riku gave him a wink, making Stefano's insides clench. "I've set this for thirty minutes on a light massage, since you've already seen me once this week. I'll be done with my patients around the time the program completes, and then I can drive you home."

Stefano wanted to spend more time with this man, and that terrified him.

Shit, hadn't he just promised God? *You vowed not to return to Thirteenth and Walnut.* He ignored the excitement racing through him at hanging out a little while longer with Riku. "Nah, I can Uber or call—"

"You already agreed to let me take you home." Riku's Dommy way gave him no chance to argue and at the same time removed his will to want to do anything other than what Riku asked.

He forced himself to overlook the incredible feeling of doing the right thing, but he agreed with a nod.

"If you want to watch nature, that's channel one, various landmarks two, and art is on channel three. Or you can close your eyes and take a nap." Riku took a blanket from the folded pile and covered Stefano. He gently tucked the edges of the blanket around him, making Stefano feel stupidly special.

"Thanks." The chair tilted back all on its own and started to run through its massage program.

"I'll see you when the massage ends." Riku slipped out of the room and gently closed the door.

Stefano sagged into the kneading, vibrating serenity. He clicked to the art channel and relaxed as some of his favorite artist's work came on the screen.

His father's voice sliced through his mind. *You deserve to die for being such a faggalot.*

No! God hadn't punished him for his behavior. He didn't have HIV, nor anything of the other things the doc tested for....

He shook his head. This was what one of his Mistresses had called faulty thinking. Why did he think God would punish him, yet he didn't believe people with HIV or AIDS had been singled out for God's abuse?

She had pointed out that he kept a different standard for himself than others and attributed everything that happened to him in the most negative way possible.

But his father's words chewed through his rational thoughts until he wondered if his father had been right. Maybe he didn't deserve to be alive.

No, he was going sit back and enjoy the works of art. There was too much beauty in the world to see it all, but it didn't stop him from adding many more must-see paintings to his list as the chair loosened his muscles.

Just as the chair ended the thirty-minute program, returning him to an upright position, Riku peeked in. "You okay?"

Stefano started pushing off the blanket. "Yeah, fine. I don't want to be a bother to you. I can call—"

"Enough, Stefano. I'm taking you." Riku's Dom voice laced through his words, triggering Stefano's need to obey him.

He gave a jerky nod and got to his feet.

Doc meandered out of his office and stood in the doorway. "Riku, I saw your car in the lot. Oh... I'll lock up."

"Thank you." Riku nodded to Doc and gestured for Stefano to head out.

Riku was on his heels. "You live in the Mill Ridge complex?"

"Yeah." How did he… ah, the medical information forms.

The conversation died, and Stefano wished his fascination with Riku had. He couldn't rip his gaze off Riku's grip on the wheel, his efficient moves that navigated the car through the traffic on Route 202.

Stefano believed you could tell a lot by how someone drove.

Riku was confident, decisive, highly skilled, and patient.

And fuck, why did that make Stefano hard?

Stefano's brain didn't even raise its hand to answer. Riku had a way about him. He was smart, and the whole Dom thing wasn't something he put on at the club. Taking charge and protecting those around him seemed to be ingrained in who he was.

"Um, I just want to apologize one more time about how I sounded in the museum. I'm really not homophobic." Stefano wasn't sure if Riku believed him, but he had to say it again.

"I'm glad. Sometimes we're fed so much prejudice it seeps into us. Acknowledging it, watching it, and correcting it is all we can do. It sounds like you've gotten some flack around orientation, so sometimes overcompensation can come out as homophobia."

"Yeah. Again, sorry." Ha, Riku didn't know the half of it.

Riku nodded but didn't take his eyes off the road.

Stefano appreciated the calm that being next to Riku gave him.

All too soon, Riku turned into the townhome community. Stefano should be happy to be home, not disappointed they would be parting company soon.

Riku pulled into a spot close to Frank's townhouse.

"Thanks, I—" Stefano started to open his door.

As soon as the engine was off, Riku jumped out of the car. He held open Stefano's door.

The little happy dance Stefano's heart made for having someone take care of him forced him to say, "I can get it."

"I'll walk you to the door. You don't need to balance the crutches, just focus on walking normally."

As Murphy's Law would have it, Frank pulled into the lot and got out of his car. "How's your ankle?"

"Good. The doctor said I can go back to work and walk without crutches with the Aircast as needed."

Frank gave Riku one of his lawyery assessments and then stuck out his hand. "I'm Stefano's brother, Frank Rossi."

Riku gave Frank a firm handshake. "Riku Tao. Nice to meet you."

"He's my chiropractor," Stefano added so Frank was clear.

"Door-to-door service," Frank commented with a slightly arched eyebrow.

Riku shrugged. "Nah, I was going this way, so there was no need for your brother to take an Uber."

"Well, the least we can do is get you something to drink." Frank made the determination, opened the door, and simply expected them to follow.

Stefano wanted Riku to come in, but he reassured him, saying, "You don't have to if you've got things you need to do."

Riku gave him that small but devastating smile. "I've got nothing I'd rather do than share something to drink with you… and your brother."

Stefano released the breath he'd been holding and trudged up the cement stairs into the house.

"Wow. This is amazing." Riku shut the door behind them and rushed over to the abstract sculpture on the left side of the fireplace.

"Isn't it an incredible piece?" Frank smiled at Stefano.

"I love life without crutches." Stefano tried to think of a way to steer the conversation and, as usual, failed.

"Local artist?" Riku asked.

"A very talented one." Frank smirked and pointed at Stefano.

Stefano rolled his eyes as his ass found the couch. "Frank and my sister exaggerate way too much."

Riku studied the piece like they were in a museum. "This is incredible. Are these engine parts?"

"Scraps from cars and found metal. I like combining different shapes and textures." Art was a hobby, just something Stefano did in his spare time.

"Here. Sit. Drink." Frank set down a tray of water, soda, and iced tea.

"Thanks." Riku chose a diet raspberry tea.

Frank took a swig of his soda. "So, are you from Bucks County?"

"Born and raised in Philly. My best friend and I opened our practice over in New Hope.

"Girlfriend?"

Riku shook his head.

"Boyfriend?" Frank asked with the same tone. It always amazed Stefano how Frank and his sister had somehow escaped their father's homophobia and prejudice.

"Not for many years." Riku drank his tea.

"Ah…. Yeah, hard to find a soul mate." Frank gave Stefano a strange look.

Soul mate? Stefano had never heard his brother talk like this.

"How about you?" Riku asked.

"Nah, still establishing my career, but hopefully I'll find that special someone." Frank sighed. "Would you like to stay for dinner?"

"I can't. I've got dinner with my parents, but I'll take a rain check, because whatever is cooking smells delicious." Riku turned to Stefano.

"Frank's a lawyer by day and a master chef in our kitchen at dinnertime." Stefano tried to fist-bump with Frank.

Frank waved him off, then shook hands with Riku. "It's just a soup I'm cooking in the Crock-Pot. It was nice meeting you. I'm going to go shower and change into sweats before dinner. Have Stefano bring you back sometime, and I'll gladly cook for you."

"Thanks. I will." Riku sounded like he meant it.

Frank took the stairs two at a time.

The silence hung between them. Stefano wanted to say something, but nothing came.

Riku frowned. "I'm sorry, but I really should get on the road."

Again, why did Riku think he would care? "Okay."

Bigger question was, why *did* Stefano care?

STEFANO HAD lost his damned mind.

That had to be the only explanation as to why he sat in the New Hope Diner. It was the café closest to Riku's office, and he finally had to admit to himself he hoped to see Riku, even at a distance. When had he become a fucking stalker?

"You want any more coffee, honey?" a waitress younger than Stefano asked.

"Yeah, thanks." He pushed his cup forward. After three hours, he should probably call it a night. "Could I see the menu to order for takeout?"

"'Course. Here's the Tuesday night specials." She handed him a plastic card.

There were only five choices. "I'll have two orders of grilled chicken and vegetables."

Hopefully, Frank would like it, because he'd texted saying he was working late. Stefano offered to grab them dinner since cooking wasn't his thing. He texted Frank: *Grill chicken and vegs. Anything else?*

Nope. Thanks. I'll be home in an hour.

Time for Stefano to finish his eighteenth cup of coffee, get the food, and head home. He sent *Ok* and stared out the window.

His body roared to life with excited energy. Jesus, there he was.

Riku's confident walk was more like a strut. Even in scrubs there was no mistaking his dominance. If Stefano wasn't sitting, his knees would have buckled in reflex and he would have landed on his knees with hopefulness.

What? He had researched BDSM-orientation. Maybe, based on his reaction to Riku, that fit him.

Riku crossed the street. Did he see Stefano?

Stefano focused on his phone like he wasn't staring at the screensaver. He should scroll through texts or something, but his fingers froze.

Fuck, he should duck down.

Oh yeah, hiding would be really mature. There was no possible reason for him to be up this way when there were plenty of diners in Jamison.

Tap. Tap. Tap.

Oh God! He's at the window. Stop acting like a fifth grader. Look up and pretend to be surprised or at least confused. He's coming inside the diner.

"Stefano! What are you doing here?" Riku beamed a thousand-kilowatt smile.

Stefano didn't pull off startled, because his lips had turned up, returning a grin. "Hey."

Riku hurried directly to the table. "What are you doing in town?"

The sound of Riku's deep voice eased him with quiet stability Stefano hadn't felt since Riku left the townhouse five days ago.

"Frank is working late, so I figured I'd pick up something healthy for dinner." There, that sounded reasonable.

"Well, I'm glad to see you." Riku slid into the booth's other bench.

"Why? I mean—"

"I've been thinking about you."

Stefano was bright enough to press his lips together before he could ask anything dumb. As much as he wanted to know, he was afraid of the answer.

Either Riku didn't notice the awkwardness or just wanted to move past it. "How's your ankle?"

"Fine. And yes, I'm taking the medicine Doc put me on."

Riku continued to smile and stare. "Good."

Stefano didn't look away from the dark brown eyes that seemed to see all of him. The strength and security he found there made Stefano feel he could do anything. He could—

"Here's your food, honey." The waitress set a paper bag and the check down in front of Stefano.

He held in his annoyance at her timing.

"Well, I should let you deliver Frank his dinner." Riku stood and moved toward the door. "But hey, you should come back here on Sundays after the lunch rush, around one thirty. It's quiet, and they make this delicious apple pie."

Was that an invite? Would Riku be here on Sunday? "Yeah... maybe I'll do that."

SHOULD HE or shouldn't he go to the diner on Sunday? That was the question.

Stefano didn't ask why he'd obsessed over the question for the last couple of days. He'd gotten good at not analyzing his actions. He didn't want to know. If he didn't know, he couldn't be held responsible for them, right? But he was.

If he went, would Riku think he would be there to see him? Would Riku even be there? Why did so much seem to be riding on this decision?

Not until he hopped onto his bike, skipping out on his ma's Sunday dinner early, did he realize he'd decided. As he got onto the PA Turnpike, he admitted there had never been a real question. He had to go and maybe figure out why he wanted to see Riku again.

When he'd announced he needed to go, he didn't have to make up an excuse. Everyone just assumed Marco's constant picking on him was getting on his nerves. Guilt wrestled with excitement as he pulled into the diner's parking lot.

He shoved his hands into his jacket pockets and trudged up the steps to the side entrance as he tried to block out his ma's disappointed expression.

Why had he disappointed her? For what... a chance to—

There he was!

Riku traced the menu with his long fingers as he stared out the front window, frowning. He looked good in the brown sweater he wore. It highlighted his powerful arms. His straight hair was full, and a chunk fell artfully over his left eye.

At almost thirty years old, Stefano shouldn't be sneaking around on the off chance of seeing someone, but the nervous thrill of simply thinking about Riku had become addictive.

Riku turned from the window, and his frown became a big smile. "Stefano. I didn't expect to see you. I hoped, but.... Join me."

Stefano banged into a chair but made his way to the booth. He hung his coat on the hook nearby and slid onto the bench across from Riku.

The excitement still rocked through him, but a sense of serenity like a protective cocoon felt draped over him. He studied the menu as though he didn't know what he was going to order.

The waitress came over. "What can I get you two?"

"I'll have apple pie and tea. Stefano?"

"May I have a piece of cheesecake and coffee?"

After the waitress left, Riku tilted his head, which made his hair slide over his shoulder. "Cheesecake? Oh, I thought you came for the apple pie."

"I don't like apple pie." The words were out of his mouth before he understood what he'd admitted. He could feel his face turn warm.

"Oh, well, I'm glad you're here."

Riku was *glad* he was here. That simple—probably just polite— statement shouldn't feel like a warm hug, but it did. Stefano opened his mouth and nothing came out.

The waitress returned with their drinks.

Quietly sipping his coffee, he stole glances when he was brave enough, and every single time Riku's gaze locked on to his. Being Riku's sole focus of attention was exciting, frightening, and, well, hot as fuck.

Riku's long fingers traced the rim of his teacup. The gentle strokes mesmerized Stefano. What would those elegant yet confident fingers feel like brushing over Stefano's skin? Gentling through his hair, caressing his cheek, tickling behind his ears, teasing his—

"How's work going?" Riku leaned forward.

Shaking himself back from a fantasy he would never be allowed to enjoy, Stefano grabbed on to the question as if it could save his life… or at least stop him from looking like a jerk. "Good. I'm still doing inventory, but the boss is happy with me and some of the improvements I've suggested. The other guys aren't too bad. I think I even have a shot at getting the open full-time position. How about you?"

"Very well. Thank you for asking."

Shit! The smile spreading across Riku's lips didn't hide the fact he appeared well aware of how he affected Stefano. Jesus, Mary, and Joseph, the kicker was he wasn't even trying to be distracting.

God appeared to do Stefano a solid when the waitress brought their desserts immediately.

Until Riku took a forkful of pie into his mouth and gave a soft moan. *Fuck!*

The moan was a simple "this is good pie." However, the noise gut-punched him. Stefano couldn't help but wonder how close the deep sigh of satisfaction was to how Riku sounded during sex. The echo of Riku's pleasure bounced around Stefano's brain and zipped down to his cock.

He tried not to squirm as he adjusted himself. But damn, watching Riku eat was—

"Is something wrong with your cheesecake?" Riku pointed with his fork.

Stefano glanced at the triangle topped with a strawberry. "No, why?"

"You haven't touched it."

"Oh, um…." Stefano shoved a piece into his mouth. The cool creaminess coated his tongue. "It's good."

"Probably not as good as the Italian bakeries of South Philly, but passable, right?" Riku lowered his voice.

Stefano swallowed and got lost in Riku's gaze. He shook himself out of his stupor. "No, it's good. Really good."

They ate in silence.

Keep your eyes on your food. Don't look at him. Fuck!

Resisting temptation wasn't Stefano's strong suit. How could he not look? Every time he glanced across the table, Riku gave him a sexy grin, making him want to smear the cheesecake all over Riku and lick it off.

Stefano needed to get out of there, so right after the last bite, he started to slide from the booth. "Great dessert. Thanks for the suggestion."

"Glad you could come...." Riku seemed to have a small sadistic streak, because he let that word just hang out there, blocking Stefano's escape.

Stefano sagged back into his seat and became hyperfocused on the word *come*. Come... yes, Stefano would like to come. What sub wouldn't? Boy oh boy, he needed to reel his *never going to happen* fantasies back. Maybe he should—

Riku set his fork down. "I come to this diner a lot and usually do so alone. It was really nice to have your company. Thank you."

Stefano's insides did a weird little fluttering thing. He barely squeaked out a "Welcome."

The waitress meandered over with more hot water for Riku's tea and topped up Stefano's cup of coffee. "Together or separate?"

"Together," Riku claimed at the same time Stefano said, "Separate."

Together. What would that look like? Cheesecake-smearing aside....

She set the check down with a smile. "No rush. You two decide."

The conclusion was there wasn't anything to decide... but together would have been nice. It didn't have to mean anything more than friendship.

Friendship would be nice. Stefano stared at Riku for a moment before pulling out a twenty. "This should cover both of us."

Riku simply gave him a nod. "I'll get it next time."

Next time? They were going to do this again?

Stefano got trapped in Riku's gaze, getting lost in possibilities that couldn't happen in reality, but he nodded nonetheless.

BETWEEN HIS fevered dreams of Riku and his constant replaying of his every interaction with him, Stefano was ready to break. Maybe if the dreams were pure sex, that would have been understandable because Stefano missed some of the things he'd done at Thirteenth and Walnut—

but his dreams centered around kissing Riku, snuggling up, and watching movies.

When Thursday of the next week rolled around, Stefano was a hot mess. He entered the Wellness Center's office with shaking hands, and... Riku wasn't there. His office door was open but empty as Stefano passed by.

The disappointment crushed him more than Wendy Fucarolli saying no to prom did, which was crazy 'cause he'd had a major crush on Wendy since third grade.

Doc said, "Stefano, did you hear me?"

"Um, yeah. I mean no. What?"

"I'm releasing you back to full duty at work. Try not to overdo it, because even though you only had a bad sprain, it can turn into more if you continue to reinjure."

"Got it, Doc. So is this my last appointment?"

"Well, for your ankle. But I can still follow up with you for the Descovy."

"Yeah, that would be great." He nodded but didn't move off the table.

"Anything else?"

"I, um, didn't see Riku—I mean Dr. Tao, today."

Doc gave him a shit-eating grin. "He's got the day off. Can I pass on a message?"

Fuck! Good Lord, Doc probably thought he was a stalker. Riku probably took the day off so he wouldn't have to see Stefano's creepy ass. Going to the diner on Sunday was clearly a huge mistake. "Um, nah. Just wanted to thank him."

Stefano escaped out the door. He wanted to get the hell out of— *oomph!*

"I got you." Strong hands clasped around his arms and stabilized him. It took everything in him not to melt into the warmth of Riku's solid body.

Shit! Shit! Shit!

"Riku, um, hi. I was... um.... Doc released me back to work." His voice had gone embarrassingly soft.

"You got cleared? Good for you."

Right, this was only professional concern. Stefano stepped back. "Thanks. I was just asking the doc to pass on my appreciation to you."

"Hey, let's go to an early dinner to celebrate."

"Um…." Stefano bit his lower lip to keep from screaming *yes!*

"Unless you've got to go back to work. But it's four thirty, and by the time you get there…."

More time with Riku. Should he? He forced himself to look into Riku's eyes and say thank you but no. This needed to end.

Although what came out of his mouth was "Thanks, I'd love to."

A FEW minutes later, the waitress smiled at the two of them. "Back again. Glad to see you both."

She took their orders and slipped into the kitchen.

Yes, back again. It was official—he was a stalker. Stefano wondered if there was a club he should join.

You think he'd be interested in a sick little maggot like you?

He countered his father's voice with *I like spending time with him. There's nothing wrong with that.*

Riku was great at making small talk. He covered news of New Hope's businesses, a funny story about his first patient, which was a rabbit, and finished up with the next exhibition coming to Philadelphia. "You know, Devon says I need to enrich my appreciation of art beyond the Philly Art Museum."

"You listen to everything Doc says." Stefano didn't mean for it to come out snippy.

"Only when he's right, which is most of the time, but don't tell him I said that." Riku smiled and a dimple appeared in his cheek.

Stefano couldn't help himself, he chuckled. "Your secret is safe with me."

"Well, I was wondering if you'd be interested in going to the Rodin Museum on Saturday."

Stefano swallowed his desire to immediately scream *fuck yeah*, and said, "Sounds good. Text me if you want to meet there or—"

"I'll pick you up at 8:00 a.m. at your house, and we can have breakfast beforehand." Riku laid the details out like this was an actual planned thing.

Say what now? Stefano nodded but said, "I don't want to trouble you."

"No trouble. I'm looking forward to it. It's a date." Riku sipped his tea like he hadn't just said it was a date.

Nervous excitement skated through Stefano, but Riku moved the conversation on to movies they both loved from last year.

After dinner Riku walked him to his bike as he finished the story of how he and Devon barely escaped an irate puppy and a furious father.

Stefano got on his bike and waved to Riku. "See you on Saturday."

Why hadn't he clarified it wasn't a date?

Because you didn't want to.... The voice didn't sound like his father's, but almost like his own.

CHAPTER 8

"THANK GOD it's Friday," Riku muttered as he collapsed into his office chair. Today had been nonstop patients, and in between, Devon continuing to bust Riku's chops about him *not seeing but seeing* Stefano made the day even longer.

Although not even the immature razzing could take away Riku's smile or anxiousness to see Stefano again.

Why did tomorrow morning feel so far away?

Checking his stereotypes and expectations when it came to Stefano would be essential. Stefano was far more than a sub in need of a Dom. He listened, though he wasn't a talker, but when he spoke it mattered.

Riku had to get a grip on his desperate longing to guide and steady Stefano before he abandoned his own good sense. But Stefano needed—

"Riku? Riku!"

Damn. He glared, having been caught daydreaming. "What, Devon... Devon... Devon?"

Devon snorted in his good-natured way. "I didn't think you heard me."

Riku shrugged and stated the obvious. "I didn't."

"It's Friday night. You want to go to the Edge?"

"Eh." Did Riku want to go and possibly see Stefano with a Mistress? Or maybe not see him at all? Maybe he could go to the diner on the off chance Stefano might show up there.

Devon sat on one of Riku's aqua chairs. "What's up? You're not indecisive. Is pining over Stefano confusing you?"

Riku let his head drop back on his office chair and swiveled side to side. "I took your advice. I'm seeing him tomorrow. We're going to the Rodin Museum."

"A date? Way to bury the lead. When did that happen?" Devon leaned toward him in that spill-it-now way he'd perfected.

Riku smirked. He'd get the bastard back. "Last night when we went to the diner to celebrate him being fully healed, and it's not a date."

A date required both people to consider it one, and wishing a meetup was a date didn't make it one.

"You really are seeing him a lot. What do you talk about?"

Shrugging, Riku admitted, "Nothing major. Just being in the same space seems to relax him… and it's more than enough for me."

"I see."

Probably far too much. "No, you don't."

Devon tilted his head. Before he could say anything, his phone gave an alert. He checked the screen. "Got an alert from the Edge. You're going on a date before the rope demo? Usually you like—"

"What? That's this Saturday?" Riku checked his calendar, and sure enough, he had down he would be doing a demonstration Saturday night. "I completely forgot."

"Yeah, well, you should text Tom to make sure he's still willing."

"Good point." He and Tom had dated briefly, but they were incompatible when it came to the scene, except for ropes.

Riku shot a quick text to Tom and then asked Devon, "If no club, how about dinner? We can discuss *your* date."

"Yeah, but I'm not letting you off the hook. I want more details on plans for *your* date."

"Yeah, yeah. The usual place at seven?" After a nod from Devon, Riku did a reservation through OpenTable. "And the museum is not a date."

"If you say so…."

AFTER AN enjoyable dinner, his body buzzed with anticipation, but he wasn't in the mood for the Edge tonight. Riku gave Devon a hug. "Dev, I'm not going to the club, so give it up."

"Fine. I'll let you know if he's there." Devon hurried to his car before Riku could lie and say he didn't have to do that.

The walk home did nothing to calm him down, so he got on his treadmill and ran. As he was cooling down, Devon texted him.

Stefano's not here either.

Ignoring the thrill that wound its way through him, Riku texted, *See you tomorrow night.*

I asked around about Stefano….

And? Riku didn't like asking for gossip, but he certainly wanted this intel.

Bad case of sub shame.

Makes sense. The sub shame screamed off Stefano every time he fought his instincts to give in to his need to obey.

Several Mistresses thought he wanted humiliation and gave it to him. Others believe he's bisexual but deep in the closet.

No doubt the humiliation reinforced his internalized biphobia and contributed to his inability to reach subspace. None of the Mistresses' approaches were going to help Stefano accept himself.

Dev, I don't know what to do.

Have fun on your date.

And just like that the conversation ended. Devon wanted him to figure out what he wanted without interference.

"It's not a date," he muttered to himself. He wasn't sure what was happening between him and Stefano, but did continuing to say it's not a date make it so?

Riku took a shower and went to bed.

When sleep wouldn't make an appearance, he started to play out scenarios with himself and Stefano involved.

All ending in disaster.

THE NEXT morning, Riku smiled as he pulled into the townhouse's parking lot. Stefano waited for him outside. Maybe Riku wasn't the only one looking forward to this outing.

Stefano went to the driver's side and handed Riku a travel mug. "Here, try my brother's latte recipe."

Once Stefano was in the car, one sip had Riku agreeing. "Really good. Thanks."

Probably trying to hide his beaming smile, Stefano ducked his head. "I hoped you'd like the taste. I love them. Frank makes one for me every day. I asked him to show me how so I could make one for you."

Fearing Stefano would backpedal, Riku swallowed down how touched the simple gesture made him feel.

"I appreciate it." Riku drove out to the road. "For breakfast I thought of the Le Pain Quotidien."

"That's the restaurant downstairs from the fancy apartments, on museum row. Sounds great."

"Yeah. How was it going back to work full duty yesterday?" Riku wanted to keep the conversation light.

Stefano shrugged. "Great. I was happy to get out of the stockroom."

"Ah." After Stefano didn't add to the conversation, Riku asked, "So what did you do last night?"

Stefano picked at a hangnail. "Not much. Watched a couple of movies with Frank."

"You didn't go to the club?" Why was he asking when he knew the answer? Or at least he thought he did. Maybe Devon missed him.

"Nah." Stefano bit his lip, then asked, "How about you? Did you go?"

"Nope."

Stefano looked out the window. "Oh, you only go on Sundays?"

"No, I just wasn't feeling it."

Stefano shifted in his seat and stared at him. "How come?"

A question that cut to the heart of the matter. Riku glanced at Stefano while they were at a red light. "Sometimes I wonder what the point is, you know?"

"But all the subs want to be with you. You could have your pick."

Riku contemplated how to answer, but as always, the truth won out. "Not all."

Stefano ran his fingers along the seat belt. "Most. I still don't get why you don't have a sub or subs."

Turning onto the road, Riku shrugged. "I've had two. Demos are easier."

"Those two subs didn't work out?"

"Not even a little. Disasters would be the best description. One wasn't interested in exploring BDSM and didn't want a Master, which always confused me as to why he was looking for a Dominant. The other took too much joy in being a brat. He wasn't serious in the least. Honestly, I'm too old for nonsense and wasting time."

"I'm sorry it didn't work out." Stefano frowned and turned back toward the window.

"We all play the hand we're dealt." Riku reached out to squeeze his forearm but dropped his hand without making contact. "Thanks."

Stefano sipped his latte, but his ghost of a frown reflected in the window. "You know, you don't have to treat me like spun glass."

"Got it." Everyone was different when it came to the aftermath of abuse, but he never wanted to make Stefano uncomfortable. This time when he reached out, he gave Stefano's forearm a quick squeeze.

The silence grew loud, but Riku understood Stefano needed time to process.

This early in the day, Riku was able to find metered parking, and they hoofed the block to the restaurant.

After they ordered, Stefano asked, "So why physical therapy?"

He wanted to reward Stefano's attempt at conversation, so Riku rambled. "You might have noticed Devon's gait is uneven at times."

"Yeah, he limps occasionally."

"When we were teenagers, I drove us to the movies, and on the way home one night, another car crashed into us. I lost control of the car. He needed several surgeries, but it was the physical therapist who got him walking. That woman never let him lose hope, even when the medical doctors didn't give him the brightest prognosis."

Stefano gave him a smile of approval. "So you wanted to help people like that?"

"Yes. And Devon became a doctor."

Stefano tapped the table to the beat of the song playing in the background and then asked, "Were you two ever…?"

Riku didn't fist-pump or grin at Stefano's extremely interested tone. He simply answered the question as casually as possible. "In high school we fooled around a bit, but we always knew we weren't the right fit for the other."

The waitress set their plates in front of them.

Staring down at his plate, Stefano's lips moved, so Riku asked after he stopped, "Do you say grace before meals?"

Stefano shrugged. "Sometimes… most… yes."

"I think it's important to take a moment and reflect on the good in the world. Like a plate of pancakes and bacon on a Saturday." Riku took a moment and thanked whoever or whatever was out there for having the privilege to spend more time with the man across the table.

"YOU PAID for breakfast. I'll get this." Stefano set down his credit card for their museum tickets.

Riku didn't argue. "Thank you."

As soon as his wallet was tucked away, Stefano asked, "Want to see *The Gates of Hell* first?"

Riku nodded and wished he'd thought to research Rodin and the museum, but it seemed Stefano knew his way around. "You've been here before?"

Stefano gestured toward the door and led the way. "Yes, it's a small but great collection, with about one hundred and fifty pieces of Rodin's best."

"The *Gates of Hell* are outside?"

As they rounded the corner of the covered porch, Stefano pointed to the huge bronze doors. "Right over there."

"Wow." Riku pointed out the seated figure in the middle on the top of the door, looking down at all the suffering. "Is that *The Thinker*?"

"Some believe it's Adam staring at the sin he burdens mankind with by biting the apple, or it's God. Others think it's Rodin contemplating his own work. And some believe it's Dante."

"Dante? The one who wrote Dante's 'Inferno'?"

"Actually, 'Inferno' was one of three parts of Dante's *Divine Comedy*, which was an epic poem." Stefano shoved his hands into his jean pockets.

Trying to keep his surprise to himself, Riku went with "You know a lot about this."

"My mother made us read the *Divine Comedy* in the original Italian." Stefano's cheeks tinted a light pink, making him adorable, or as adorable as any man in a leather jacket could look. A blushing Stefano appeared open and made Riku wish for things he shouldn't.

"You're fluent in Italian." The man continued to shock him. Usually Riku wasn't a fan of unpredictability, but in this case, he liked it… a lot.

Stefano shrugged. "Don't be impressed. It wasn't a decision. In my house only Italian was spoken, with some bits of English, until I graduated high school."

Riku pointed to the thinking figure on top of the door. "Who do you think it is?"

"It's always been hard for me to make sense of God sitting by with all this suffering in the world. I get the free-will argument. I just don't buy it. I guess I'll go with Rodin appreciating his work."

"I think so too." They crunched through the garden, amid the fallen orange-and-red leaves, admiring Rodin's other works before heading inside.

"A copy of *The Kiss* is on display." Stefano unzipped his jacket and hurried to the piece.

The Kiss screamed of the deliciousness of erotic surrender. A woman submitting everything she was to her lover, the man appeared to have abandoned all sense, giving in to his need for the woman's lips. Although that might be Riku's projection, there was a fluid urgency that swept the viewer into the passionate embrace.

Stefano studied the piece from every angle, with an expression of deep-seated longing. "It's gorgeous."

"Yes, she's stunning. I think beautiful works of art transcend gender and orientation, touching all of us."

"Yeah, sexuality doesn't play into—you want to get that?" Stefano pointed to Riku's buzzing pocket.

Riku hated his phone interrupting what Stefano was going to say, but it might be a patient, or maybe Tommy finally calling him back. "You sure you don't mind?"

"Why would I?" Stefano wandered to a bronze pair of hands.

His caller ID cued him in. "Hi, Tommy. You set for tonight?"

Stefano stared at him and then quickly turned away.

"Nah, man, I can't. I'm not doing too well." Tommy sounded hungover or sick.

"You okay?" Riku became concerned.

"I think my new boyfriend got me sick." Tommy fake-coughed.

Of course. "Tommy, this is rather short notice. Where am I going to find someone for the demo tonight?"

Stefano moved around the piece, but he seemed to be watching, maybe listening to Riku's conversation, if he went with Stefano's ever-changing facial expressions.

"I know, man. I'm sorry. I hope it works out." Tommy giggled and tried to cover the merriment with a pretend sneeze. "I've got to go. See you around."

Why hadn't he expected this from Tommy? He shook his head. "Damn."

"What?" Stefano appeared by his side and tilted his head. Beams of gold from the skylight illuminated strands of bronze mixed in with Stefano's dark brown hair. He licked his lips as he stared at Riku.

At that moment, Riku's heart filled with a desire to have Stefano any way he could... any compromise—

Not good. Not healthy. Not relevant.

Riku shrugged. "The sub who agreed to help with the demonstration tonight canceled."

Stefano frowned. "Oh, no. Really. I was hoping to see you—I mean...."

All good sense told Riku he shouldn't. This was too soon. But Riku's wish was out of his mouth before he could stop the words. "You wouldn't be willing to—"

"Me? You want to tie me up?" Stefano spun away from Riku.

"It's some simple kinbaku." As if somehow that would relax Stefano.

Stefano turned and stared at Riku with his big brown eyes. He licked his lips, and his breath hitched. "But kinbaku's not like shibari."

It had been crazy to ask. "True, kinbaku is erotic bondage, the act of using knots and ropes to highlight the beauty of the sub."

Stefano shook his head. "I'm not beautiful."

"I disagree, and I'd bet I could bring you to subspace." Riku didn't want to make promises he couldn't keep, but he believed that.

Pushing his hands into his jacket pockets, Stefano asked, "Is it true the placement of the knots is like acupuncture?"

"It can be." Not everyone was skilled at the practice, which was why he did these demos.

"And since you're a physical therapist, you probably know how to do it right." Stefano shivered.

At that moment, Riku wasn't sure if he was encouraging Stefano so he could finally find subspace or because Riku desperately wanted to be the one to guide him there. But he wouldn't lie. "Yes, I do."

"Oh." Stefano exhaled with a tiny shudder.

"Demonstrations aren't scenes. Will you be my kinbaku canvas so I may show you how truly incredible you are?"

"But I... I...." Stefano started breathing hard.

He shouldn't push. "It's okay. I just thought—"

"But what if I screw it up?" Stefano bit his lower lip.

"You don't have to do anything. I will guide you into the positions I will bind your body in. I'll tell you what I'm doing, and you can always safeword if you don't want to continue." Riku kept his voice even, though his heart raced with the possibilities.

Stefano paced over to a bench and sat. He stared at the floor.

Riku joined him but remained silent.

Five minutes passed, and then ten.

Stefano twisted his hands. Finally, he peered over at Riku through his hair. "I would like to offer myself to be your canvas."

Riku swallowed hard and kept his cool. He wasn't completely sure if Stefano could go through with it. "I appreciate your faith in me. I'll happily accept your offer and thank you for being willing to attempt to push beyond your usual boundaries."

"You should probably know I can't be blindfolded, and I might need some reassurance it's you tying me if I can't see you."

"Understood. I'd like the scene to have open communication. I don't use a mic, so anything you say will be only for me to hear unless you project your voice."

Stefano inhaled and nodded.

"Anything else you'd like to share right now?"

Studying his fingers, Stefano carved off a piece of cuticle. "Um, well… you know this is just for the… um, the demonstration, right?"

"Of course. It's not meant to be sexual, only educational."

"Though it might be. Erotic bondage and all…."

Riku sensed no homophobic fear; still, he wanted to be clear. "True. A physical reaction wouldn't mean—"

"I know. And that's okay," Stefano was quick to add, like he needed to reassure himself as much as Riku.

"However, I will insist on you letting me provide aftercare." Riku had some nonnegotiables too.

Stefano shrugged as if it was a foregone conclusion. "I won't need any."

"There's no pressure. Even without subspace, ropes can be enjoyed. But I need to end each scene with aftercare." Truth was, he required the quiet focus as much as the sub. He'd rather not do the demo than miss the opportunity to revel in the intimate connection with Stefano.

Stefano's lips twisted into a frown, but he finally nodded.

"Shall we continue looking at Rodin's genius?" Riku wanted to draw Stefano back to his comfort zone.

"Yes. We haven't seen *The Awakening* or *Balzac*. I wonder if it's still on view or has been rotated out." Stefano's whole being seemed to uncoil.

"Lead the way." Riku grinned even though he heard the warning bells.

"NICE! YOU got your leather out of mothballs and even shined it up," Devon snarked at him when Riku entered the Edge.

Riku ran his fingers over the soft buffed leather. "Feels good. Right, you know."

"You're in such trouble."

"What? For the leather?" Which he hadn't worn in years, but Stefano inspired him.

Later, when Stefano swaggered into the bar, Riku let go of the breath he'd been holding. He could have found someone to take Stefano's place on stage, but this one time Riku didn't want to just go through the motions. His longing to deepen their connection was self-indulgent folly, but mark him down as keeping his internal reservations in check.

Stefano stood in front of him with arms crossed and total attitude.

"You okay?"

Stefano opened and slammed his mouth closed. Finally he hissed, "Of course, why wouldn't I be?"

"Usually overcompensation means concern or worry." A strap snapping rang out, followed by mournful screams again and again. The rhythm was too fast and not—

Devon brushed past them and groaned. "Newbies gone rogue. I've got it."

Uncrossing his arms, Stefano unzipped his jacket. "I borrowed Frank's biking shorts like you suggested."

"Good." No sense in Stefano being naked if it created unnecessary discomfort.

The strap stopped.

Stefano's shoulders sagged as he exhaled hard. "You're one of the good Masters, I can tell."

Not knowing what to say, Riku went with "Thank you."

Stefano shrugged out of his jacket and wiggled down his jeans.

Riku dropped one of the lengths of rope. He snatched it off the floor and set the coils on the stage.

A red T-shirt joined the neat pile Stefano had made of his clothes to the side of the stage. He didn't seem uncomfortable showing his back, but maybe in this environment it was understandable.

Stefano's body didn't have gym muscles but actual work muscles, which Riku found… stimulating.

"Would you allow me to massage your muscles to relax you?" Riku held his breath, but he didn't miss the flash of heat in Stefano's eyes.

"What? Here?" Stefano glanced at the people milling around, who were not paying them much attention.

"Yes. Usually a light massage grounds the sub, as well as me."

Frowning, Stefano shrugged like it didn't matter. "Um, yeah, sure… I guess."

Riku smoothed his hands over Stefano's shoulders and down his arms, loosening the muscles as he moved with slow, steady hands.

"I want to make a point about how injuries can affect pain tolerance. Do you mind if I mention your injury?"

"Um, no." Riku used his hands to relax him.

When he massaged Stefano's hand, a gasp escaped Stefano, followed by a moan. He did the other and slid his hands up Stefano's chest. Stefano stood still, allowing Riku to soothe the muscles with a deeper massage.

"Turn around. I'm going to massage your back." He needed to check Stefano's willingness to participate fully.

Stefano nodded as he turned around.

The mess of gnarled skin could have easily brought tears to Riku's eyes, but he focused on relaxing Stefano. He tried not to let murderous hate into his heart, but he hoped if there were a God, Stefano's father should be burning in eternal torment.

He finished the massage. "There."

"Thanks." Stefano turned around to face him, and his cheeks were a bit red.

"I'd like to do some breathing with you." Riku hoped the exercise would help him refocus and continue to soothe Stefano's jitters.

"I'm fine."

"I know, but it's part of how I can get us both in the right mind space for what we're here to do tonight."

Stefano rolled his eyes. "Whatever. You know best, Almighty Dom."

No missing that Stefano was looking for ways to test putting Riku in the Dominant role.

"When it comes to relaxing people, call me the Dominator."

Stefano stared at him before cracking up.

"Good. Laughter is a wonderful way to release tension. Now, feet shoulder-width apart. Inhale, exhale," Riku stated.

Finding his own center, Riku took a couple of minutes to breathe with Stefano. Their inhalations synced into a slow rhythm that resulted in a yawn from Stefano.

"Oh, sorry." He covered his mouth.

Riku smiled. "No, that's good. Yawns are signals that your brain is turning off and shutting down. Let's keep going for another minute or two."

Five yawns and three minutes later, Stefano leaned against him and tipped his chin up.

Even though Riku was a head taller, their positions put their faces very close together. The height difference made him feel even more protective toward Stefano.

Breath mixing, the perfect balance of harmony between them synchronized.

The trust Stefano already showed him went straight to Riku's head. He had never felt this completely in sync with a new sub, ever. Maybe it was topspace taking over his brain. Whatever it was, he didn't want this rare connection to be severed.

"Shall we begin?"

CHAPTER 9

"PLEASE" WAS the only thing that came out of Stefano's mouth when Riku asked if they should begin. Maybe Stefano should be worried the word sounded like a desperate plea, but he wanted this too much. He felt boneless, submissive, and ready to give his body as Riku's canvas.

What he now recognized as internalized biphobia—*thanks, Google, for the education on how we screw ourselves up*—tried to raise its ugly head, but the potential of what he was about to do allowed him to shove it to the side.

Thankfully, Riku didn't comment and only asked, "What's your safeword?"

"I don't need one." Even as he said the words, he knew someone who taught BDSM classes wouldn't accept that answer.

Riku set his jaw and arched one of his perfect eyebrows in that Ice King way of his and asked, "Do you really believe I would do a scene or demonstration without one? That word is for me as much as it is for you."

Stefano wanted to fight, but unlike some of the Mistresses he had played with, Riku would never agree. He avoided staring into Riku's kind eyes because he didn't want to break. "Fine, but I won't use it."

"Not unless you need to." Riku nodded frustrating encouragement.

"*Sacerdote.*" His choice tasted of pain, hurt, and anger. He swallowed to get the sour out of his mouth.

"That's Italian. What does it mean?"

The memory ripped the present to shreds and changed Stefano back into a thirteen-year-old who just wanted God's love… anyone's love would have done.

"I told you to call me sacerdote. Now stand still," Father Lucca demanded as he yanked down Stefano's jeans.

This couldn't be happening. Stefano must be misunderstanding. Something cold and wet was slapped into his ass crack. "No!"

"I am your priest. You will do as you're told." Father Lucca pushed him flat.

Pain ripped through Stefano. He must have deserved—

"Stefano, I'm here. You're safe. I'm with you. You're at the Edge." Riku's deep, calming voice pulled him back to the present. With his thumbs, Riku wiped away the tears that dripped down Stefano's face.

Blinking to clear his vision, Stefano whispered, "Sorry, Master."

"You're shaking. We don't have to do this. Why don't we go get some coffee? Break down and have a pumpkin-spiced something," Riku offered, as if it would be nothing for him to walk away from this planned and scheduled demonstration.

The kind understanding ate into Stefano's gut, but he wouldn't let his stupid reaction ruin the night. Besides, he *did* have to do this, if only this once. God smite him down but he did. "No! I mean no. I really want to do this… with you."

Riku rested his hands on Stefano's shoulders. "If you're determined to do this demonstration, then I need you to tell me what I can do to make this easier for you."

He forced himself to look into Riku's eyes. The connection dragged him back completely from the edge of his private abyss, allowing him to shove away the fear of getting sucked into his pit of hell and never being able to return. Riku's gaze made him believe everything could be all right, if only for a bit.

Stefano greedily drank in the kind attention, and dare he even believe there was acceptance in Riku's gaze? Begging to have his embedded memories taken away wasn't possible. Instead he asked, "Talk to me so I know it's you. I need to focus on you."

Riku squeezed his shoulder and then rubbed. "I will do that. Does my touch help?"

Stefano swallowed and nodded. How did he admit Riku's touch erased some of the terribleness, stabilized him, and planted him firmly in the here and now? He didn't want to think too hard about what that meant, but there it was.

"I suggest you choose another safeword." There was nothing in Riku's tone that made this a suggestion. This was a direct instruction.

But Stefano couldn't ignore Riku, because he was right. Having a safeword was a good idea, but what could he pick? He racked his brain for the right term, something he would hate to use, and rubbed his temples, hoping for inspiration. When he thought too hard, he felt like one of the paintings by Munch, *The Scream*. That's it. "*Munch*."

Stefano imagined the person screaming but no sound could be heard. People were coming after him, not to help him but to punish him.

Tilting his head, Riku's face lit with recognition. "As in Edvard Munch?"

He enjoyed that Riku understood how his mind worked. "Yes."

"I love his work. My favorite is *The Vampire*."

Stefano couldn't help himself and corrected, "Isn't that called *Love and Pain*?"

"Oh, you're right. He never titled the painting 'Vampire.' Though *Love and Pain* works well in a BDSM setting."

A rush of heat swept over Stefano. Maybe the stage lights had gotten hotter? "Well, the pain part… at least does."

Riku licked his lips. "The love part can also work if—"

Devon poked his head into their huddle. "Hate to break up this cozy stage-side chat, but folks are getting restless."

Stefano looked over his shoulder. Shit! How could he have forgotten he was on stage in biker shorts, waiting to be tied up?

"You good?" Riku asked.

He really was and he could do this. "Yeah."

"Make sure you *Munch* me if you need to stop." Riku's expression left no room for misunderstanding.

The command, along with how serious Riku was, really aroused Stefano on a primitive level. He wanted to expose his neck and surrender to this Master.

Devon looked between the two of them and said, "Alrighty, then," as he backed off the stage with slow, deliberate steps.

Stefano snorted, giving Riku a smirk.

Riku winked at him and then turned toward the crowd. "Hello, I'm Riku Tao. This is Stefano, who kindly stepped in at the last minute."

"Master Riku, I'll volunteer for you!" someone in the audience shouted.

Stefano's hands tightened into fists, and he glared at the unknown volunteer.

Waving them off, Riku said, "Thank you, but Stefano is all I need."

All he needs. It was dumb. Riku didn't mean the words literally of course, but the idea made Stefano feel special. How incredible would it be to be everything someone required? Granted, that was some fairy-tale shit right there, but…. He ignored the fluttering in his heart those words caused and focused his attention on Riku, who paced back and forth across the stage, going through the basics of bondage.

Holding up a pair of shears, Riku took a length of rope and cut. "Make sure your round-edge scissors work. Use them if you need them. When in doubt, cut them out. Rope can be replaced, but your sub can't."

Riku coiled the rope. "On the Edge's site, you can find information and recommendations on various types of rope and how to keep it clean between scenes, or just use fresh rope. If my assistants could bring up the web?"

Devon and someone Stefano didn't recognize carried a standup six-foot wooden frame and placed the device in the center of the stage. A spiderweb of ropes spanned the entire height, inviting a Master or Dom to tie their willing partners to it.

"Thank you, gentlemen." Riku inspected and adjusted each of the knots on the device. "As you can see, I tied the web earlier, because I wanted to focus all my attention on Stefano. Though you can pre-tie, you should always double-check right before use."

Almost time. Stefano stopped himself from rocking side to side.

Riku grinned at him. "Are you ready, Stefano?"

Was he? The precipice of now or never tried to drown him. "Yes, Master Riku."

"What's your safeword?" But Riku… Master Riku was there to catch him.

"*Munch.*" He shared a small grin with Riku.

After a quick nod, Master Riku turned toward the audience. "Again, safewords are for the Dominants as much as they are for the submissives. We can't push limits if we can't trust our subs to use their safeword, so that means Doms and Masters out there better ensure they have one."

Stefano rolled his eyes at Riku.

His lips twitched, but he gave no indication that Stefano's complaint had been registered. Riku guided him to the frame with a firm but gentle hand on his shoulder. "Let me know if there's anything you need."

Everything about this scene felt different to Stefano... *because it's Riku.... No, probably because it's only a demonstration... and Riku's doing it.*

"Show him how much you can take, Stefano," someone shouted, but Stefano didn't recognize the voice.

Riku cleared his throat. "Bondage, BDSM... isn't about just taking it. This is a power exchange where Stefano is trusting me to give him sensations. Keep in mind, personal limits are unique and vary based on the individual sub's experience and needs."

Inspecting the first length of rope, Riku added, "Not to say testing limits or pushing boundaries is a bad thing, but I'm someone who thinks it shouldn't be the *only* goal all the time, and it is certainly not our goal here tonight."

The slow cadence of his deep voice relaxed Stefano.

He continued to project his voice, "Tonight, I'm going to display how beautiful Stefano is by using kinbaku, which is the art of erotic bondage. The ropes will help me highlight him as a work of art."

Me? A work of art? Stefano's breath caught in his lungs. Riku glanced at him, and he immediately let out the air with a sigh. He forced himself to find a comfortable position and received a smile from his Master... um, Master Riku, for his efforts.

"Since this is a beginning class, we're going to do a simple chest harness. Find the middle of your rope and loop it. Take the doubled rope and wrap along the chest. For women, place above the breasts, and for men, right along this line."

The rope glided over Stefano's skin, following the path Riku traced with his finger.

Riku positioned him so he faced away from the audience. "Now, put the two loose ends through the loop. Don't pull through too rough, and always watch the tails of the rope to give the sensation you wish."

Stefano shivered as the ends caressed his skin, raising goose bumps. He was glad he'd jerked off twice when he went home to change.

"Remember, the ropes should always have room for two fingers to slide between lines and skin. Wrap the rope under the breast area right about here, and continue to the back. Tuck the ends into the previous section here."

Riku's words drifted into the distance for Stefano as the ends of the rope traced up his leg, over his ass, and across his back. The noise in his head started to fade further until only Riku's voice remained. Though only some of the words registered, the cadence of his voice became something Stefano's heartbeats followed.

Secure and safe, all he had to do was stand there.

More knots were tied, and Master… Riku? Stefano had gotten to know the man beyond the capable doctor and the confident Master. He really liked Riku.

Though right now it was Master Riku who was probably explaining how to do so, but the knots weren't Stefano's concern. He was the canvas awaiting his Master's paint, which was the rope.

His Master….

The ends of the rope rode over Stefano's shoulder, and Riku turned him in a fluid motion, as if they were dancing. Warm fingers traced over his chest directly over his heart, and the rope tucked over the lower binding and teased his nipples.

Even as the ropes bound him, the melody of Master's voice unwound deeply coiled things inside of Stefano. *Unwinding while being tied…. That's funny.*

Riku's eyes twinkled as he leaned toward Stefano's ear. "Something amusing?"

Stefano managed a smile that probably looked goofy as hell, but whatever.

After a nod, Riku said to the audience, "As you can see, I can simply wrap the rope over his other shoulder and tie it off, but we're making art. Feed the rope around this line several times to make the separation of the muscles more pronounced."

As the rope trailed across Stefano's chest, it dangled and teased his nipples again. His body arched toward the sensation without his help. He wanted more of the teasing drag.

The audience might have missed the movement, but Riku's smile widened, confirming he hadn't. As Riku fussed with the ropes, getting them perfect, the loose ends continued to brush over Stefano's skin in the most maddening way.

Stefano felt himself start to get hard. Damn, these latex biking shorts didn't hide a thing, and at that moment, he began to separate from such worries. Hard or soft, he was a canvas for Riku, and if Master wanted Stefano to become aroused, it was out of his control.

Riku ran the rope over his shoulder and turned him so his back was to the audience. "I simply tucked the rope here."

The rope caressed Stefano's back, and the ends tantalized his ass, making him wish to be bent over and fucked or even simply whipped with the rope. Something—

Anything.

"And you make a circle with the rope. Keep checking to ensure there's space between. Draw the rope through the loop and finish with another over knot." He spun Stefano around and whispered, "How are you doing?"

"Fine. Just fine." Stefano's voice sounded faraway to him, but he was right there.

"Ready for more?"

"Yes, Master." So ready for so much more. He caught sight of the audience and cleared his throat. "Um, yeah."

"Good. I want to do a simple hip harness, okay?"

Hip harness? The ropes would be around his—Riku would be near... ropes and fingers would touch him.... He squeaked out, "'K."

"Use your safeword if anything becomes too much."

Stefano's bigger fear was begging for more.

"I'm going to use a simple shibari hip harness. It mixes nicely with what I want to do." Riku wrapped the rope around Stefano's waist and turned him, tracing a path with the rope. "Make sure the rope lays flat and isn't twisted."

Rotating him forward, Riku began to explain about the importance of rope tension, bights, friction, and knots, but Stefano only heard the melody of Riku's voice. The deep tranquility soothed him like a warm bath.

The ropes danced over his thighs, and a knot was tied over the front of his biker shorts. Riku discussed safety and pressure, though Stefano's thoughts narrowed down to the glide of the ropes over his body.

The gentle touch and checks Riku made burned him with heat.

"I'm going to continue down his legs." Riku's fingers ghosted over his junk as the rope swooped. The thin barrier of the bike shorts did nothing to prevent shivering as even Master's breath tantalized him.

Stefano let Master Riku guide him into the required positions. Each slow, rhythmic transition into the next position allowed Stefano to let go of his concerns and worries, and the voice in his head remained silent.

Life was simple. Stefano's body throbbed with anticipation of the next touch, and his mind floated in a peaceful place of sensation and safety. He was decorated with rope, doing his Master's bidding. All was right in the world.

The music of Master Riku's voice tethered him to the earth, allowing Stefano to simply be.

"Stefano, you are doing very well."

Stefano tried to answer, but only a purr came out of his mouth.

"So beautiful." Master Riku ran his fingers through Stefano's hair to get the strands out of his face.

No words, only a sigh, came out of Stefano, but it was enough.

"I'm going to attach you to the web, Stefano." Master didn't ask this time, he only informed, which was good because Stefano wasn't about the decisions right now.

No, he was in a place where he only had to be. He owed nothing to anyone. Sheltered, free of all troubles, and happy.

"Is this a comfortable position for your arms, Stefano?"

His arms? Oh, he had been attached to the web by his hands and elbows. Yawning, he said, "Yes, Master."

"No tingling or burning?"

"No, Master. It's so good." Was he slurring his words?

No matter. Master understood him and would give him what he needed.

"I'm going to press on the various knots. Stefano is still healing from an injury, so his pain tolerance might be lower. Always take the physical well-being of your partners into account." Master Riku traced the lines of rope and pushed on various knots.

The added sensation made Stefano groan, but not in pain, not really. More in acknowledgment of the attention. He was his Master's art. There was nothing to do, simply be enjoyed.

Master Riku put two fingers under the top of the hip harness and pulled the rope away from Stefano's body, relieving one pressure but increasing it from the knots farther down. The knot in front of his dick rubbed across him.

Stefano's eyes drifted closed. So good. He wanted… whatever his Master gave him. His cock throbbed with arousal, but as a canvas, and not even his erection mattered.

He was grateful the ropes held him upright, because surely he would have fallen to his knees.

Master Riku whispered, "Such a good sub."

Stefano melted deeper and leaned on Riku. The adrenaline kick had to be better than any drug available anywhere.

"More, Master. More." Stefano wasn't sure what he pleaded for, but he hoped Master Riku did.

"I'm going to hug Stefano, which allows me access to more than one knot at a time."

Stefano dropped his head onto Riku's shoulder and tucked his face into Master's neck. He might have pressed his lips into Master's shoulder.

"How are you feeling?"

Liberated. "Wonderful, Master."

"I'm glad. You deserve to feel good. You're an incredible sub."

Stefano drank in the praise and floated away on contentment.

Riku began answering questions, but his hand remained on Stefano. He wasn't forgotten.

"I'm going to unwrap each and every rope and loosen all the knots. If you have any other questions, please add them to the Edge's online board under the topic of Demo and I'll get back to you. Please do not applaud. I don't want to startle Stefano." Master Riku slowly unknotted and untucked each and every loop.

Stefano probably had a stupid smile on his face, but he didn't fucking care. Master thought he was an incredible sub… incredible.

Master Riku was talking—oh, to him. "…And I'm going to leave your arms attached while I undo your legs. I don't want you falling."

"'S okay. Master." Stefano would simply stand there for more.

"I'm going to use my body to hold you up against the web as I remove the ropes on your arms." After a heavenly forever, Master said, "And finally I'm going to unwrap the chest harness."

"Yes, Master. As you want…." His words were less slurred, but he felt free. No second-guessing, only easy acceptance of his thoughts and a euphoric feeling that made everything seem awesome.

"He's rope drunk." Devon's voice broke into his bubble and made Stefano look in his direction. Oh, he was holding the frame with someone else on the other side.

Stefano chuckled. "I am." Was this subspace?

"Damn, he's a real rope bunny, Riku," the other man said with a tone that screamed compliment.

"Yup." His body slumped forward into his Master.

As if by magic, Stefano was in a borrowed pair of sweats and his T-shirt was back on.

Master wrapped him in a blanket and took most of his weight as he carry-walked him outside.

Devon said, "Dreamy needs help. Get in the back. I'll drive."

Stefano stumped over onto his Master. "I feel so good. Like really good. Is this subspace? I like it a lot."

"Good, because you were an amazing sub. You were so beautiful, just like a work of art." Master held him tight and ran fingers through Stefano's hair, extending his bliss.

CHAPTER 10

DEVON USED the key Riku had given him before he'd even moved in to open the townhouse.

Riku wrapped his arms around Stefano and guided him out of the car. He maintained a firm grip so as not to lose the blanket or Stefano to the ground.

As he got to the front door, Riku said, "Thanks, man. I've got it from here."

Smirking, Devon nodded, then hung Stefano's leather jacket on the coat closet's doorknob and set his folded jeans on the floor. "I'm sure you do. Call me if you need me."

"Talk to you tomorrow." Riku eased Stefano through the doorway and kicked off his shoes.

"Night." Devon shut the door and used the key to slide the bolt into place.

"I'm going to lay you down." Riku maneuvered the unsteady Stefano to Riku's bedroom.

"Sure. Hey, how come if your name is E-Ku, with the silent R, you let people call you Ric-ku?"

"How do you know that?" He leaned Stefano against the bedroom wall.

Shrugging, Stefano paced over to the bed and mumbled, "Google translate."

How oddly sweet that he'd taken the time to find out. *No! Stop.* "Ric-ku is fine."

Stefano kicked off his shoes and grumbled. "Now that I know, I'm calling you by your real name."

"If you say—careful!" Riku tripped over Stefano's shoes and landed right on top of him on the bed.

Stefano started laughing.

"Oh, so sorry." Riku scrambled to get off, but Stefano held him for a second.

"Thank you. I don't think I've ever felt so relaxed and free." Stefano sighed.

"You're welcome. I really didn't mean to tumble onto the bed with you." Riku had tried to be so careful and here he was, falling on Stefano. He stood. "I promise I wasn't trying to push an agenda. I know you don't want—"

"Who says?" Stefano's eyes still had that dreamy subspace cast to them.

What? "You do?"

"Oh, um…."

Riku noticed the borrowed sweats did nothing to hide Stefano's interest, but he was too damned old to be a convenient port in the aftermath of a horny BDSM-created storm. "Look, why don't I give you a few minutes to sort things out, and I'll come back to check on you?"

"Wait…." He could almost hear Stefano's wheels turning. "Aren't you supposed to stay with the sub?"

Riku felt his mouth opening and closing like a hungry koi. "What are you proposing? That I… watch you—take care of yourself?"

Stefano glared at him. "No, I—what do you normally do with subs who touched subspace?"

"Make sure they're hydrated, warm, talk to them, hold them…." Riku left out "take care of them sexually if the mood was right and we both want that."

"Could you hold me… please?" Stefano's uncertainty bled into his words.

Riku hesitated. It was the first time Stefano had reached subspace, and Riku should give him complete aftercare if he requested the attention. "I don't want to make you uncomfortable."

"I know, but I think it would help."

Riku's heart raced at the simple request. All he needed to do was wrap his arms around the man and lie there with him until Stefano drifted to solid ground. As Devon would say, no big, but it felt huge. Was he going to hold him because he longed for that or because it was what Stefano needed?

Go back to the beginning. A Master's focus should be on the sub's needs, and if the action would benefit and not harm them, do it.

Glancing at Stefano's needy expression, there was no mistaking he wanted Riku to hold him.

I can do this.

He reminded him, "Tell me if this isn't working for you."

"Thanks. I keep floating in this dreamlike world where nothing is bad and everything's going to be okay." Stefano stood and pulled his T-shirt over his head.

Riku averted his eyes. Even though he'd tied Stefano to a web, shirtless, this seemed more personal. "I'm glad."

"Argh. Help. I'm in self-bondage." Stefano chuckled as he struggled with the tie on his sweats, adding knots instead of untying them.

"May I?"

"Please." Stefano frowned as he tied another knot.

Riku unknotted the first and second knots, and finally the original bow. The pants slid down Stefano's narrow hips over the bike shorts.

"Thanks." Stefano grabbed his Vans and trudged barefoot to the corner of the room. He tucked the shoes under the chair and folded everything, a little less neatly this time, but somehow Riku found that endearing.

Riku untucked one side of his bed.

Stefano stumbled over his own feet but caught himself before Riku could get to him.

Yeah, Stefano needed to come down a little more. Riku guided him to the bed.

"Did you get to topspace?" Stefano asked as he slid under the covers.

Stefano was in his bed. His bed! The white sheets and pillows surrounded him, highlighting his dark waves, his dark eyes, and those beautiful lips.

Riku paced as he cleared his throat. "I usually don't when I'm doing a demo, but I have to say it was a struggle to stay focused on teaching. So I guess I did get there too."

"Why?" Stefano patted the bed next to him.

Riku shrugged, sat with his back against the headboard, and gave him honesty. "I got you to subspace, and you were stunning."

Stefano frowned and gave him a nod. "Oh, I guess it's like making a woman come with your dick."

Or a man, but Riku bit his tongue. Was that Stefano's attempt to remind Riku of his orientation? Message received. "I'd imagine so."

Stefano rolled into Riku, tucked his chin into Riku's shoulder, and threw an arm around him. He breathed a sigh of relief. "Ah, I don't think I've ever felt this good. It's like nothing is weighing me down or holding me back."

The clarity of Stefano's message was now scrambled. How in the world had this happened? Seriously.

Normally, Riku would run his fingers through a sub's hair. But was the desire to do that to comfort Stefano or enjoy it himself? They were still in the dynamic of an exchange, so would that be impinging on Stefano? Why did Riku want to touch him so much?

"I'm going to pet your head, okay?" That didn't sound insanely paranoid at all.

"Yes, I'd love that." Stefano pressed flush against Riku's side.

The position allowed Riku to feel Stefano's heartbeat through his erection. He really should give him time to—

"God, I'm horny. Is that normal after subspace?" Stefano shifted his body and pouted.

"Sometimes." Riku left out how some subs needed to orgasm or make their Master orgasm—or both—in order to stabilize quicker.

Stop making a BDSM porn scene! He's not gay, and even if he were open, he's not into you. A part of his brain screamed, *Stefano's bisexual and he is totally into you.* The other part yelled, *He hasn't accepted his sexuality. Run!*

Riku started to slide off the bed. "I should go. So you can…."

Stefano latched on to Riku's arm. "No, please don't, Master."

The title carried way too much meaning coming out of Stefano's mouth for Riku to move. "But—"

"Aren't you supposed to stay with me?" Stefano's eyes pleaded that Riku not abandon him.

"You're back to yourself." Mostly, though making requests that had the potential to kill Riku was a level of sadism he'd never played with before. "You don't want me here when you…."

Pointing out the obvious should have rained the cold reality down on Riku's ardor. Instead, Stefano's heavy-lidded smile gave him too much hope. "But what if maybe I do want you here?"

The warning bells turned into a siren's call, luring Riku to dangerous places. Men who struggled with their sexuality could become violent, though Riku didn't think Stefano would hurt another….

What if Stefano wanted to test the waters and himself? Or maybe he was horny and needed an orgasm? Could he help Stefano explore without getting swept away?

Yes!

No!

Stefano gave him a needy gaze through his inky long lashes and won the battle over Riku's good sense.

"Okay."

Stefano pressed closer. "What do you normally think about when you masturbate?"

All parts of Riku's brain silenced. He must have misunderstood the question. "What?"

Stefano gave him a delightfully sexy smirk. "I think you heard me. You're just surprised I asked."

He tried to block out his most recent fantasies of Stefano being Riku's plaything, lover, and... again, a not realistic submissive. "I don't know. What about you?"

A charming blush tinted Stefano's cheeks. "Lots of things."

Did he not expect Riku would ask, "Like?"

"BDSM stuff, blowjobs, and stuff." Stefano shivered as he rutted his erection against Riku's leg.

Lascivious excitement skittered through Riku as thoughts of Stefano's fantasies went right to his own erection. Perhaps it had been too long since Riku had been with someone, and even longer since he'd exchanged blowjobs.

"Receiving fellatio, I'd imagine, is typical fantasy of most men, gay, straight, or bi." Riku sat against his headboard. Certainly, if he had one of his sex wishes come true, Stefano would be on his knees for him. And then he'd be on his knees for Stefano.

Riku needed to shut down those desires before he did something they would both regret.

Stefano turned over in the embrace and lay on his back. He rubbed his bulge through the biker shorts. "Mmmm, yeah. You know, sometimes I think about people I know."

"Are you sure you don't want privacy?" Riku's head might explode with what Stefano appeared to want to do, but it didn't stop him from wrapping his arms around the man and pulling his back against Riku's chest.

Riku had never felt more like a masochist than at this moment.

A rightness he had no right to feel encompassed him. He combed his fingers through Stefano's chest hair, and his hand itched to skate lower.

Stefano thrust upward as he glanced over his shoulder. His smirk screamed that he knew exactly what he was doing and he intended on doing more. He palmed his bulge and proclaimed, "I rather like you touching me."

Riku traced his fingers down to Stefano's lower stomach. The muscles jumped as Riku ran his fingers along the hair that trailed beneath Stefano's shorts. How Riku wanted to cup Stefano's erection, which begged for his attention, but he didn't. He let Stefano take the lead.

Stefano froze.

Had he felt Riku's arousal?

Wiggling directly against Riku's erection, Stefano asked, "Mmmm, isn't that my job?"

"What?" Riku squeaked. What was he suggesting? "Just 'cause we did a demo doesn't mean—"

Stefano turned over so he faced him. Determination flashed over his face, and he slithered against Riku, inviting him to imagine what Stefano's lips would feel like. "Doesn't it? You've taken care of me. Shouldn't I—"

"No! Kiss me first." This idea might not make sense in the light of day, but somehow a kiss felt like an appropriate litmus test. Someone who looked only to get off any way they could would be less inclined to kiss if they weren't attracted to the other person, right?

Stefano's eyes widened, and he stilled. "What?"

"I think you heard me." Riku gave him a bit of snark, trying to bury his craving, but every fiber in his being wanted to experience Stefano's lips on him.

"I've never kissed a guy. You really want my mouth on yours?" Stefano choked out.

Riku's heart screamed, *Yes!* Why was that even a question? "Only if you want—"

Stefano lunged forward on a whimper, his mouth crashing onto Riku's. Stefano pressed his soft lips against Riku's. The culmination of Stefano's suppressed passion infused the kiss with an urgency Riku had never tasted before.

Pleasure and desire hummed through Riku's veins. He let himself be ravished by Stefano's desperate need, and for a heartbeat, he worried he couldn't give everything Stefano required. By the next, Riku vowed he'd do almost anything to ensure Stefano got what he needed.

Riku caressed Stefano's face, appreciating the stubble, and some of Stefano's frantic writhing slowed.

Taking control of the kiss, Riku dialed down the desperation to sexy, gliding his lips over Stefano's, seeking permission.

There was no hesitation. Stefano surrendered, becoming pliant. His entire body telegraphed submission.

Trying to ignore the charge of power that shot through him, Riku zoned in on Stefano. He trailed a hand down Stefano's back to his waist.

When he did nothing, Stefano thrust his bottom out.

Riku skimmed his hand over Stefano's rounded ass. The muscles weren't overly pronounced, but the cheek Riku rubbed felt perfect in his hand.

Stefano shifted them until his bulge was against Riku's. He groaned and rutted his hard-on against Riku's, issuing many promises of pleasure. Stefano thrust his ass under Riku's palm.

"May I, Master?" Stefano licked his lips, making Riku even more confused.

Master? Right. Master. He needed to step up and make sure Stefano was ready for this. "Stefano, we don't have to do this. I don't want to be a regret."

"Only regrets are the things I haven't done." Stefano inched lower on Riku's body.

Swallowing hard, Riku tried to block how magnificent Stefano's tongue and lips would feel wrapped around his erection.

"I want this, Master…. Riku, I need you." Stefano's voice broke into a moan on Riku's name.

This beautiful man who continued to deny his sexuality begged to suck him off. Common sense should be enough to forbid Riku from even considering this insanity. "I—"

"Please. It's been so long since I… and I really want to." Stefano's face was above Riku's zipper, so close to his erection that Riku's imagination teased him with the fantasy of feeling Stefano's breath through his leather pants.

"This is madness!"

"I don't care. Please let me suck you off." Stefano's eager eyes, filled with hope, pleaded with Riku.

Riku caved. He slid out from under Stefano and stood. He opened his bedside table. Behind the box of lubed condoms, he located the unopened box of flavored condoms Devon had gotten him as a joke. Not so funny right now. He grabbed one, then peeled off his pants and toed off his socks.

Stefano's breath hitched as he stared at Riku with yearning. His pupils were blown, and he squeezed his erection through the biker shorts.

How could Riku be sure this was the right thing to do? What if Stefano panicked? All the what-ifs crashed down on him.

"Riku," Stefano groaned.

Regrets and mistakes would be for tomorrow. Riku longed for this moment with Stefano, and for once he would throw caution to the wind.

Or at least he tried to. He glanced at the condom packet. There was a line between carefree and careless. "Wait, you're not allergic to latex or strawberries, are you?"

Stefano licked his lips and shook his head. "I love strawberries, and they taste delicious with cream."

How could anyone be endearing, sexy, and in need of protection all at the same time? "Good."

Feeling foolish that he wore a shirt, Riku added the silk, along with his pants, to his hamper. He climbed back into bed.

"Your safeword is still *Munch*, but *stop* will also work." This wasn't a scene. Why was he rambling? He couldn't seem to stop himself. "We can end this any time you want and—"

Stefano placed his index finger to Riku's lips for a moment. "If you don't want to do this, you can say so. No safeword is required."

Not want to do this? Riku's erection throbbed at the thought of aborting this mission. "No, I… I mean, I want to make sure you're comfortable."

"I will be. I want to take care of you. Lie back and let me have you."

Have him? That's exactly what Riku craved.

Forget sex. Had Riku ever had a sub take care of him? Everyone thought Masters were always taken care of first, and maybe in some dynamics that's how it worked, but Riku was always concerned— possibly overly so—that the submissive got everything they required. He didn't burden the sub with his desires.

Stefano pressed on Riku's chest as if to ensure Riku stayed put.

He settled back onto his plush pillow and spread his legs, making a space for Stefano to crawl into. *Oh damn!*

Stefano clambered into place on his knees. The accomplished submissive roared to the surface, falling into his role flawlessly. He grabbed the condom still held in Riku's fingers and rolled it on him. "May I suck your cock, Master?"

Fluttering eyelashes be damned. Every need in Riku was being fulfilled. "Yes, Stefano, use your mouth to please me."

Stefano blew hot air over Riku's shaft. Riku could only imagine how incredible that would feel without the rubber barrier, though the visual filled in the sensation and was almost enough to make him come.

It had been a long time since he'd gone this far with anyone. The concept of getting head enthralled him, but having Stefano being the giver made the act heavenly.

Groaning, Stefano started to lick Riku's erection from root to tip, thrusting one hand down his shorts and stroking himself. Pushing his lips down toward Riku's base, Stefano teased Riku's scrotum with his tongue. He dragged his lips to the tip and lashed Riku with fast licks.

This wasn't Stefano's first time giving head. Stefano purred as he licked Riku's shaft and writhed against him. He didn't appear subspace dreamy anymore but still seemed happy and content.

Stefano moaned as the hand in his biker shorts started moving faster. His ass popped and wiggled.

While that was an incredible sight, Riku felt exceptionally greedy. "Stefano, don't come. Wait for me."

"Yes, Master." Stefano groaned his approval and dropped his lips over Riku's cock.

When Stefano's head started bobbing, the barrier between the heat of his mouth and Riku's flesh disappeared. Riku tried to prolong his pleasure, but he couldn't and didn't want to.

Locking gazes with Stefano might have been a mistake, because the image would be embedded in his mind for all eternity.

Stefano staring at him with such longing in his beautiful brown eyes. A craving for things beyond the physical, all while sucking on Riku's cock. Stefano's cheeks indenting with every suck and his dark pink lips stretched around Riku. His very own submissive angel happily debauching himself for Riku's pleasure.

Riku's heart expanded with affection at their connection. He longed for completion but wanted this moment with Stefano to last forever.

He ran his fingers through Stefano's hair and brushed the strands off Stefano's forehead. "Such a wonderful sub. You're so good, Stefano."

Stefano's eyes sparkled with the praise. He sighed and then redoubled his efforts and quickened the grinding of his lower body down onto the bed.

Riku only had time to mutter, "I'm going to come. You wait, Stefano."

Stefano moaned but stopped humping. He stroked Riku's shaft. The basic but quintessential sub move of foregoing their pleasure for their Master's short-circuited Riku's brain.

The restlessness Stefano displayed as he struggled to make Riku come intensified every sensation.

Riku stiffened and hung suspended over the edge until Stefano desperately moaned around him as if begging for his cum.

"Stefano," Riku gasped as the pleasure radiated out from his center and spread. The condom might have taken away some of the feeling, but he barely paid attention. Riku shot everything into the lips dragging up and down his shaft.

Stefano bobbed his head in time with the pulses and increased the suction. He swallowed around the filled condom and finished Riku off with perfection.

Riku blissed out on the bed, basking in the tremendous physical relief. Trying to ignore the emotional connection, he attempted to blank his mind except for the sub who brought him to this carefree place.

Finally, Riku stretched and cracked his back. When he opened his eyes, Stefano sat back onto his knees. He wore a satisfied smile, and his erection made a nice budge in the biker shorts.

Ah, they weren't done yet. Riku hurried into the bathroom, dealt with the condom, and cleaned the fluids off himself.

He strolled back into the bedroom to find Stefano on his back in the middle of the bed. His arousal stood free of the biker shorts.

Delicious. "You were so good. How do you want to come, Stefano?"

A strangled groan came from deep inside Stefano. "Any way you want me to, Master."

Riku never gave any mind to the titles subs bestowed on him—Sir, Master, Dom—until tonight. He wanted Stefano to use the word *Master* with him… *my* Master would be even better.

"You're perfect." Riku grabbed another flavored condom from the container and read the packet. "Vanilla good?"

"Yes," Stefano squeaked.

Riku put Stefano's ass on a pillow and rolled on the condom.

Stefano thrust into Riku's fist. "I won't last long."

"You don't have to," Riku assured him.

He licked the vanilla condom, getting the rubber wet, and peeked at Stefano.

Stefano studied him with his eyes opened wide. Immediately their gazes locked, and Stefano's mouth dropped open. His fists tightened on the bedding as if that would hold him together.

"You have permission to come whenever you want." Riku put his mouth over Stefano's shaft and went to work.

He pushed away the affection that twined its way around his heart and tried not to make more of this than what it was supposed to be. Stefano had submitted with beauty and grace, and he deserved a breathtaking orgasm. Riku concentrated on the activity and not the emotions that couldn't be put in check.

After sliding off the tip, he licked Stefano's condom-covered shaft.

Stefano trembled and whimpered, "Please."

Not being able to resist, Riku mouthed him and added quick strokes with his hand.

"Oh, Riku!" Stefano pulled at the bedding, writhing.

Riku sucked him deep once, twice, three times.

Stefano stiffened, threw back his head, and panted. "Master, I'm coming. Oh, God. Master!"

Adding more suction, Riku made Stefano bow off the bed and practically howl.

Stefano shivered and filled the condom as he thrust an inch or two into Riku's mouth.

When Stefano finally sagged into stillness, Riku took the condom to the bathroom, brought back a wet washcloth, and tenderly wiped him clean. He threw out the empty packets and placed the cloth in the hamper.

Did Stefano want him back in bed?

"Master? May I rest with you on the bed?" Stefano answered the unasked question.

Riku tucked Stefano in and stood over him.

"Please?" Stefano turned down the bedding nearest Riku.

Hiding his uncertainty, Riku retrieved a cold bottle of water from the mini refrigerator in his closet. "Drink this and I'll join you."

Stefano arched a haughty eyebrow.

Riku folded his arms, making it clear there was no negotiation about hydration.

Sighing dramatically, Stefano drank.

Riku had never seen anyone drink a bottle of water that fast.

Smirking like an imp who'd won a battle, Stefano handed him the empty bottle and patted the bed next to him.

CHAPTER 11

STEFANO PRESSED closer to the warmth. He tugged on the covers over his shoulder and snuggled his face into the crook of a neck. Strong arms wrapped around him, making him feel safe. Talented fingers ran through his hair.

He'd never stayed overnight with a Mistress—

Strong arms?

Blinking, Stefano opened his eyes, only to be blinded by the sun seeping through the drape. A man lay next to him. He was cuddling with a man!

Master Riku…. Riku stopped carding his fingers through Stefano's hair. "Good morning, Stefano. Did you sleep well?"

Fuck, Riku's deep voice set Stefano's heart to pounding. "Morning—wait! What time is it?"

"A little after nine. Why?"

Slapping a hand over his face, Stefano explained, "Shit! I've got to go!"

"Work?"

"No, it's Sunday… church." Stefano bounced out of bed and stumbled over to the chair to get his clothing.

"You go to church?" The man who mastered his world sat upright, and his disbelief echoed his own. The blanket dropped to his waist, giving Stefano a good look at his toned and manly torso.

"Every week with my ma." Stefano shivered and turned away from the unholy, delicious, but totally mouthwatering sight.

Holy fuck! He had submitted to Riku, finally got to subspace, exchanged blowjobs, and then cuddled until morning.

"Interesting," Riku added.

How was that fact interesting? Stefano didn't have a freaking clue, but whatever. He grabbed his shirt off the chair. Fuck, he couldn't embarrass his mama by wearing a wrinkled T-shirt and borrowed sweats to church.

Shit! He paced back and forth, balling the shirt up further. "I don't have time to go home and change."

Riku stepped in front of him and put two firm hands on Stefano's shoulders. "I think I have a button-down that will fit you. Go take a shower."

The Master tone Riku used with complete success last night had Stefano's feet moving toward the shower even before he smelled their night on him.

Getting into the shower, he got right to work. How could he have overslept? How did—

Got to go.

Stefano had never spent the whole night with anyone. Usually he craved his own space far too much. *No time to overthink!* He soaped, rinsed, toweled dry, and used a finger to brush his teeth with a bit of swiped toothpaste.

As he stepped back into the bedroom, Stefano tried not to be disappointed that Riku wore jeans and a red long-sleeved thermal shirt that clung to his muscles. So casual yet so goddamned pulled together and hot!

Riku handed him a white button-down. "Here, you can wear this."

The guy was tall, lean, and powerful. There was no way in hell his clothing would fit Stefano. "I don't think it'll fit."

"It was part of a Halloween costume Devon tried to convince me to wear, but I didn't. Let me go put your jeans in the pants press to refresh them."

Stefano slipped the shirt on. "Thanks. This is a perfect fit."

"Good. Feel free to keep it." Riku disappeared into a walk-in closet. Within a minute, he came back with Stefano's jeans looking like they were new, and they even smelled fresh.

"Thanks for grabbing these from the club." He accepted the jeans. Riku really took care of him. No, Riku took care of people in general. It wasn't like he was special or anything.

"Oh, here." Riku spun around to give him privacy he didn't quite need, especially after last night. "I'll take you to the Edge so you can get your bike."

He didn't have time for an Uber. Besides, he could tell by the set of Riku's jaw that he wouldn't win the argument if he tried. "Great. I appreciate it."

"Can I get you a quick breakfast? I can make—"

"I'm sorry, but I really have to go." Stefano couldn't look at Riku. Why did leaving like this hurt?

"You should eat." Riku led him to the front door.

The Master tone made Stefano long to comply. "I will, but my ma will be worried. I'll be lucky if I get there before mass is over."

"Come on." Riku held out Stefano's jacket.

Stefano should grab his jacket and throw it on, but he craved this last bit of caring Riku offered him. He pushed his arms in and tried not to sigh. "Thanks."

Riku grabbed his own leather coat. Jeans and leather. Fuck! He looked good. Stefano wouldn't say it out loud, but he needed to stop lying to himself. His Master—no, he wasn't that! But Riku was a gorgeous man.

He let Riku open the car door for him.

The silent car ride gave him too much time to think of last night. Riku's mastery of the ropes, Riku giving him everything Stefano craved, him getting to subspace for the first time, and then the mind-bending blowjobs.

Unlike in the past, he knew whose dick was in his mouth. He wanted to suck because of who he was with. The blowjob wasn't about derogation or punishing himself, but of exploring and maybe even celebrating. And that kiss—never mind those soft, demanding lips….

Riku pulled into the parking area of the club.

No time to dissect this. He had to go.

But what should Stefano do? What did Riku expect him to say? Did he kiss him goodbye? Maybe he should—

"Thank you for a lovely evening." Riku's deep voice surrounded him. *Say something! Anything!*

Stefano stared at the dashboard. "Thank you. I, um…."

"Go. You don't want your mother to worry." Riku rescued him one final time.

Nodding, Stefano stumbled out of the car and to his bike. He gave Riku a wave, grabbed his helmet out of his locked box, and strapped it on. Sitting, he started the engine. He adjusted his mirrors, and… why was Riku still there?

He rolled over to the car. When Riku lowered the car window, it allowed him to ask, "Is everything okay?"

Riku nodded. "Yes. Drive safe."

Stefano waved one more time before getting on the road. He glanced back. Riku still hadn't moved his car.

Why the hell did that make Stefano feel lonely? Maybe the guy was texting or something. No. He wasn't.

Zipping along the backroads to South Philly, Stefano counted on them having less traffic.

Shouldn't he be happy? He got to subspace, received, and got to give an incredible blowjob. His ma was making his favorite spaghetti and meatballs for Sunday dinner. He should be farting sunshine, but his heart was all gloom and confusion.

Fuck feeling lost! He sped right to the speed limit, hoping the wind rushing past him would allow him to unwind, but the empty feeling grew.

After finding parking in the church's backlot, he hurried around to the front. He stared at the cement steps leading to the church's door.

Shit! He swallowed hard.

Stefano didn't have time to stand outside of St. Anthony's and gawk. What the fuck was he waiting for? An invitation from the Pope?

Hiking up the steps, he tried to convince himself he could do this as he did almost every single week of his life. He took a deep breath, pushed open the door, and ignored the dread crawling over him.

The building was immense, with thirty wooden pews polished to a high gloss on either side of the long aisle. Relics of gold were displayed on the white marble altar, catching the midmorning sun. A riot of color cast from the huge stained-glass windows decorated the stone pillars with vivid sparkles. Incense hung in the air.

He dipped his fingers into the holy water and blessed himself with the sign of the cross.

Several people turned to smile at him. He gave them a grin and a mouthed "Sorry." Of the sixty people in attendance, most had been there to celebrate his first Holy Communion and his Confirmation.

He spotted his mother. She sat with Marco in their usual pew, three rows from the altar on the left side. She had even left space for him to sit on the aisle.

Stefano hurried down the aisle. When he got to his ma's pew, he made the sign of the cross and gave a quick bend of the knee before sliding into the open space.

She didn't look at him but smiled and patted his knee.

Father Giovanni was already at the lectern, giving his sermon, so Stefano had missed at least half the mass.

"Remember, the 1986 Letter reads, 'Although the particular inclination of the homosexual person is not a sin...,' and it goes on to state homosexual persons are called to chastity. Does that seem harsh in today's society?"

Fuck yeah, it does! Father G was a decent guy, but wow.

Father Giovanni shrugged. "God has a plan for each of us. When I felt the Lord calling me to priesthood, I've got to say, chastity seemed like an impossible sacrifice."

A sprinkling of uncomfortable laughter echoed around the arches and walls.

He continued with a smile, "An aspiration I'd never be able to meet."

Chastity was only something Stefano did when put on denial.

But last night had nothing to do with foregoing anything. It was all about indulging in some of the fantasies that plagued him. *Stop! Not in church!*

His mama leaned over and whispered, "Are you okay? Do you have a fever?"

He didn't look at her but gave her a head shake.

The priest went on, "These letters specifically give guidelines for how a gay man or woman can still have God's love. It calls them to be holier than others. He asks for them to sacrifice so they do not sin."

Sin. Stefano had grown up knowing he'd been born into sin through Adam and Eve, but he was much worse. He was a sinner. Maybe that's why Father Lucca did what he did to him.

Stefano had tried so hard to be a good person, to follow God's commandments, but he often fell short. He didn't want to believe chastity was the cost of Heaven. Guilt seeped in at hoping he could find a loophole.

In the past, when he couldn't take not having what he needed, he'd found himself on Walnut, and it was then impossible not to go to the cross street of Thirteenth. Within fifteen minutes he would find someone to give him what he needed to survive, and then he dealt with the fear and guilt for months.

Father Giovanni cleared his throat and continued, "However, the doctrine commands us to accept and respect everyone regardless of orientation. It's not our place to cast stones, right?"

What Father Giovanni didn't say was implied. If you were gay and acted on your desires, you weren't going to Heaven. Forget the whole BDSM thing—going to Hell for that was a given.

No matter how good Stefano tried to be, he would be tossed into the abyss. No ifs, ands, or buts.

What he'd done with Riku hadn't made him feel dirty. It made him feel alive and right in all the ways he'd never experienced before. How could that be a sin?

The sermon went on. Father Giovanni explained exactly how living the "gay lifestyle" was an abomination. Stefano supposed Father G had never heard Lady Gaga's "Born this Way."

Stefano allowed his gaze to drift over the stained-glass windows of various saints. As usual his gaze stopped on St. Sebastian. The saint was naked save for a loincloth draped low. He was tied to a tree, and arrows pierced his torso.

How many hours had Stefano sat in this very pew drooling over St. Sebastian? The image in his prayer book had given him his first erection. Stefano had never been clear whether it was the saint in bondage, enduring the pain of arrows, or the fact that St. Sebastian had a rocking bod that did it for him.

So why do I keep claiming I'm completely straight? Other than being beaten for luring a priest into sin—*yeah, like I wanted to be hurt like that by an old... by... him.* His own father certainly had given him no pity when he'd tried to tell him what happened. *How could I want that now and risk everything for it?*

He flashed back to last night. Sucking off Riku and coming in his mouth. The subspace—it was all too much and somehow not enough.

He refocused on the panes of stained glass. Maybe it had been St. Sebastian's ability to surrender and accept his punishment, however unjust, that got Stefano's motor revving.

Everything was jumbled in his head. Unlike the other men he'd been with, he was attracted to Riku. He liked everything about the guy. With Riku, Stefano's surrender hadn't been filthy or shameful—he felt liberated, cared for, and even beautiful. Somehow *beautiful* was no longer an insult, but something that was okay to be and feel.

"Let us rise and say the creed." Father G put out his hands and raised them.

Stefano was on his feet, muttering the words and going through the motions until the end.

Finally he could lead his mother down the aisle toward the door. Marco stepped on the back of his heels twice.

Stefano shot him a "what are you five years old" look over his shoulder.

His brother resembled his father in a scary way. Marco bit out, "You look like a bum. Coming to church in jeans."

His mama glanced down and patted Stefano's hand of the arm she had latched on to. "That's just fine, as long as you're here."

Once Stefano helped his mother into Marco's huge truck, he jumped on his bike and drove through the streets of his old neighborhood filled with row houses with sloping stoops, and for the first time he felt out of place. He didn't belong here.

He had changed. Maybe it was living in Bucks County with his brother. It might be finally working at a job he loved or maybe more recent *events* that affected him.

After pulling into the tiny spot in front of Marco's truck and the next-door neighbor's junker, he parked. As soon as he entered his childhood home, there was a predictability about Sundays that comforted him.

Marco had already plopped in his father's old recliner, watching the Eagles, and Ma scurried into the kitchen, pausing only to give his sister a quick kiss on the head. "Thank you for setting the table, Angelina."

His sister and Frank went to the Unitarian Church. Their service started earlier, which meant it ended before their Catholic mass, so they beat them to the house every week.

Angie rushed over and gave him a big hug. "Hey."

"Hey." He inhaled the happy vanilla scent she always wore.

She pulled back and studied him for a moment, then looked over his shoulder toward the living room. The television blared the football game. Still, she whispered, "What's wrong?"

How could she tell? "Nothing. I'm good."

She gestured toward the football zombie. "Did the jackass say something to you at church? I'll take him out. I just need a reason."

"That makes me glad you like me." Stefano bit back a smile, because his sister was even shorter than him but certainly would not appreciate his amusement. "As much as that would please you, there's no need."

She waved her finger at him. "I know something's up with you. You know I'm here and you can tell me anything, right? Me and you, unconditional love. Got it?"

Could he? Maybe. But there was nothing to tell... not really... well, maybe some. "Yeah. Same goes for you."

Angie crossed her arms over her chest. "I'm serious."

"Stefano, could you start bringing the food to the table?" Ma called out from the kitchen.

Whew, saved by a chore. He patted Angie on the shoulder and darted into the kitchen, coming to stand next to the old Formica table speckled with black dots and scratches. The tabletop always looked like someone had spilled the pepper. There were seven well-worn pleather-cushioned yellow chairs tucked underneath.

He waited for further instructions and enjoyed the smell of his ma's homemade spaghetti sauce.

The Rossi family kitchen had always been headquarters. Everything from cooking and medicine-taking to every important discussion that ever took place in this row house happened here.

Ma had refused to upgrade her appliances to stainless steel because the ones in harvest gold from Sears worked just fine, and they matched the flowers on the wallpaper.

"All these go to the table, Stefano." Ma pointed to the dishes containing smells from the comforting parts of his childhood.

Stefano carried the garlic bread, salad his sister and Frank insisted on, the pot of meatballs, and a huge dish of pasta to the dining room.

The dining room was a crush. Their grandmother's huge cherry table, chairs, and hutch she'd shipped directly from Italy took up the entire room. Family pictures in black frames filled the walls.

"Dinner," his ma bellowed loud enough to be heard over Marco's game.

"Ma, can I eat in front of the TV?" Marco called out from the living room.

"No, you may not. Come and sit down with your brothers and sister." Her voice carried the same surprise it did every week he had the gall to ask.

Marco pushed himself out of the chair. "Whatever. The team the Eagles are playing is so gay."

His sister growled, "What do you mean by that?"

Marco rolled his eyes. "Nothing. Jesus, even in my own home I've got to be politically correct?"

Frank cleared his throat. "Actually, there's nothing political about being accurate. The Eagles are choking like they usually do against the Giants."

Stefano pressed his lips together so he didn't crack up. His sister took no precaution and giggled.

"Horseshit, the Eagles—"

"It's a good practice to respect every group, even if you're not in it, since you don't want to insult customers down at the shop," Frank nicely reminded Marco.

His sister continued to chortle, earning one of Ma's frowns.

Angie pointed at Marco. "He started it. Tell him it's not right to use the word *gay* to describe something bad."

"Or maybe the other team had a talent for kicking the Eagles' ass and he was trying to express how wicked good the other team was playing." Sometimes Stefano couldn't keep his mouth shut.

Marco glared at him. "Leave it to Stefano to start talking about asses. Talk about gay."

He wasn't—Stefano stared down at his empty plate—yet how did he explain last night? But he really didn't find most men attractive, only Riku and St. Sebastian.

I'm not completely straight? Wanting to spend time with Riku and resorting to being a bit of a creepy stalker....

"Marco, stop immediately," Frank snapped.

Marco scoffed. "What, you *gay* now too, Frank?"

"Well, if I was, I'd expect respect from *everyone*." Frank's words were said in a tone to pacify Ma, but his glare let Marco know he'd best shut the hell up.

"It's wrong and against God's law. The priest was talking about this very thing." Marco sputtered and hit the table with his fist.

Stefano jumped, fear took another bite of his insides, and he tried to become invisible. *Dammit! I'm a grown-up.* But the desire to hide fed his anxiety. *If they see me, they'll know....*

"God's law, huh? And which Bible are you going with? Sections have been added, subtracted, and altered throughout the centuries. How do you know it wasn't distorted from the original intention?" His sister had always been smart like Frank. She worked for Philadelphia's

Department of Human Services doing some big important job that helped lots of people.

"Children." Ma clapped her hands.

Marco wiped a hand over his face. "See, Mama? This is what happens when you let them go to that make-believe hippy church."

"Marco, you will stop this right now. Frank and Angelina are adults. I don't *let* them do anything. I raised them to make their own decisions. All I care about is that they're happy."

Marco waved her off. "Well, if they followed God's laws—"

Angie laughed without humor. "Wow, that's rich coming from a divorced man who cheated on his wife. Seems like you only follow the rules you like, Marco."

Pointing at the crucifix hanging above the hutch, Marco said, "The Bible says homosexuality is forbidden. End of discussion."

Ma cleared her throat and bowed her head. When everyone followed suit, she prayed, "Thank you, Heavenly Father, for the food we're about to share. Thank you for bringing us all together. Amen."

Ma handed Stefano the pot of meatballs and pasta swimming in her fabulous sauce. She whispered, "Your favorite."

"Thanks, Ma." Stefano's stomach knotted, but he took a helping of spaghetti from the dish and two meatballs, then passed the pot to Frank.

Stefano didn't want to believe a loving God would send him to Hell for the times he couldn't stop himself from being with men, but that fact had been literally beaten into him.

Frank shook his head. "Actually, the word homosexuality wasn't used until psychoanalysts started the practice in the late 1800s."

Say what, now?

Marco grimaced and shook his head. "Well, I don't know about all that."

"I know, that's why I'm sharing, to increase your knowledge of your religion. In biblical days, people didn't have a concept of sexual orientation, so the mentions of same-sex behavior really relate to the worshipping of idols, treating people unfairly, and violence. Similar things were said about men and women, and no one believes that the Bible is condemning relationships between men and women."

What? My head is going to explode.

Angie leaned back in her chair, folded her arms, and glared at Marco. "Funny how it's only against people who are attracted to the same sex, huh?"

His mother passed him the salad bowl.

"Thanks." Stefano scooped some onto his plate and passed the bowl on. How had he never heard any of this? Truth be told, he wasn't a big thinker and certainly didn't focus too hard about how he was destined for Hell.

Frank piled his dish with lettuce and tomatoes. "By the way, the story of Jesus and the adulteress—"

"Casting the first stone bit?" Angie asked.

"Yeah, that story doesn't appear in the Bible until the twelfth century."

Holy shit!

Frank continued as if he were prosecuting a case, "And add to the fact that people can't even agree on how many books make up the Bible—"

"What do you mean?" Marco held up his hands.

Frank smiled his "I'm sorry I dropped you when you were a baby" smile. "Well, think about it. The Catholics and Eastern Orthodox have half a dozen more books in the Old Testament than—"

"What!" Marco clenched his fists and looked like he might try to make Frank take back the information he'd shared.

With these facts, Frank took a hammer and chisel to all Stefano had been brought up to believe.

What else don't I know?

Angie nodded.

His ma remained silent, but her mouth had dropped open during some point of the conversation. She slid the basket of garlic bread at him.

He took a piece and passed the basket.

Frank pushed Marco, and anyone could see Marco was on the ropes. He grinned and took a piece of bread but didn't let up. "Don't you want to know about the other five books, Marco?"

"The food is getting cold. Please start eating as you talk." Ma's demand came out as more of a suggestion.

The conversation crashed over Stefano, overwhelming him with a sense of confusion.

Frank continued to toss so much information at Marco on Catholicism, orientation, and a variety of other topics that trying to hold the information felt like using a strainer to carry water. Pieces of information that made Stefano hopeful that God might not hate him slid away before he could grasp on to them.

He never was all that great in school, so he focused on food until his sister said, "Religion shouldn't heighten homophobia, transphobia, or biphobia."

"Biphobia?" Shit! The first word he uttered confirmed Marco's assessment of him. Stefano squeezed his hands into fists so they would stop shaking.

"A prejudice towards people who identify as bisexuals." Angie touched his calf with her foot.

Ma cleared her throat, and instead of asking for an end to the conservation, she asked, "Bisexuals are people who like both men and women, right?"

How did she know that? His ma never struck him as someone who would have such information, but he didn't ask.

Angie gave her a big smile, one which shouted pride in Ma. "Basically. They are attracted to two or more genders."

Marco gave a bitter laugh. "They're just people who are greedy and—"

"Why, Marco, you sound rather biphobic." Frank gasped and pretended to be shocked.

"There's a surprise," Angie scoffed. "That's why people internalize this bull—I mean, negative stuff about their orientation and have problems accepting who they are. And for the record, bisexual doesn't equal polyamory."

Why did Stefano feel like maybe he should understand all of this better?

You know why!

"How come you two are so full of gay details?" Marco filled the words out with his snide tone.

Frank pretended not to notice but answered as if he couldn't help himself. "Glad you asked. Actually, two of our members are getting married next month, so Pastor Jean wanted us up on details."

"Two queer boys?"

"No, two women who've been together for twenty years."

"Twenty years?" Marco's mouth dropped open.

"Their relationship has lasted eighteen years longer than your marriage," Angie growled.

Of course, Stefano knew same-sex marriage was now legal, but for how long? He grew breathless, imagining two people of the same sex, standing together in front of God and everyone, declaring their love was equal to a man and woman's.

Stefano's brain was twirling, so he didn't stay for dessert. He needed to be alone. After he cleared the plates, he made his excuses to his ma and fled into the afternoon traffic.

HE IGNORED his desire to stalk the diner on the off chance Riku might be there. He went directly home and took the stairs two at a time. After locking himself in his room, he texted Frank, *Early work tomorrow. Night.*

Hopefully his text would be enough to reassure Frank and buy Stefano some alone time.

He got undressed and carefully folded the borrowed shirt. He'd take it to the dry cleaners tomorrow.

After grabbing his computer, he crawled under the covers.

He started researching bisexuality. A voice that sounded too much like his father growled, *See? You are a little freak!*

Angie had mentioned internalized biphobia, so he searched that. He wasn't much for psychobabble, but he realized he had taken all the negative shit about being anything other than straight, swallowed it as fact, and over time the negative bullshit ate his soul and made him hate that part of himself, so he saw his needs as bad and dirty.

Doing more clicking around, Stefano found a site that said some men liked sex with men but were not attracted to guys. It was simply physical pleasure, getting off together. Bisexuals, however, could feel romantic attraction toward both men and women.

Stefano got a bit lost on the discussion about the spectrum of sexuality. The picture of a sliding scale helped. It showed people could have a leaning preference toward women or men to varying degrees. All the way to one side and you were completely into the same sex. However, landing on the other side meant you were completely attracted to the opposite sex, but it wasn't an all or nothing. You could fall anywhere in between, more or less attracted to the opposite sex and more or less attracted to the same sex.

He did find some men attractive, though he was mostly attracted to women. Riku happened to be one of the exceptions. All Stefano knew was he really enjoyed last night... a lot.

His dick started to chub up at the memory of Riku's perfect mouth sucking him. Those full lips lit the craving deep inside him. Kissing Riku had been a revelation. Hot and sexy, and then it morphed into sweet and almost caring.

Feeling the stubble beneath his fingertips when their lips met sent him reeling with a desperate need. Sucking him, well, that was like going to subspace all over again. Then that mouth sucking on his cock. Damn, he hadn't lasted more than a minute, but fuck, who could have?

Yeah, he was definitely attracted to Riku, which meant he was bisexual. What did that mean? Maybe nothing. Though it helped explain more about himself.

Stefano slipped out of bed and went to the bin he kept in his closet. Buried deep within the box of odds and ends was a book. He opened the book, revealing a tool from Super Discreet Pleasure hidden in the cut-out pages.

Running his fingers over the dildo, he decided the device was about the same size as Riku.

His mouth watered, and his ass clenched, wanting to feel it.

Jesus, what was wrong with him? All his religious upbringing and on a Sunday, hours after church, contemplating....

He needed to shove the thing back where it belonged. Staring at the fake book, he slowly reopened it.

Well, it was already out... and he was horny.

CHAPTER 12

RIKU'S ALARM rang, and he immediately reached for his phone. For the hundredth time in the last four days, he checked for messages. Still no response from Stefano. He turned off the incessant beeping.

He reread again the words of the text he'd sent Stefano.

I appreciate you doing the demo on Sat night. You're an incredible submissive. Thank you —Riku

Maybe Riku should have called him? But wouldn't that be too much if Stefano hadn't responded to his text? Wasn't that an answer to the question he should never be asking?

Or maybe he shouldn't have listened to Devon. It wouldn't have been desperate to check in with Stefano. It would be being a responsible Dom. He needed to set a higher standard. Perhaps Stefano had subdrop or he reinjured his ankle or….

Riku let his gaze land on the pillow, where the perfect excuse lay. He'd found Stefano's biking shorts kicked under the bed and his T-shirt in the bathroom. Returning Stefano's T-shirt and biker shorts would give him a reason to reach out.

If he was going to return to them, he'd have to put them through the wash while he exercised. After grabbing the clothing, he brought them to his nose and inhaled. Wow, he didn't consider himself a clothing sniffer, but damn, Stefano's scent was embedded in both fabrics.

Setting the clothing back on the pillow, he rolled out of bed, made the bed, and started his day.

RIKU SIGHED as he sat for the first time all day. He pulled a nutrition bar out of the stash he kept in his desk and took a bite.

His phone buzzed. Restraining a groan, he pushed the intercom. "Yes, Janie?"

"Um, I think one of your patients is pacing out front on the sidewalk."

Riku took a sip of tea and opened the blinds enough to see Stefano take two steps away from the office and stop. Then he dragged himself three steps toward the door before turning back around. He carried a hanger with Riku's Halloween shirt.

Riku had told him to keep the shirt. Dare he hope Stefano scrambled for an excuse to see him?

Stefano paced in a hesitant stop-start loop several more times.

The intercom buzzed again. "Yes?"

"Um, Dr. Tao, should I ask if I can help?"

"No, Janie. Let him alone." It had to be Stefano's decision to come to him, though that didn't stop Riku's heart from racing.

Riku watched for eight minutes. Stefano paced and smoked a cigarette. Finally he dragged his feet all the way to the door.

Come on. Open the door and come in. Please.

The door buzzer went off and seemed connected to Riku's heart.

Containing his excitement was impossible, so he gave in and went with it.

Stefano's voice drifted back to his office, sending tendrils of happiness and want through him.

Janie buzzed him. "Dr. Tao, Mr. Rossi would like to speak to you."

"Of course, Janie. Send him to my office."

Riku centered himself and opened the door. He expected to see Stefano ambling down the hallway. Instead, Stefano stood three feet away. "Hello, please come in."

Stefano didn't make eye contact. "I don't want to take up your time."

Riku said, "No worries. Please give me a reason to sit down," as his heart begged, *please talk to me.* He closed the door, giving them some privacy.

"I just brought the shirt back to you. I, um, guess I should go. I don't want to bother you." Stefano hung the shirt on the door hook. He reached for the knob.

"You're not bothering me… ever. Besides, I don't have any more patients today. Sit." Riku added the steel to his voice that Stefano appeared to need in order to take a chair.

Stefano sat and glanced around the office.

Riku waited.

Gliding his fingertips over the arms of the chair, Stefano frowned. "I don't know why I'm here."

"Maybe you wanted to see me again." Someone should take a leap.

Stefano's gaze landed on him, and the answer resided in his eyes, but Riku was certain that kind of admission wouldn't come out of his mouth anytime soon.

The silence grew between them.

Riku cleared his throat and stepped up. "I don't need to know what made you stop by. I'm happy you did. When you didn't answer my text...."

Stefano shrugged. "I didn't know what to say."

Reviewing what he'd texted, maybe it wasn't as open-ended and inviting as Riku had hoped. "I'm glad you're here."

Squirming in his seat, Stefano glanced around the room again.

"I'm going to head home in a few minutes. If you don't have previous plans, would you like to come over for dinner?"

"Yes," Stefano blurted out, then wiped a hand over his face.

Riku gave him an out. "You want to think about that? The look on your face—"

"No! I think too much. So if you really meant to invite me, I'd like to come—I mean, I'll be there." Stefano's face got adorably pink, but he shook it off enough to ask, "What can I bring?"

"Just yourself. Give me about thirty minutes. Do you want to use the massage chair or—"

"Nope, text me the address and I'll meet you there." Stefano rushed out the door before Riku could even stand.

Would he show?

WHEN RIKU couldn't make sense of any of this, he marched into Devon's office. "He could barely look at me. Why did he bring the shirt back? I said he could keep it."

"What now?" Devon shut his door and then sat back down.

Riku paced. "Maybe he returned the shirt to be done with me completely and he agreed to go to dinner so he could escape."

"Who are we talking about?"

Giving him a fast update irritated Riku. His emotions were too close to the surface. He tried to center himself while he waited for Dev to give him sound advice.

Devon folded his arms over his chest. "Riku, what the fuck do you expect? That the King of Narnia is going to be all settled after a night in your ropes and a bounce in bed with you?"

"I never said—"

"Do I look stupid? Please, he melts like ice cream on a summer's day for you. And frankly, you've been a hot mess ever since—"

"I haven't—" Riku stopped the lie.

Devon snorted and cracked his knuckles. "Tell tales to yourself, not to me."

"Fine! I might have been out of sorts. I'm all up in my head. This is why I don't go down this path." Riku didn't mean to sound bitter, but relationships always had a way of slicing him in two as they imploded.

Devon's eye roll might have been heard in Philly. "You can't pretend he doesn't flick all your switches. He's physically your type. He's not a pushover, wants badly to submit, and he needs so much of... well, of everything."

And Riku craved being able to provide some of what Stefano needed, even if it was only temporary so Stefano would have time to figure out who he wanted to be.

"Yeah, but why did he give me back the shirt? Probably to get rid of any evidence of our time together."

"Wow. Asked and answered. Step back. It's not always about you. The man is probably questioning things he always believed about himself, or at least wanted to. It's not surprising he's not ready to grab on and ride the Pride Bus to Fire Island with you. Give him a minute."

Devon was right, but the truth didn't make reality any easier.

"But what if he never is?" Riku hated to voice his true fear.

Devon shrugged. "You won't know unless you try. Go make him dinner."

Riku gave his fear voice. "If he shows."

Instead of reassuring him, Devon shrugged. "If he shows."

NO NEED to freak out when Stefano didn't show, Riku would—

"Oh, you came?" No way to keep the shock out of his voice. In all Riku's mental gymnastics, he hadn't thought about what to do if Stefano came.

Stefano jumped off the steps, a pink bakery box in his hand. "Um, you did invite me for tonight, right? I mean, I can go—"

"No. I didn't know if you'd come." Riku went with honesty.

"Well, it takes a little more than *that*, but if you ordered me to...." He gave him a teasing grin.

Riku covered his snort with his hand. He shook his head and unlocked the door. "You're the master of mixed messages. Please come in."

Stefano must have noticed Riku slipping out of his shoes, because he stepped out of his boots. He set the box on the hallway table and helped Riku off with his jacket. Then he hung Riku's along with his in the coat closet.

Riku stared. He wasn't used to having someone consider his needs. Odd, since he was a Dominant, but there it was.

Clearing his throat, he tried to shake the nonsense out of his head. "Do you like stir-fry pork and vegetables?"

"Sure. These are for you. I got them from the new bakery." Stefano smiled.

Riku accepted the box. "Thank you. I've been meaning to stop in there."

He led Stefano through the house.

"I got a variety of cookies. How can I—wow. I love this kitchen. It's so open, and the red shocks you after all the whites and creams of the rest of the house."

Riku washed his hands and took the marinating pork cutlets out of the refrigerator. He had planned on cooking and freezing, but now he'd share a meal with Stefano.

As Stefano washed his hands, he said, "Put me to work, Mas—Riku."

His heart skipped a beat at Stefano almost calling him Master, but Riku kept it together. "Of course. You can start by washing and chopping these vegetables."

The awkwardness slipped away, and a comfortable silence descended as they cut the vegetables.

Riku cooked, and Stefano cleaned and set the island with plates and glasses of filtered water with lemon.

These domestic activities together gave Riku a level of contentment he'd never experienced.

When they sat, Stefano piled vegetables and pork on Riku's plate and then his own. "Thank you. It smells delicious."

"Thank you for serving me, Stefano."

Heat and excitement flashed in Stefano's eyes, and Riku's body responded.

The moment hung there, neither saying a word but almost daring the other to do something.

Riku came to his senses and gestured to Stefano's plate. "Eat."

Stefano bowed his head and his lips moved silently except for the ending, "Amen."

They ate and shared stories of their day like this was the most natural thing in the world, except for the elephant in the room. "So tell me, why did you stop by my office? It wasn't really to return the shirt."

Stefano shrugged. "No, I guess not. I'm just trying to put things together. Figure things out, you know?"

Setting his utensils down, Riku asked, "And you needed someone to talk to?"

"Yup." Stefano stood, took the plates to the sink, and rinsed them.

"Do you drink wine?"

Stefano nodded. "Yes, my sister is trying to expand my palate from beer."

"Let me put the leftovers in the refrigerator. We can open a bottle and talk." Riku got to work saving the food while Stefano efficiently placed all the dishes, including the wok, into the dishwasher with an amazing ability to use all the available space.

He guided Stefano over to the sofa. After sitting with stemmed wineglasses in their hands, Riku raised his glass. "To you."

"*Salute.*" He clinked glasses and drank the entire contents of his glass.

Riku tasted some of his. The white wine was sweeter than he was used to, but the candied taste was perfect for after dinner. He poured a small amount in Stefano's glass, because he'd be driving home later on.

Silence hung between them. Gone was the easy chatter from the kitchen.

Stefano cleared his throat. "I guess I used to play dumb."

Big realization to start off with, so Riku figured it was best not to go with *what do you mean* and asked the simpler, "Why?"

Staring at the fireplace, Stefano shrugged. "Frank always says to admit you have knowledge means you have responsibility."

Trying to gently probe, Riku encouraged with an "Oh?"

Stefano wrung his hands and then rubbed them on his jeans. "I think I'm bisexual."

Riku kept his mouth shut and waited for more.

Sighing, Stefano continued, "You know, there were times I found myself on Walnut and Thirteenth looking for someone to use and hurt me." Stefano threw out the words as carelessly as he allowed himself to be treated.

"Hurt you?" Riku was gutted by the idea of someone harming Stefano in such a manner. Originally, Riku had believed Stefano's actions were more about having sex with men, but could the desire also be connected to BDSM?

Stefano took a big sip of the wine. "People who are into quick hookups aren't always considerate with the other person. Sex with other men always made me feel dirty and used."

So many things were wrong with that statement, Riku didn't know where to begin. "I can only imagine."

Shaking his head, Stefano said, "I don't think you can."

Riku leaned forward. He wanted desperately to understand. "Can you trust me enough to explain exactly what you mean?"

"I'll try." Stefano finished the rest of his wine. "I was thirteen. There was a priest—"

Riku tried not to react, but his breath caught.

"I was asked to be an altar boy. My family was proud I'd been picked to serve the Church." His voice had gone monotone.

Riku struggled to remain silent when he could guess where Stefano's story was headed.

"Which turned into hell. It was my fault. I didn't stop him… couldn't stop him. When I told my father… well, you've seen my back." The words came tumbling out, devoid of emotion. Stripped of their horrifying impact, as if Stefano spoke about someone else.

Riku's brain tried to push out the horror Stefano's story etched into him. "Stefano, it wasn't your fault. You were a child."

Tears ran out of the corners of Stefano's unfocused eyes. "It couldn't be happening. He was a priest. But I already knew by that time I was *different*. Sometimes I found men attractive… some."

There were no words that could be said to make this better, so Riku just listened.

Stefano grimaced and added, "But not him. Never him. But how could he…? Maybe my father was right—there was something wrong with me."

"Nothing is wrong with you." Riku couldn't emphasize that strongly enough, though he knew it wouldn't be easy to change Stefano's ingrained thought.

"Father Lucca had asked me to stay after mass to help clean the sanctuary. I shouldn't have had my back to the door. I didn't hear him come in, and then it was too late." Stefano's voice had gotten softer.

"I'm so sorry." Riku buried his rage at everyone failing to protect Stefano.

Stefano turned his attention onto Riku. "So, having all that happen, how could I possibly want more of *that*? How could I be so broken that I'd want more of that?"

Riku's heart screamed that Stefano wasn't broken, but Riku didn't want to invalidate him. He didn't need to be a psychologist to see Stefano's teenaged mind must have connected rape with the desire to be with men. That harmful thought resulted in biphobia, reinforced by everything around him. All Riku could come up with to say was "It must have been devastating."

"I'm broken." Stefano straightened his spine. He shrugged like his words didn't matter. "I just hate how it's still affecting me."

From what little Riku knew of abuse, it had to have touched every part of Stefano's life. His expression had gone blank during the telling. Stefano's lack of expression and dismissal suggested he buried the pain in order to function. "How can I be here for you?"

"I don't know. I feel lost. I don't even know if I'm really gay or bisexual. I never looked too deeply before. There was no reason to."

Not wanting to try to parse out whether Stefano was referring to Riku being the reason, Riku said, "Avoiding something that has brought you such pain is understandable."

He pushed away the urge to hold Stefano. He needed to give Stefano what he needed, and right now his stiff body suggested space.

"If I'm truly honest, I think part of me has trouble figuring out my orientation, because if it's anything other than straight, it would be like wanting what happened to me."

How did Riku disagree with this well-honed belief without minimizing Stefano's pain? But with that as a thought process, how could Stefano ever have a healthy relationship, regardless of his orientation? Though it might explain why he went to Thirteenth and Walnut. No questions were asked.

Stefano sighed and continued, "And BDSM, talk about a mind fuck. How could I want to hand over power to someone when that only results in hurt... except during the demo."

That confession eased something in Stefano, so Riku confirmed, "You didn't feel like that with the demonstration we did?"

"No, I felt worshipped almost, cared for. You saw me. When I hurt, you acknowledged my pain and pressed more on the knots, telling me how good I was to endure the hurt. And then you got me through to the other side and made me feel like I could do anything."

Stefano needed therapy, but in this moment, he didn't need Riku telling him that.

Though Riku had to know. "How did the sex feel afterward... with me?"

Stefano stared at him for a long moment. "Usually being with a man makes me feel terrible, like everything my father and Marco had ever called me and more is true. But I wanted to suck on you, not to punish myself. Because with you everything I wanted to do felt right and good."

Riku nodded because he didn't trust his voice. At least they were on the same page.

"Afterward, I should have called, but I was all up in my head about admitting I was bisexual or gay and what that all means. I've been researching...."

No wonder Stefano didn't text back. "Exploring your orientation is a huge deal. Doing that is very brave of you."

"But I have this voice saying how stupid I am to want that after what happened." Stefano's voice was no longer monotone, and he sounded more like himself.

Internal voices could be brutal. Riku added, "And the Church reinforced the negative beliefs you had about yourself, bisexuality, and homosexuality. Anything other than heterosexual is presented as wrong."

"Though not all churches do. Frank and my sister go to a UU church, where they're even having a wedding."

Riku was happy two people in Stefano's family seemed open-minded. "Same-sex couple?"

"Yes, and the two women have been together for twenty years." His words held a wistful tone.

"Amazing." It wasn't the time to confess he always hoped to find someone who fit him so well he wanted to spend forever with them, so he'd keep the wish to himself.

"You know, when I kissed you after the demonstration, that was the first time I'd ever kissed a man."

Under the circumstances, it wasn't surprising, but it saddened Riku's heart. Keeping an even tone, he clarified, "You didn't kiss any of the men you were with?"

"Nah, no one I let pick me up was there for that." Stefano's grimace said he hadn't been there for kissing either.

Ignoring his own pain on behalf of Stefano, Riku asked something much simpler. "Did you like our kiss?"

Turning red, either from the wine or the question, Stefano grinned. "I did... and if you'd let me, I'd kiss you some more."

Here was where ground rules needed to be made. Maybe after all Stefano said, Riku shouldn't push, but out of self-preservation for his own feelings and Stefano's, this needed to be kept in check. "It's probably not fair to ask you right now, but what are you looking for?"

Pressing his lips together, Stefano shifted away from Riku. "I don't know. I mean... I really don't know."

After a minute, Stefano gave him a small smile and rested a hand on Riku's thigh, hardening his cock.

Riku wanted a chance to see where this went. He had to be honest. "I'm too old to go back in the closet."

Shaking his head vehemently, Stefano quietly informed him, "Don't expect you to, but I'm not ready to come out."

Riku knew that, he did, but it still didn't stop him from hoping for a very different answer. "That's understandable."

"What?" Stefano must have read him.

He longed to say nothing and just follow wherever this went, but he couldn't. "Honesty is necessary for a reality check. I've got to say, you scare me."

"Me?" Stefano leaned back and furrowed his brow.

"Yeah. I'm afraid I'll get caught up in you and you'll never be ready." *To fully be mine* was left unsaid.

Stefano took his hand off Riku and stared straight ahead. "I know that's not fair to you."

Riku would be putting his heart on the line while having no control over the outcome. It wouldn't be a matter of working harder on the relationship if one of the people involved couldn't admit they had a relationship.

He'd played that game in his early twenties. Expecting the other person to come out or to want things out of BDSM they didn't was folly. Hadn't he learned? How could he even consider going down this route again?

Stefano frowned, and tears gathered in his eyes. "I'm sorry. This is probably a terrible idea."

Everything in Riku longed to give Stefano what he craved, even if just for a little while. How could he deny him? He couldn't stop himself from asking, "What?"

Shaking his head, Stefano said, "Nothing."

"Stefano?" Riku's commanding tone slipped out. He wanted to know and wasn't above reminding Stefano of who they had been to each other. Who they could be—

No.

Twisting his hands in his lap, Stefano peeked through long lashes. "I can't help it. I want to kiss you so bad."

Such a soul-melting admission. Against Riku's better judgment, he leaned in and glided his lips over Stefano's.

The bliss-filled sigh that escaped Stefano lit places deep inside of Riku, spreading a warmth he craved.

Maybe common sense wasn't all it was cracked up to be.

Riku guided Stefano onto his lap.

Pliant and willing, Stefano slid into what appeared to be his rightful place. He licked his lips and parted them, waiting for Riku's bidding.

Ah, what a good sub. A charge of dominance zipped through Riku at witnessing his lesson was learned. Stefano understood who was in control of the kiss. Riku rewarded him with a toe-curling kiss.

He licked into Stefano's warm mouth, tasting the sweet wine, and maybe a little bit of smoke from his cigarettes. The soft mewls of surrender that came out with the kiss screamed out, making him want to conquer Stefano for his own. He deepened the kiss.

Riku's heart tried to open and allow Stefano in, so he pulled back.

Stefano's clinging lips didn't make the task easy.

"There." Riku didn't mean to be cold, but taking this further would be foolish.

Riku asked without truly knowing the answer, "I need to ask again, Stefano. What do you want?"

"Whatever you do… *Master*." Stefano's eyes had a dreamy look, and his pupils had spread into the soft brown.

Stefano must know the power in that word. How could any Dominant refuse to accept what he handed over? At the same time, it was impossible not to want to protect him.

Time and space would help give them both perspective. "Would you like some of the cookies you brought?"

"Um, yes." Stefano climbed off him and stood. "I can put them out."

How could Riku refuse Stefano's desire to serve him? "Thank you. I'll show you where the plates are. Would you like tea or decaf coffee?"

Riku opened the cabinet holding his plates and serving pieces.

"Decaf coffee would be nice. Thank you, Riku." Stefano arranged the cookies artfully on the small oval platter.

Back to *Riku*; the *Master* title had vanished. Riku didn't like how his name twisted into some kind of inaccurate title that suggested distance and lack of ownership. It shouldn't eat at him, but it did.

Though he was the one who had pulled them back. Could he blame Stefano, who was already so unsure, if he did the same?

Riku made him a decaf coffee and himself a rose-and-chamomile tea. He gathered napkins. "Do you take anything in your coffee?"

"Nope. Milk or sugar in your tea?"

Gasping, Riku shook his head. "Never."

Stefano chuckled and carried everything to the coffee table. "Got it."

Riku followed, trying not to imagine the luxury of having someone to share things with. Quiet evenings, binge-watching bad TV shows, meals, talking about all the little and big things. He studied Stefano, who arranged the beverages, napkins, and plates. "We really need to figure out what you want, Stefano."

"I want more of you. Everything is new and confusing, but when I'm with you, it's not. Things make sense." He calmly sipped his coffee like he hadn't set off a bomb.

New and confusing—that was an understatement, considering he'd just gotten to subspace, started to question his sexuality beyond having sex with other men, and was dealing with both physical and sexual abuse.

Riku wanted to help him. Anyone would.

Bullshit!

He longed for so much more, and for some reason his heart seemed determined and set on Stefano. "Have some cookies."

Stefano picked one chocolate-dipped madeleine and a rose-topped white-iced petit four. He devoured the madeleine in two bites and caught Riku staring. "Don't you like cookies?"

"I do." Riku picked a blue-flowered chocolate-iced petit four and a rose-topped one. "But these are my favorite. More cake than cookie."

"These are lemon-poppy and a lavender sugar." Stefano put two other cookies on his plate.

"Lavender sugar, yum." Riku took a bite of each. "Thank you for this. I rarely take the time to go to an actual bakery, but I do have a bit of a sweet tooth."

"You'd never know it." Stefano gave him a slow perusal, along with a lust-filled smile.

Pleased that Stefano noticed, Riku admitted, "I'm up by 5:30 a.m. every day to exercise."

"I need to start."

Stefano wasn't fishing for compliments, but Riku had to say, "You look like you get plenty of exercise."

Stefano looked away and appeared charmingly embarrassed by the compliment as he munched on the cookies. "Thanks, but I should do some cardio."

Only sips of warm beverages and bites of cookies broke the comfortable silence between them.

Stefano glanced over with fuck-me-now eyes. He seemed completely unaware of how well he charmed Riku.

Meaning Riku needed to cut to the chase. "Stefano, I really like you. I think I could like you a whole lot, given the chance. You're an incredible submissive who checks everything on my Dominant wish list, but maybe we can just hang out as friends until you figure out what you want."

Stefano slumped back against the couch, frowned, and nodded. "I guess that makes sense."

Riku buried the disappointment of how easily Stefano agreed.

"I should head home, but I'm afraid to leave your side."

"Why?"

"Everything is perfectly clear when I'm with you, but when I'm alone I get lost. I'm afraid I won't find my way back to you." Stefano kissed him on the cheek and left.

CHAPTER 13

FOR THE last two nights, Stefano hadn't slept well, though he had clarity on what he wanted. If he were honest, he'd figured out a couple of weeks ago what he needed, but now maybe he could have a bit of it.

He wanted a good person who could be a strong Master and didn't shrink away from the shards that resided in Stefano's mind. Someone who could help him be the submissive he was meant to be. The fact Riku was hot as fuck happened to be a bonus.

Riku being a guy didn't bother Stefano like he thought it might, but he still had a fuck-ton to clarify in his brain.

He hoped doing this might help him figure things out. When he checked his watch again, finally the numbers read 5:35 a.m.

Stefano rang the doorbell and dropped to his knees.

Go big or go home.

Riku opened the door. His eyes went wide, and his mouth dropped open. He stood there, dressed in gray sweats and a black T-shirt with the image of yellow marshmallow chicks in bondage gear. Sneakers in hand, his feet were bare.

In a moment his face morphed into what Stefano thought of as a Master's mask. Some were better than others. Riku's stare wasn't indifferent but was all about confidence and control and scorched Stefano from the inside out. The gaze stripped him naked and made him long to get a reaction out of Riku.

Trying not to grin at Riku's T-shirt, Stefano straightened his back. Who knew Peeps were into BDSM?

"Stefano, please explain." Riku's calm tone suggested having another man kneeling on his porch was just a usual start to every Saturday morning.

"I figured out what I want… *Master*. I'm not good enough to be your sub, but if you'd let me, I'd like to try."

"Are you ready to come out?"

Stefano dropped his head. "Not yet, but I plan to. Can you give me some time?"

"I won't force you to come out, but I can't go back in. Let's give this six months and then see where we are, but I have conditions." Riku seemed to have thought about this possibility. Did he hope for something to happen between them as much as Stefano had?

"Yes, Mast—Sir." He shouldn't assume. Staring up at the Master he most wanted to worship and knowing he wasn't worthy, he waited.

"We will work together on you quitting smoking, and once you have full-time benefits, I want you to work with a therapist—"

"But Sir, I don't need therapy." Did Riku think he couldn't handle himself?

"Stefano, I want nothing more than for you to call me Master, but if whatever this is between us ends in heartbreak, I would have our time together truly mean something. Those two things are my nonnegotiables that will be worth any future pain." No sugarcoating his expectations of this ending in disaster.

Stefano didn't know what to make of the fact both things Riku demanded were for Stefano's betterment. He'd always wanted to quit smoking, though therapy... not so much. But he needed to ask, "Why do you think this is doomed even before we begin?"

"In the past, several subs found my kind of BDSM intrusive, and my need to be out and open was an insurmountable obstacle. I can't assume this won't be the same."

You was implied. Why did the assumption hurt Stefano? He didn't want to fail the way others had. Riku deserved... no, *his Master* deserved better.

"Please allow me to try... Master." He might not have earned the right to call Riku that beyond their demonstration, but he was going to do so until Riku asked him to stop.

Riku considered him for a long moment and then asked, "What's your safeword?"

"*Munch*, Master." Each time the title felt better and better coming out of Stefano's mouth.

"Give me your hands, Stefano." Riku reached out with both hands and helped him off his knees.

"Thank you." Stefano didn't hesitate, because accepting the help made Riku smile. He held on a little longer than necessary, absorbing the stability.

"I was headed down to exercise. Would you join me?"

Was he serious? One look at the arched eyebrow gave Stefano his answer. "Yes, though I don't have—"

"You're already in sneakers. I have some shorts and a T-shirt you can wear." Riku hurried toward his bedroom.

The things Stefano expected to find, like an unmade bed or clothing on the floor, he didn't. What he saw gut-punched him. The biker shorts and T-shirt he'd worn the night of the demonstration were folded and lay on the bed... on top of one set of pillows.

Riku came out of the walk-in closet and stopped as he must have realized what Stefano was staring at. He handed him a set of workout clothing and grabbed the pile of clothing on the bed, along with the pillowcases. "I guess I can wash those now."

What the fuck did that mean? Why would he sleep with Stefano's clothing? Shouldn't this creep Stefano out?

He studied Riku. The answer was in his new Master's eyes. Riku cared about him. The affection ran much deeper than either of them was comfortable acknowledging, so Stefano stated, "I'll get dressed and meet you downstairs."

"Yes. I'll leave the basement door open."

When he arrived downstairs, wow! The basement was just as impressive as the rest of the house. One side was a home theater, and the other was a workout place.

Riku put down the weights he held. "Why don't you start a basic workout on the bike?"

"How does it work?" Seemed fancy, and he didn't want to bust the thing.

Riku showed him and set the program. He grabbed two bottles of water from a black refrigerator Stefano hadn't seen next to the popcorn maker. Riku put one in the cup holder for him. "This will run forty-five minutes. Hit Start when you're ready."

Swallowing hard, Stefano nodded. It was just water, but to him the bottle meant his Master was looking out for him, and that was everything.

Stefano jumped on and followed the instructions on the screen, which showed a pretty country road.

His eyes kept drifting over to the better scenery of Riku running. Goddamn him, but he'd never seen such a firm ass in sweats before... and Riku's toned arms pumped.

Riku glanced over and gave him a grin. Oh, the bastard knew. "Drink some water, Stefano."

"Yes, Master." Forcing his eyes away so he would stop drooling, because erections were not helpful when pedaling a bike, he did as he'd been instructed.

"Well done." Riku gave him a nod of approval.

Crazy, but praise for drinking water felt like an A+ that needed to be hung on the refrigerator. He absorbed the positives even if he felt silly to crave the praise. And Riku still hadn't corrected him on the "Master," so maybe that was okay by him.

You're silly and stupid and unworthy. There was no defense against the truth. He pedaled harder and faster.

Riku's run turned into a jog. "You've done great for your first workout on the bike. The program should be going into cooldown in another minute or so."

I've done great. Riku's words silenced the nasty voice. *I've done great. I've done great.*

The bike's resistance eased, and Stefano followed the cooldown path. He drank the rest of his water, and when the program finished, he jumped off.

Stefano led him in a few stretches. His body felt good, loose, and ready.

"Let's go take showers."

His "yes" dried to dust when Riku led him to another bathroom not connected to the master bedroom. Riku pulled out towels. "Shampoo, soap, and conditioner are in the shower. I store extra toothbrushes, pastes, brushes, along with hair products, in this drawer. Use whatever you want."

"Thank you." Stefano tried to cover his disappointment. He had expected to serve Riku in the shower.

He took a thorough shower, brushed his teeth, and wished his sister were there to show him how to use the hair products. Figuring mousse was his safest bet, he ran that through his hair. Clothing! How could he have forgotten? Wearing a towel, he opened the door and found the pile of his clothing outside the door.

Grabbing the clothing off the floor, he hugged the pile to his chest. His Master thought of him. He sniffed and…. He dressed and followed the delicious smells to the kitchen.

His Master had prepared a feast of eggs, turkey bacon, low-carb wraps, and black coffee, making his heart rev like someone pressed the accelerator on a classic car.

Stefano hurried to set the counter. "Thank you, Riku… Master. When should I call you what?"

"I'm not hung up on names or titles. I'd rather you do what feels right to you. Then I'll gauge my behavior on you."

Huh? "But you're the Master. I should gauge my actions on what you want."

Riku set his cup of tea on the counter. "No one said those two agendas have to be exclusive. We can both try to provide for the other."

"You're really not like most of the Mistresses I've been with." Stefano wasn't comfortable with this concept. He was a sub; he was meant to serve.

"I expect they were giving you what they thought you needed. I'll do the same after breakfast."

Stefano's dick lengthened. "We're going to do a scene?"

"Of sorts. Are you okay with allowing me to give my submissive what I believe he needs?" The words rolled off Riku's tongue but got stuck in Stefano's brain.

My submissive… his submissive….

"Stefano?"

"Oh, sorry." He shook himself back from the sub serenade.

"Looks like you were headed toward subspace with your own thoughts," Riku teased.

"I might have been. I'm looking forward to finding out what a 'scene of sorts' means." Stefano hoped Riku was hard on him, punished him, denied him, and maybe even humiliated him, putting him in his place.

WHEN BREAKFAST was finished and cleaned up, Stefano stood next to Riku, shifting from foot to foot. "What should I do, Master?"

"Use the bathroom. It's a Washlet so the water can clean you, and there's even warm air to dry you. The remote is above the toilet paper. There are guest toothbrushes in there as well. Then undress."

"Yes, Master."

Stefano used the toilet and played with the remote. The temperature of the water was set to warm, and the damn thing could pulsate and even oscillate. The dryer gave a new meaning to the word "blowjob." He washed his hands, brushed his teeth, and made sure his curly hair had dried without frizzing.

He folded his clothing and took a deep breath. Was he ready for his first official scene *of sorts* with his Master?

Shouldn't this feel more foreign to him? He waited for what he now knew was called internalized biphobia to strike as he stared at the mirror.

The light shadow on his face and his sprinkling of chest hair did a reasonable job of making him look manly. But that wasn't what made him a man.

The voice remained silent. Stefano was prepared to do anything Riku said, so he left the bathroom, clutching his clothing.

"Put your clothing on the stool in the kitchen." Riku's black leather pants clung to his powerful thighs and cupped his junk just right. He wore a black leather vest with a red dragon scrolled on each side.

Stefano felt the chill of the floor on his feet, but his cock only received heat from his Master's observation.

Riku waved him into the living room.

Instead of finding crops, restraints, and paddles, there was a massage table covered in a towel and several bottles of essential oils.

Confused, he had to ask, "You want me to massage you, Master?"

"Not today, Stefano. I require you to simply be." The words were laced with enough steel to make Stefano shiver.

"Yes, Master." How did one just be? Rule number one of being: don't beg to be beaten or fucked up the ass with no lube. He pressed his lips together.

Am I simply being now?

"Please lie facedown on the table," Master commanded.

Stefano did, but the chaos in his mind swirled. *How would this be a scene? Why didn't Riku let me service him? What about—I need to trust my Master and simply be.*

"Good," Riku commented, as if able to hear Stefano's twists and turns. Did he understand the crazy this scene caused? They hadn't even started, but at least when he lay down, there was no gasp of pity at his messed-up back.

His Master's praise centered Stefano.

"Your safeword is *Munch*, correct?" The words were calming and even lulling.

"Yes, Master," he muttered to start the scene. He braced himself to find out how his Master would punish him.

"I'm going to worship your body."

Huh? Stefano struggled to push onto his elbows. "I don't understand."

Riku put a hand on his upper ass. "I know. Please lie back down."

The Master's tone zapped Stefano back into sub mode. Not his place to question or even think right now. "Yes, Master. I'm sorry, Master."

"Stay as still as you can. I'm going to touch you and cherish your skin."

Stefano gasped. "You're going to what?"

Riku didn't respond to Stefano's not very sub-like outburst as he spread a sweet-smelling orange oil over Stefano's back. "This is the oil I used on you at the office. But that's where the similarity of your experience ends. This will be nothing like that visit."

Talented hands and fingers danced over Stefano's back, unwinding coils of tension as easily as if they were ropes.

"Your scars have a harsh beauty to them."

"Nah. They're fucking ugly." Stefano wished he could hide all the disgusting parts from Riku.

Riku patted his butt. "Nothing about you is ugly. You're a survivor. You're strong, rather magnificent, and quite beautiful."

His Master continued to loosen the muscles under the scars.

Stefano sniffed. Maybe he was getting a cold. "That's nonsense."

"Are you calling me a liar?" He didn't have to see Riku's arched eyebrow; Stefano heard it.

Was he? There was no way Riku could actually think that. But.... "I don't know, Master."

"I understand." Riku rubbed oil on every section of Stefano's back with his warm, talented hands.

Stefano yawned and fought the relaxation threatening to overwhelm him. "I like that scent, Master."

"Good, we're going to do this a lot." Riku made the decree as if Stefano would say no. Even though this felt nothing like a scene—

Riku buffed his hands over Stefano's ass. "I want you to say, 'I'm beautiful.'"

This was stupid. He should just safeword and end this bullshit.

Fine. Whatever. He could mouth the words, and he wouldn't even roll his eyes. "I'm beautiful."

"Well done, Stefano." Riku's tone suggested he understood how Stefano tried to play him, but for whatever reason he let it slide.

Dammit, Stefano wanted to earn the praise; otherwise it grated, showing his flaws.

Riku massaged his arms, releasing more tension Stefano didn't know he had. Then he lightly caressed trails up and down Stefano's arms.

How was this a scene?

Stefano tried not to fight the shivers the caresses gave him as waves of pleasure shot through his body. The relaxation turned into sweeping erotic feelings and raced down to his now very erect cock.

He shifted, trying to rearrange his dick so—there. Nope, now it throbbed against the table.

His Master rubbed and relaxed Stefano's legs, but all that did was give a bit of friction to his already needy cock.

Stefano released a quiet moan. "What are you doing?"

"Cherishing you. You deserve someone to see you as the treasure you are." Riku's words sliced into Stefano's heart, letting some of his pain pour out.

His eyes welled with tears. He should safeword and stop this fuckery.

"I know you could endure all the pain in the world. I see your scars and can only imagine what you survived. Right now I want you to tell me you'll be my treasure—at least for the next six months. I know we haven't agreed to anything longer."

Stefano didn't know what hurt more, the expiration date or having to say he was a treasure when he was anything but.

His Master kneaded his ass. He didn't deserve such pleasure.

"Stefano, I know we've not spoken of the consequences of your disobedience, but trust me when I say I'm fully capable of disciplining you. Now tell me or use your safeword."

How could he make Riku understand how broken and awful he was? Wiping his eyes on the towel, Stefano forced out the words. "But I'm not a treasure."

Riku patted his ass. "I know right now you don't think you are. You currently don't have a reliable view of yourself, so I'll ask you to take on mine even if you don't quite believe how I and others see you yet."

Right then, while Stefano didn't believe he was anything other than a lot of baggage, he did want to be Riku's. "Yes, Master. I will be your… *treasure*."

"I'm going to touch you and ask you some questions. I would like you to be honest. If you can't, I expect you to safeword, understand?"

"Yes, Master." Stefano squirmed, and the fucking friction went right to his cock.

His Master massaged Stefano's back, making him boneless, and then glided lower, polishing oiled hands over Stefano's ass. He rubbed in slow circles, making Stefano relaxed and excited all at once. "Do you want me to touch you?"

The parting and closing of Stefano's buttcheeks brought to mind how long it had been since Stefano had been fucked. "God yes, Master."

He was rewarded with Riku's thumbs digging deeper into the crack of his ass as he massaged. "How does it make you feel when I do this?"

"Good, but sometimes bad, but always back to good." Stefano gasped the last word as Riku rocked Stefano's hips against the table. If he kept doing that, Stefano would come.

"Turn over." Riku gave him a too-light tap on his ass.

Begging for a harder smack wasn't a sub's place. He rolled over as Riku was there to guide him onto his back and protect him from finding the floor.

"Why?" His Master circled his finger over the glistening tip of Stefano's erection. "Why does my touch feel good, then bad, then back to good?"

Jesus, that one finger was going to make him come. "I feel like my head is fighting what my body wants."

His Master spread Stefano's wetness around the crown and ran that wicked finger along his shaft. He circled the base and traced a vein back to the top. "Why?"

"I don't know."

The touch stopped. Sadness, anger, and confusion ripped through Stefano. He didn't want to say the words.

Riku caressed Stefano's cheek, encouraging him to open his eyes. When he did, Riku said, "Sometimes naming the demons helps. Can you try? What makes you fight what your body wants?"

Anger faded and tears slipped out of the corners of his eyes. It seemed impossible for him not to give Riku anything he asked. "The Church, my father, and… with what happened…. How could I want this?"

Stefano's voice broke into silent sobs that racked his entire body. He curled into Riku, wanting to merge with the person who seemed to bring all these confusing feelings to the surface. He wanted more, yet he kept waiting for the voice inside him to torment him for longing to have a man… a Master… Riku.

Strong arms wrapped around Stefano, stabilizing him, allowing him to vent a little more of the poison from his guts.

Gentle strokes on his face along with soft sounds helped bring him back from the pit of hell. The words started to register. "It must be terrible to have gone through so much at such a young age."

Stefano tried to agree, but his voice didn't work. He nodded jerkily.

"When you went to someone who was supposed to protect you, he abused you and blamed you for it." Riku's words were soft but shredded him.

Sobs racked his body because people who should have protected him didn't. Riku saw him and everything he'd been through and said he was a treasure.

"I want to be here for you any way I can."

Long minutes later, when he had control of himself, Stefano confessed, "I hate that I'm broken."

"Life may have bent you a little, but you're not broken." Riku kept one hand on Stefano and grabbed a blanket with the other. He wrapped him up and half carried, half walked him to the couch.

There were no words. Riku held him while Stefano clung, depending on his Master to keep him safe.

AN ETERNITY later, Stefano was wrapped in a blanket, still in Riku's arms. Riku appeared to have dozed off with him as they lay on the sofa.

There was no denying Riku was strikingly handsome. He had an elegant, sophisticated way about him that made Stefano remember how far out of his league Riku was.

I'm his treasure. Maybe if he repeated that enough it would seep into his brain.

Such dominance, yet kindness, shattered Stefano.

Riku's body was a work of art: lean but not perfect—exactly why it couldn't have been made even by the best sculptor.

Stefano's dick hardened and pressed against Riku's thigh. Fuck, those muscular thighs. He tried to readjust his cock, but that rubbed his dick on the blanket, sending pleasure shooting through him.

His Master smiled at Stefano like he was special and important. "You're a wiggle worm."

"A wiggle worm? I thought I was a treasure." Stefano couldn't stop from chortling.

"Mmmm, you are," Riku said, right before he pressed his lips to Stefano's.

Stefano melted into him. The kiss deepened, sending fireworks shooting off behind his eyelids. Shooting off sounded like the best plan ever. He shifted forward and started rutting against Riku.

Stefano broke the kiss and dared him, "Master, show me why I crave this so much."

Riku's hand wrapped around his cock and stroked.

"I want to touch you too. May I?"

Riku stopped and stood. He growled as he struggled to get naked. "Erection or leather pants. One is great, add the second and there's a problem."

Stefano snorted until Riku won the struggle and kicked off his leather. He stood in front of him, nothing like the haughty Ice King Stefano once imagined.

Riku's erection was a good size and had a slight bend to the left. A drop rolled out from the tip. Stefano longed to blow him without a condom, but Riku would never allow that, and maybe that was for the best.

Right now, he just wanted to get Riku off and come himself.

He spit into his palm and glided his hand over Riku's shaft.

"Oh." Riku moaned and thrust into his hand. "Let me sit alongside you."

Riku sat, flicked his tongue over his palm, grasped Stefano's dick, and started stroking.

"Fuck." The sensation was like lighting a sparkler and wanting to touch the tip.

"Don't swear."

Stefano snorted but kept stroking. His chuckle got lost in a groan as Riku sped the tugs up. "Kiss me, please."

"You do enjoy kissing," Riku teased him.

"Kissing you is even better than getting head. Your lips make me crazy." No fronting or calling the words back. He might not be able to be out yet, but when they were alone, Riku should have no doubts of Stefano's… feelings.

"Come when you want." Riku wrapped an arm around him and pulled him close. He captured his lips and took control, making Stefano want to do all the submissive things in the world.

Instead he grunted and came. *Damn, damn, damn.*

Riku groaned into Stefano's mouth and unleashed warm cum that rolled over Stefano's hand, making him complete.

Stefano slumped back on the couch. "Well, that was quite a scene *of sorts.*"

His Master kissed his lips. "That was much more than a scene."

And it was.

CHAPTER 14

"STEFANO. EARTH to Stefano." Frank waved a hand in front of his face.

"Oh, um…. Sorry. What?" Shit! Stefano was zoning out again. Jeez, he couldn't even have dinner with Frank without daydreaming.

His brother smiled. "I asked if you could pass me a taco shell."

"Sure." Stefano hurried to hand him the empty shell he'd been holding, grabbed one for himself, and added turkey.

Shit! For the past three weeks since Riku agreed to be his Master, Stefano had been gliding through his days. His brain focused on his next visit to Riku's townhouse and not on much else.

It was weird how many things reminded him of Riku. Hell, yesterday a dumb commercial about green tea gave him wood.

His sessions with Riku even encouraged him to focus on the positive things.

"What are you thinking about?"

Riku…. "I don't know. I guess at lunch today I watched a plastic bag."

"And?" Frank leaned forward.

"It's dumb, but the wind caught the plastic, and the bag whirled and floated like it danced. Stupid…."

"Nah, it's interesting. Something no one wanted, threw it away, and you were able to find the magic in it."

You're a piece of trash no one wanted. His brain countered, *Riku wants you.*

Stefano shook his head. "Angie would be worried about the bag getting into the ocean and strangling a dolphin, so I figured when it landed I'd throw it away—"

"I bet it never came down."

"Nope." Stefano had been glad. He liked to imagine the bag gliding around the world on wind currents, touching people with its magic.

Frank grinned at him, then bit into the taco.

It was crazy how different his world had become in such a short time of knowing Riku. He wanted to share things he never thought twice about. He kept a running list of things he'd tell Riku, like today when he'd stood up to the other mechanic who kept offloading the shit work onto him, or about the new scrap part he'd collected for the piece he was trying to finish.

Was this what happy felt like?

Frank studied him over the top of his glasses. "So, will you be disappearing again tonight?"

The time slipped by between accidentally-on-purpose diner meetups and scenes.

"Yeah, probably. You?"

"Early court tomorrow." Frank kept staring at him.

Stefano tried not to wiggle like a bug under a magnifying glass. "What?"

"Just wondering who you're seeing."

"I hang out with Riku sometimes. I told you we're exercising together and… stuff." Yeah, that didn't sound guilty.

The eyebrow of a well-schooled attorney rose. "You've been seeing a lot of him."

"So?" He tried to dial back the defensive tone and failed. "Yeah, he's a good guy."

"Well, invite him over so I can give him the dinner I promised."

Terror whipped through Stefano. Keeping his worlds separate allowed this to work. "No… I mean… it's okay. I'm sure he's forgotten."

"Well, I haven't, and he seems like a nice guy. It would stop Angie getting bent out of shape that I don't do anything but work."

"But you don't." Not for nothing, but Frank had to get a life.

Frank grimaced at the reality, but then in a flash he grinned his practiced victory smile. "So for everyone's sake, invite the man to dinner."

Outmaneuvered again. Stefano gave a noncommittal nod and focused on eating.

"And are you seeing anyone about those nightmares?"

Stefano swallowed and opened his mouth to deny—

"I heard you last night. You were asleep when I checked on you, so you might not even remember."

How could he forget? His dreams shoved him right into the darkest parts of his brain he tried to avoid. The brighter his world was during the waking hours, the harsher his dreams became. Last night he'd been held down and hurt by a zombie. He didn't require a therapist to explain the dream to him. *You shouldn't have been there alone… it was all your fault* whispered through him.

"…and we'll have pound cake and strawberries for dessert. How's that sound?" Was Frank talking about what he'd make for Riku?

Um… no clue what his brother planned for a menu, but he agreed. "Great. I'm sure he'd like that."

With effort, Stefano finished his dinner, avoided agreeing to see a therapist, and helped clean up before he escaped to the blissful oblivion that awaited him in Riku's arms… and, um, BDSM of course.

THE USUAL bite of worry grazed its fangs over Stefano's heart as he paused before knocking. He balled his fist but left his hand hanging in the air.

Each time he came to Riku was a choice. *Was it?* Could he ignore his desire to spend as much time with Riku—his Master—as possible? Yes, he could, but he didn't fucking want to deny himself.

Knock! Knock! Knock!

Riku answered his door with a warm smile. Even in bare feet, wearing olive lounge pants and a baggy T-shirt, he still appeared more put together than Stefano ever hoped to be.

"Shall we begin?"

Stefano gave him a nod. "Yes, Master."

He entered the house, took off his shoes, and handed Riku his jacket.

Riku hung the leather jacket in the coat closet right next to his own, making Stefano's heart calm with the rightness. His Master turned and pulled Stefano into a full body embrace, making him feel welcomed. "I missed you."

"I missed you, Master." Stefano melted into the strong body pressed against his.

He swallowed back the fear about what that meant, but for now he allowed himself the luxury of being Riku's… sub.

The greeting ritual began to work its magic, easing him. These moments of transition from one world into a fantasy where only he and Riku existed were precious to him. He was at the start of his time with his Master.

Riku led him to the powder room off the entryway to treat Stefano's hands.

Stefano had learned fussing about doing this was useless. It didn't matter that he'd already scrubbed his hands at work.

His Master checked and adjusted the temperature of the water, and when he was satisfied, he pumped soap into his palm and took Stefano's hands in his.

The tender gesture made Stefano swallow past the lump of emotion in his throat.

"These hands have worked magic. They make broken things work again. We should appreciate them, right?"

Shit! On the surface, handwashing didn't appear to have anything remotely related to BDSM, but the fact Riku demanded they start their time together with self-care somehow pointed Stefano down the path to subspace.

"Yes, Master."

He washed both of their hands with orangey scented soap and rinsed. "Taking the time to do self-care reminds you how important *you* are."

Stefano had learned not to roll his eyes or reject his own importance. In truth, this hand-cleaning ritual relaxed him and reconnected them. Granted, the focused attention turned him on, but maybe he did start to feel like he mattered… at least to Riku.

Then Riku squeezed a dollop of blue soap onto an ornately carved nail brush and buffed Stefano's fingertips until they were soapy. Riku rinsed Stefano's hands and then patted them dry.

As if that wasn't enough, his Master pumped an orange-and-basil-smelling moisturizer into his palm and massaged the cream into Stefano's right hand, then his left.

When he was done, he touched his forehead to Stefano's and their breathing started to sync. As usual, all of the loneliness Stefano shoved down deep came to the surface and evaporated like water on a hot engine.

"If you're ready, let's have tea and talk." Riku guided him to the sofa.

Tea, cups, and sweets were laid out on a tray.

Stefano knelt at the coffee table, the plush rug cushioning him into position. "May I serve you tea, Master?"

"Yes, that would be lovely. I stopped at the bakery and got you those cookies you like."

Eyeing the lavender-iced lemon cookies with the bits of lavender seeds on top, Stefano smiled. "Thank you, Master."

He used to think the big heavy scenes were what mattered, but it was the smallest things that meant so much. Knowing which cookies he liked, taking the time and preparing for him... these were things he didn't know mattered, but they did. His Master expanded his view of BDSM.

Stefano poured the tea into handleless black cups.

"This is Longjing tea. It's grown near where my father's family is from in China. I think you'll enjoy the freshness."

Neither he nor Riku shared much about their families, reinforcing that their time was outside the bounds of the real world. This information wasn't unwelcome. He liked knowing more about Riku and his life, but since he wasn't reciprocating, it wasn't fair to ask.

He filled the second cup, and Riku patted the seat next to him in invitation.

Stefano sat close to his Master, causing their thighs to touch.

Riku handed him a cup of tea and then smelled his own. "Inhale the fragrance."

Doing as instructed, Stefano sniffed his cup. "Smells green. I mean—"

"It does. Try a sip. If you don't like it, we can make you Lipton's green tea."

Stefano had gotten more adventurous with trying new foods and drinks when he was with Riku. His Master hadn't steered him wrong yet. He took a small sip.

The fresh, clean flavors exploded in his mouth. He sipped some more. "Mmmm, I like it."

His Master smiled and handed him a plate containing one of the light purple iced cookies.

"Thank you, Master." Stefano eased against Riku's side, drinking in the pure calm and peace his Master gave off.

Riku held up the text Stefano had sent. "So, you achieved your exercise goal for the third week in a row."

He had exercised with Riku, and on the days he hadn't seen him, he worked out for at least forty-five minutes on his own. He also went for walks on his lunch break, so yeah, he was proud of his accomplishment. "I did."

"Very good. Do you think you'll keep at it?"

Stefano nodded. "I feel better, so yeah, I'd like to."

"Wonderful. What would you like as your reward?"

"For you to fuck me." Stefano hadn't meant to blurt out his request like that, but he'd thought about it a lot. He hadn't been with anyone for a long time, and he was anxious to be used as a cock sleeve.

Riku frowned and shook his head. "Stefano, I will never *fuck* you."

"Why the fuck not?" *You're not good enough—*

"I will be inside you, I will cherish your body, but I will never treat you with the casual disregard a fuck suggests." When Stefano didn't make anything come out of his mouth, Riku continued, "You want it rough, and I can give you that, but you deserve not only that but more."

Swallowing around the nervousness that closed his throat, Stefano couldn't count the many things Riku had left unsaid. Was it about his words? Fine! He'd use other words. Grasping for clarity, he asked, "So how about you being inside me as my reward?"

Riku bit back a smile and shook his head. "When it's time."

"When will that be?" Screw leaving indignation out of his tone, though he did add, "Master."

Sighing, Riku patted him on the knee. "When you realize you're worth more than what you can give me with your body."

Sounded like some philosophical bullshit way of saying no fucking. Maybe he could—running a teasing finger up Riku's thigh—entice him. "Is that a firm no?"

"Unfortunately for both of us, yes. I have control." Master caught his fingers and kissed each of them, forcing more need into Stefano.

Frowning, Stefano grabbed his cookie and slumped back on the sofa. He took a bite of cookie and tried to pacify himself. The lavender-lemon creation didn't come close to compensating for not getting fucked.

"But you did meet your exercise goal, so what is your reward? Other than that, what have you earned?"

Should he ask about bathing Riku again? He had done that in the past with his Mistresses without issue, but when he chose that for his first reward with Riku, he came in his pants almost as soon as the bath began.

"If you're considering asking to bathe me, I think we'll have to use a cock ring." Riku must have read his face.

Stefano felt the delicious warmth of embarrassment creep through him. His Master was an expert at giving him exactly what he craved to build arousal and get him to admit to things he'd rather not.

"No, I...." He what?

"Do you want to try a ropeless predicament scene?" The way his voice dropped suggested Stefano didn't want to miss out on such a treat.

"Um... okay?" Sounded hot... though everything Riku did melted his brain from the inside out.

"Is that a question, Stefano?"

"No, Master. I'd like to try a ropeless predicament scene, please."

"Come to the kitchen." Master turned on his heel and strutted to the kitchen.

"Now that is kinky," Stefano joked, hoping to ease his nerves as he trailed after Riku.

Riku turned and his lips twitched, but he didn't join in the amusement. Instead he ordered, "Put one hand on the island and the other on the countertop."

Stefano's hands were on the granite even before Riku's delicious Master voice reached his brain.

In a quick move, his Master pulled the hem of his T-shirt behind his head, giving complete access to Stefano's chest. Master skimmed his hands across Stefano's midsection in a ghostingly light touch down to the waistband of his jeans, making Stefano harden faster than if he stroked his cock directly.

"Can you keep your hands on the counter no matter what I do?" Riku's eyes sparkled as he issued the challenge.

Even though Stefano didn't think he'd succeed, he had to try. "Yes, Master."

Master raked his fingers through Stefano's hair. Slow and rhythmic again and again. "I love your hair. The curl and this length are perfect."

Stefano yawned. Mortified, he sputtered, "Oh God, I'm sorry... Master."

"No worries. Remember that's your brain disconnecting and relaxing. You know I'll watch out for you even if it's only for a little bit." The deep voice lulled him further.

Stefano unplugged from everything other than his Master to a place where only Riku's touch and words mattered. He didn't have to think; he could just be.

Riku unbuttoned Stefano's jeans and teased the zipper down. His underwear met the floor with Riku's help. "Step out."

Stefano clutched the counters and kicked away his clothing. Fuck folding them, he didn't have the coordination anyway.

"You look stunning." His Master's voice reminded him of his nudity while Riku remained clothed.

This situation made him hot with embarrassment and turned him right the fuck on. Clothed Master, naked sub—that had to be a thing, and if it wasn't, it should be.

Stepping back, Riku studied him. "Look at you. You're all submissive in my kitchen, naked except for your socks and a T-shirt that appears to be a fabric harness."

Stefano couldn't help but whimper. His Master's voice had dropped into that deep Dominant tone that made him ache with expectation.

"And why are you standing there like an obedient sub?" Master dragged teasing fingers in a line across Stefano's chest, making his nipples peak in need of being pinched.

"Because you asked me to, Master." Stefano's voice was barely above a whisper, but it still cracked.

His Master stroked his face and gazed into Stefano's eyes. "That's right. You're a wonderful and obedient submissive."

Not even Stefano could doubt the sincerity of the words.

Ducking under his arm, his Master stood behind him.

Stefano didn't look, but couldn't stop himself from giving him an inviting twitch of his butt.

His Master caressed hands over Stefano's back, down to his ass.

The gentle rub made Stefano long to be spanked. A moan escaped with "Please, Master."

Soft pats were the only thing he got. The yearning built. Did his Master think him too weak for real discipline? That he couldn't handle some discipline?

His Master dropped low, breath caressing Stefano's ass, adding more fuel to the fire, making him shiver. Just the whisper of a tongue across his ass, and then the wet sensation was gone.

"Open your eyes," Master commanded.

When had he closed them? He opened them. Master was in front of him.

With a grin, Riku rose with his usual fluid, controlled grace, but in a quick move he set Stefano on the granite island.

Goddamn! That was freezing on his ass, though his erect cock seemed unbothered by the cold and leaked.

Riku took Stefano's hands and pressed them down on the counter. "Hold the edges."

"Yes, Master." The stone warmed under his body heat.

"Do you know I've thought about you tied to this island?"

"I didn't," Stefano squeaked out.

"The placement of the handles is in the right position for a spread eagle. Maybe someday, but right now I want you to hold on while I suck you."

Stefano tried to speak but only made a strangled noise.

His Master bowed his head over Stefano and blew. Hot, wet breath wafted over his cock.

Groaning, he thrust, because how could he not? He held the counter tighter and waited as Riku rolled a condom on him.

Riku tilted his head so he could stare into Stefano's eyes. The connection was... intense, and then he flicked out his tongue, almost touching him.

So very close, but no contact. His Master teased him with near misses again and again.

Oh dear God. The missed swipes of Riku's agile tongue had Stefano's condom-covered cock throbbing.

Master drank in every single movement and gasp Stefano made, playing him like an instrument. Even without ropes, Stefano was completely bound to the spot and unable to move. Not that he'd want the freedom to get away, but to—

Riku licked his tongue across the tip of Stefano's cock. The wetness from Riku's tongue on him thinned to a string but connected them.

Before he could do anything, his Master dragged his tongue around the tip and then traced a wet line down to Stefano's balls and back to the crown.

"Hold the counter tighter," Master whispered.

Stefano did.

Riku gave him an electric smile that made everything in Stefano clench, and then he took Stefano into his mouth.

The suction, the lashing of his Master's tongue, it was too much.

He felt himself going over the edge, but Riku gripped his cock, stopping Stefano's cum. Rhythmic waves of orgasm tried to move through him but had nowhere to go. "Dammit! Motherfucker! I was almost there… Master."

Riku's eyebrow arched. "Yes, I'm aware. Let go of the island and suck me off."

He released the island to slide off the granite and dropped to his knees. Riku's haughty demand broke through the confusing and conflicting messages his body and brain gave him. His dick throbbed woefully.

As soon as Riku unzipped and put on a condom, Stefano took him in his mouth and sucked.

Riku wrapped his fingers into Stefano's hair and tightened them.

Stefano's gut clenched as his Master used his mouth. To be used as an instrument of Riku's pleasure thrust Stefano into the stratosphere. Nothing mattered. He had a purpose.

Master worked Stefano's mouth on his cock. Instead of feeling used and dirty, he simply gave his mouth to his Master any way he wanted it. The joy of the action fulfilled a need deep inside him.

Since he had little control over his movement, he let his tongue go wild.

"Swallow around me, Stefano." Twice more Riku pulled Stefano's lips up and then down lower. He came with a low, satisfied grunt.

Hot damn! I just made my Master come. I'm the sub! It was a perfect reward.

He licked Riku thoroughly and then removed the condom and set it aside. He even zipped him back into his pants, being the full-service sub he was—wanted to be.

"That was wonderful." Riku pulled him off his knees and dropped back down in front of him.

The lack of oxygen to the brain confused Stefano. "What—"

"Hold the island, Stefano." Then Master's mouth was on his still condom-covered dick, sucking him deep.

The incredible heat of Riku's suction made it past the condom, forcing Stefano to latch on to the granite to stay upright.

His sucking was magic. Within a minute, Stefano writhed on the edge of orgasm.

"Please, Master."

Silence.

Jesus, Mary, and Joseph, this was more sucking than he'd ever gotten in his entire life.

He squirmed, trying to control the uncontrollable, but he didn't have to—his Master was in control. "Master, please let me come."

Silence.

Was his Master going to make him fail? No, he wouldn't allow himself to come without permission. No! "Please, Master. I can't. Please say I can come."

Pulling off, his Master grinned. "Come." And he went right back to stroking and sucking.

Permission. So good.

"Thank you, Master." A kaleidoscope of colors crashed as he let go of everything, trusting his Master to keep him safe.

He came hard.

Riku kept his mouth attached and busy until Stefano stopped panting.

When he was done, Riku disposed of the condoms and then said, "Let me get you to the sofa."

Nodding, Stefano would have agreed to anything. He felt incredible.

Riku maneuvered Stefano to the living room, wrapped him in a blanket, and sat down. Somehow Stefano ended up in his lap.

"Here, drink some water." Riku handed him a bottle that had been hiding behind a pillow.

Stefano drank and slowly came back to the earth after a good long while.

"Are you ready to talk, Stefano?"

Was he ever ready? Stefano shrugged and nodded.

His Master pressed his lips together as if suppressing a grin. "What is the next goal you'd like to work on?"

"Um, I don't know." Stefano didn't want to think.

"How about we work on smoking cessation?"

"So you actually think I can quit smoking?" Stefano didn't have casual sex anymore. He didn't drink more than a beer or two a week because of his family's habit to overdo it. He had one vice—Riku's arms tightened around him—well, maybe more than one. But damn!

"Yes, if you want to stop smoking, I'd like to help you quit. How do you feel about that?"

Stefano sighed. "I would like to quit, but I've never been able to. I don't know if I can."

"You could safeword." Riku dangled the out as if Stefano would actually take the easy path.

Fucking hell if he'd be made to safeword. Although maybe he should safeword. This whole thing could just vanish, evaporate like it never happened…. Stefano's lips became glued shut, but he nodded.

Riku tucked some wayward curls behind Stefano's ear. He gave a bright smile. "Okay, great. So we'll work on you quitting."

With less enthusiasm than he should have for his Master's decisions, he said, "Yes, Master."

"How many packs of cigarettes do you smoke a day?"

"About one or so." Usually it was less, but sometimes more.

"And you would like to quit?"

"No… yes. I don't know if I can. I've been smoking since I was fifteen years old." Sometimes it was the only thing that calmed him down.

"Do you smoke regular or menthol?"

"Mostly regulars."

"Good. Those are easier to quit. I hate to get up, but…." Riku shifted Stefano's weight off him.

Stefano tried to hide his frown as Riku glided into the kitchen.

He returned with an odd-looking red-white-and-black rounded egg-shaped thing with two blank eyes that stared at Stefano.

"What's that?" Stefano sat up. Maybe the thing looked familiar somehow, but he couldn't place where he'd seen one.

"My gift to you. It's a Daruma wishing doll. Something to help you reach your goal of being a nonsmoker."

"Thank you, but I don't understand." How would a doll help him quit smoking?

"Let this doll be a constant reminder of your spirit. Life is full of bumps, so it's inevitable that you'll fall. But you can get back up."

Many times, Stefano didn't want to get back up, but eventually he'd always found his feet and kept trudging onward. As he traced a finger over the blank eyes, he felt a kinship of sorts with the plump little warrior.

"When things got hard, my mother always said '*Nanakorobi yaoki.*' It's a Japanese proverb that means fall down seven times, stand up eight.

No matter how exhausting, difficult, or thankless the journey, our spirit propels us forward."

God in Heaven, Riku was so deep and profound. Stefano wanted to absorb some of that spirit and be a better person. "I like that, but how does the doll... Daruma doll, work?"

"When you have a goal or wish, you color in one of the eyes as you focus on what you want. Every day you work for your goal. The Daruma doll reminds you to stay focused. Then when you achieve your dream, or in this case you stop smoking, you draw in the other eye."

"So I should color in the eye? All of it?"

"You can draw a circle and blacken it." Riku handed him a marker.

Here goes nothing. I want—his gaze met Riku's. His heart tumbled with all the things he wished for, and none of them had to do with not smoking.

Riku smiled, warming him. "Focus on your goal of not smoking."

"Yes, Master." He dragged his head back to the task at hand. *I want to stop smoking and become an ex-smoker.* He drew a lopsided circle with the marker, correcting the shape as he filled it in.

"Keep this where you'll see it every day. Remember, it's not about the fall but the getting up and continuing down the path to achieving your wish."

With that philosophy in mind, or maybe it was his self-destructive bent, he added, "Frank wants to know when you're available for dinner."

CHAPTER 15

THIS WAS something even the shop owner of the Witch's Coven shop, a palm reader, wouldn't have been able to see: Riku sitting down to dinner with his sub and his sub's brother, who didn't know half of Stefano's secrets.

His sub. He loved the sound of that and how well they fit together.

Though was that really the case? Stefano had agreed to be his sub for six months. They'd been seeing each other several times a week for the past six weeks, if you didn't count the time he kept running into Stefano at places he frequented, but there were some major restrictions. No one knew about their relationship except Devon, and they basically never left the townhouse except to get a quick meal at the diner.

Glancing over at his vivacious sub, he couldn't help but wax poetic about how Stefano resembled one of Botticelli's angels. His dark curly hair, the full red lips, and his wide, kind eyes... but that wasn't what enthralled Riku.

No, if good looks was all Stefano had, Riku could have moved on. However, Stefano was strong, clever, creative, and he would give any art professor a run for their money when it came to analyzing works of art. And the way he yearned to serve Riku, and how that allowed Riku to access parts of himself he hadn't known existed, was nothing short of a miracle.

Where was Riku's self-control? Instead of enjoying their moments together as Devon had advised, Riku couldn't help but wonder where the relationship was going. He kept racing down the path of what-ifs.

Would Stefano fulfill his desire and simply move on? Could Riku have finally found something and someone real to explore life with?

Full stop. Realistically, what were the options, especially when Stefano wouldn't even acknowledge they were together?

After a quick grace, Frank cut into the delicious-smelling lasagna and grinned at Riku. "This is a thank-you for helping Stefano quit smoking."

He accepted a portion of what he'd been smelling since he arrived with a grin. There wasn't a way possible to finish the generous serving, but if the lasagna tasted as good as the Italian perfection smelled, he'd give devouring all of it his best shot. He gave credit where credit was due. "Your brother's the one who did all the work."

"It's only been a little over two weeks since my last cigarette. Don't jinx me." Stefano frowned.

"Well, I think it's great. Bad enough Dad was a heavy smoker. Marco smokes even more than Dad did. I'm glad you've stopped or are stopping, that's all." Frank's words were gruff, but anyone could hear the relief.

In truth, Riku was proud of Stefano's determination and happy that he lowered his health risks by quitting and exercising.

Stefano grumbled, "It's like going on a strict diet and your snack is, like, seven almonds and water. That shit helps, but you still want a big juicy burger and chocolate cake."

Frank handed Stefano a plate with a huge piece of cheesy goodness. "Well, take this for all your willpower, and instead of pound cake and strawberries, I went with chocolate cake for dessert."

"Not smoking is going to make me fat." Stefano grabbed his plate with two hands.

"There's always ways to burn off excess calories. Riku can help you with that, right?" Frank asked.

Stefano blinked in rapid succession and his mouth dropped open, though nothing came out except a tiny strangled sound.

Shoving to the back of his mind the images of glorious sexual BDSM tasks that surely burned off many calories, Riku nodded. "Um, yeah. You can simply double your workout for the next few days."

Frank arched an eyebrow at him and then glanced at Stefano. His lips twitched, but he didn't say more.

Everyone dug in.

Riku savored the first bite. The noodles were the perfect texture, and the herbed meat sauce blended with the cheese. Was that basil? "This is amazing, Frank."

"Thanks." Frank gave Riku a pleased smile.

Stefano hmphed. "Yeah, it's great. Though it's proof Grandma liked you best."

Frank shook his head. "No, she knew I loved cooking as much as she did." Turning to Riku, he said, "I'm the only one who has my grandmother's lasagna recipe."

"She willed it to him, and he won't share."

"It's part of her wishes, and I don't even have the recipe. I only do what she taught me. Though she did give me permission to share how to make this with my significant other." Frank sounded like he had repeated these words countless times.

"Whatever... though as long as you make it for me, I'm good." Stefano smirked and then shoved another forkful into his mouth.

Riku dipped the garlic bread into the perfectly blended herbed tomato sauce and enjoyed every carb-filled bite.

As the meal progressed, Frank asked, "So, Riku, I take it your work is going well?"

"Yes. New Hope is incredibly supportive of new businesses, and everyone is referring us, so we have to get another physical therapist on staff."

Frank nodded. "A great problem to have. So tell me more about yourself."

"What do you want to know?" Riku sipped some water.

"I don't know, are you seeing anyone?" Frank studied Stefano.

Stefano glared at Frank. "Nosy much?"

As Riku had told Stefano, he wouldn't reveal secrets, but he wouldn't lie either. "Yes, someone very special."

A fork clanked against a plate to his right, and then Stefano quickly grabbed another piece of garlic bread.

Frank didn't miss the reaction and was clever enough to focus on Stefano. "Have you met Riku's significant other, Stefano?"

His expression changed into a blank. "I wouldn't call him significant—I mean, they just started seeing each other."

Riku listened to Stefano's words, but he heard, or maybe projected, insecurity.

Again, Stefano needed the truth, so Riku corrected him. "Actually, I would call him pretty *significant*. I care for him a great deal."

Stefano grabbed his bottle of micro-brewed beer and took a big swig.

"Jealous, little brother?" Frank asked, like he already knew the answer.

Coughing, Stefano set down his beer and shook his head. "I guess I didn't know it was that serious."

Was Stefano serious? Did he not know that something special was happening between them? Riku shrugged. "It is... at least for me."

"Well, you'll have to bring him over. I'd love to meet him. Stefano's gone a lot. I'm still waiting for him to share who he's seeing."

Stefano shook his head at Frank and glared.

Needing to protect his sub from further stress, Riku asked, "How about you, Frank? I know when we met you weren't dating anyone, but anyone of interest?"

Frank's gaze darted between them, and he must have decided to give Stefano a break. "Nah, I'm working too hard."

"No prospects?"

"Eh, I don't even know what type of person I'm looking for."

"Someone who can tolerate your workaholic ways." Stefano seemed to miss his brother's use of *person*, not *woman* or *man*.

Frank shared a look with Riku, and then his gaze traveled to Stefano and back. Giving Riku a little shrug, he asked, "Who's up for dessert?"

"I'd love some." Stefano started collecting the dinner plates.

The dessert and the rest of the evening passed without incident. They sat in front of a toasty wood-burning fireplace and enjoyed rich chocolate cake and tea.

A half an hour later, Frank stifled a yawn. He stood and shook Riku's hand. "I'm sorry. Sad as it sounds, this is late for me. Thank you for coming over."

Riku stood and clapped a second hand over Frank's. "I appreciate the invite. I'll have to have you and Stefano over to my place."

"I'd like that. And then maybe I can meet your *significant other*."

"I hope so." Riku just barely restrained a sigh.

Frank's eyes gleamed with an understanding that appeared lost on Stefano. Possibly because Stefano poked at the embers of the fire, but more likely because he didn't want to understand.

"Night, Frank. Thanks for cooking. I'll make sure everything is cleaned up." Stefano wandered back to the sofa and sat.

"Night." Frank gave him a nod and went upstairs.

Stefano patted the seat next to him. The fire embers gave a soft glow to the room and chased shadows across his face.

Riku sat.

Melting into him, Stefano whispered, "Good evening, Master."

As far as segues went, this was as good as it was going to get. Riku straightened his spine. "Are you planning to come out to Frank?"

"Yeah, soon." Stefano's response was too quick and didn't ring true.

"Really?" All the doubts surfaced. Maybe he was kidding himself and hoping for something beyond Stefano's capacity and his own reach.

Stefano frowned. "You said you'd give me six months."

Riku bit back the "Then what?" Would time actually change anything between them, or would Stefano walk away? It had only been six weeks officially. He had to stop pushing.

"I should go." Riku stood.

"No… I mean, already?" Was that the closest Stefano could come to admitting he wanted Riku to stay?

He needed some time to recenter himself. "Yeah, I've got a 7:00 a.m. tomorrow."

"'Kay." Stefano walked Riku to the door with a frown on his face. He grabbed Riku's coat off the banister and then held it out for him. "I'll see you tomorrow night, though, right?"

The uncertainty and worry pulled at Riku's heart. He wanted to reassure his sub, but really, all he could do was confirm their next meeting. "Yes."

Stefano's gaze darted toward the stairs where Frank had disappeared, but with only a small hesitation he leaned into Riku.

His poor sub craved him even if he couldn't confess to anyone else.

That fact tore at Riku. He was driven to give Stefano what he wanted. But did he have enough control to give him what he needed?

THE NEXT day Riku was plagued by all the what-ifs and all the things he had done wrong, so he popped into Devon's office. "That was a long day."

"It was." Devon studied him for a moment and finally broke the silence with "Still obsessing, huh?"

"I don't know what to do or how to support him." Riku did know, but he also didn't want to accept it.

Devon put his feet up on the desk. "You can't force him to come out."

"I know that." Riku paced the length of Devon's office. Didn't he think Riku incredibly aware of that fact?

"And you can't settle for half of a relationship. That's not a happy way to live." Devon gazed at the far wall.

Devon was living proof of that fact. He had tried to make a relationship work with someone who wasn't available and it just about crushed him.

Even now, several years later, that fiasco infuriated Riku, watching his best friend get torn to shreds by that bastard who toyed with Devon's heart.

Here Riku was banging his head against a similar brick wall. "I know that too. We both do."

Sighing, Devon shrugged. "It's okay to set expectations. Your feelings matter in this, not only his."

Being a sexual abuse survivor, Stefano carried more baggage than Riku even knew existed. "But he's been through so much."

"Agreed, but if you settle for less, you're also letting him settle for less. Give him the choice."

"I gave him six months. It's only been about six weeks." What could he expect?

Why did he do this to himself? How did he expect not to fall for Stefano? He was stupid to have let the submissive become woven into his world in so many ways, because if—when—he vanished, there would be gaping holes in Riku.

"Dinner?" Devon dragged him back to reality.

"Yeah, the usual?"

"Great. How about around five?"

"So early?" Riku was happy to have more time to prepare for Stefano's arrival—

"I figured I'd head to the club afterwards."

"Really? It's a Thursday night."

"There's this sub...." Devon grinned a goofy smile. "So, yeah."

Oh, really? "I look forward to hearing about him. See you at five." Riku strolled into his own office.

His gaze landed on his golden Daruma doll, which sat in the middle of his bookshelves. Mother had given it to him a few days after he came out to her.

Before he was born, she had given up her family, along with their wealth and support, to be with his father, so she had always taught Riku love was the most important thing. Giving him the doll was her way of letting him know she loved and accepted him no matter who he loved. Her dearest wish for him was to find a love of his very own.

He had colored in one of the eyes as he wished to find someone willing to give up everything to share his life with him. A tad dramatic and not realistic for a kid out of Philly.

Now almost two decades later, at her suggestion, he kept the doll in his office so he'd be reminded that success in business was fine, but his true goal should be to find happiness in love.

He'd been young and foolish… and here he was again, hoping and wishing Stefano would flip his world upside down for him.

LATER THAT night, Riku used some simple ties to restrain a very naked Stefano to the bed. Stepping back, he admired his work. "You look stunning in my ropes. Any pain?"

"Yeah, right here, Master," Stefano muttered as he thrust his erection up.

Riku chuckled. He laughed with Stefano more than anyone else. "Other than that?"

"No," Stefano grumbled. He hadn't made it to subspace yet, but that was about to change.

"Good." Riku teased two fingers along Stefano's shaft and then rubbed under his circumcision scar, right over his frenulum.

Within a minute the first drop of precum rolled down to lubricate Riku's fingers. Droplet after droplet allowed Riku an easy glide along Stefano's shaft.

Stefano panted, "Please let me come."

"It's only been fifteen minutes." *Mmmm, delicious.* He slid onto the bed, almost curling into Stefano's body, and changed from long strokes to tight circles, directly paying attention to his frenulum.

Stefano moved against him while he tugged at his arms as if wanting to take the matter into his own hands. "I know. I have to come."

"No, you don't." Riku kept his tone deep and teasing.

Stefano groaned and dug his heels into the bed. He ground his ass down.

"Relax, Stefano." He drank in the struggles and loved how Stefano fought against his own needs to satisfy Riku's.

"Easy for you to say." Stefano squirmed against the ropes. "I'm so close to busting, and then it goes away."

"With a frenulum orgasm, you must be patient. The sensation ebbs and flows sometimes for as long as thirty minutes before climax." Riku kept changing the pressure so Stefano couldn't get enough.

"Thirty minutes?" Stefano voice squeaked.

"You are pleasing me. I like watching you delay your pleasure just because I asked. Such a good sub." Riku took his fingers away.

Stefano gasped and his eyes glazed over. "Master?"

"That's right, I'm your Master." Riku pushed away the sad question of for how long and found excitement in Stefano's jerks and pulls at the ropes.

He picked up the rope and waved it in front of Stefano. "I bet you're wondering what I'm going to do with this frayed end of the rope."

A strangled sound was wrung from deep within Stefano.

Riku dusted the fringe against his shaft.

Giving a long, drawn-out sigh, Stefano shivered and gave him a dreamy smile.

"You like pleasing me, don't you, Stefano?" His actions already answered, but Riku was greedy and wanted the admission.

"Yes, Master." There it was. Stefano's tone held surrender both to him and subspace.

"I promise it'll be worth it." He tickled the rope across Stefano's frenulum, caressing the skin again and again with the fringe, adding a little more pressure with each pass.

"Yes, Master." The restraints wouldn't even let Stefano clutch the bedding. His struggles stilled, and he tried to accept that all he could do was absorb the frustration and let it build.

Riku drifted on the surge of power that putting Stefano into subspace gave him. Stefano's responses to him were outstanding. This rare connection didn't happen often, and Riku was top-drunk enough to think he could help Stefano understand how good they were together.

Tilting the rope end, he secured the knot with his two fingers and rubbed directly on Stefano's spot. He made circles over the inverted V, upping the torment and forcing the physical urgency to return. "How's that?"

"Please, Master. Do whatever you want with me." Stefano arched off the bed, as if he could convince Riku he needed to come rather than receive more teasing attention.

"A little more." He loved this open and free place where Stefano didn't care about hiding; he simply wanted to be, and to come. To have Stefano give him permission to do whatever Riku wanted when Stefano's body was in clear disagreement fed a sadistic part of him. Teasing Stefano this way, all the while reassuring the kinder part of him that Stefano would orgasm harder the more he taunted him with this prolonged tease.

Stefano tugged against the ropes like the orgasm was trying to break through his veins.

"Come when I kiss you."

Gasping, Stefano parted his lips and surrendered, absorbing all Riku's attention and efforts while remaining hungry for more.

Not being able to wait a moment more, Riku found Stefano's mouth and gave him what they both craved, kissing him hard and hot. Sparks of wonderment coursed through him.

Riku muffled the moans of Stefano's completion by deepening the kiss and using the rope's knot to stroke his shaft. Stefano was so sexy, needy, and perfect, Riku lost all patience.

Stefano's body wavered with the pulses of his pleasure, but his lips remained on Riku's.

"I have to have you. Or at least join in a climax." Riku wiped off Stefano with a towel and was glad he'd had the foresight to stay away from leather pants tonight.

Without much thought he unzipped his pants and recaptured Stefano's perfect mouth.

Stefano tugged at his bonds. Witnessing Stefano's desire for him made Riku stroke himself to a quick orgasm.

He grabbed the towel he had set out for Stefano and came hard all over it.

Stars exploded behind his eyelids, and his heart expanded. How did a man completely tied up satisfy Riku so completely, on levels he didn't want to think about?

Pulling his lips away from Stefano, who didn't make it easy, he tried to catch some air. He rested his head on Stefano's shoulder.

Control. He had to find some. His abandonment of self-discipline had been unexpected.

He placed a kiss on Stefano's shoulder and zipped himself back into his pants.

Inhale. Exhale. Focus on Stefano.

Riku had to get back to being in control. He loosened each of the four corners of the setup carefully so he didn't overstimulate his completely blissed-out sub. Then he unknotted the rope and dragged the last bit gently across Stefano's belly.

Stefano laughed as he opened his eyes.

The response was perfect and pure and unguarded.

Whatever he read in Riku, Stefano's mouth dropped, but he didn't say anything.

Once the rope was away, Riku got Stefano a water and helped him drink. When he was done, he took one himself and enjoyed the cool refreshment. Then he lay on his back, allowing Stefano to curl into him.

Riku wasn't a religious man, but holding his sub close to him and listening to him breathe made him believe Heaven existed.

A GLANCE at the clock informed Riku he must have fallen asleep for an hour.

Stefano sat on the edge of the bed, probably attempting to sneak out before morning... again.

Riku asked, "How are you doing?"

"That was incredible. Thank you, Master." The gratitude in his voice showed in the appreciative smile he gave Riku.

"You're welcome. Before you go, I'd like to follow up on something you said a couple of weeks ago." He needed to stop avoiding sensation play. Many subs had been abused, and they didn't find impact play abusive. Riku had to Master-up and figure it out.

Stefano's eyes widened. "Go... oh, um, yeah. Of course. Sure, shoot."

"You said a sub wants their pain acknowledged."

Stefano shrugged and nodded.

Riku continued, "There's a theory that when a Master prepares for a scene and focuses all their energy on the sub, it shows the sub they are thought of and someone is trying to address their needs."

Stefano turned and sat cross-legged on the bed, facing Riku. "Yup, that sounds about right. I saw a demonstration once where the Mistress explained that she gives the sub pain. They suffer for her, but she sees the hurt and helps them get beyond it."

"So it's a way of validating your experience?" Riku wanted to understand Stefano better. He hated Dominants who simply assumed the rationale behind a sub's needs.

The sheet slipped lower on Stefano's torso. "Yeah, I guess you... someone witnessing my pain means it's real."

"And you think it may help some past pain as well?"

Stefano nodded.

It was beyond the time that Riku should acknowledge the truth of their situation. "I realize we aren't doing things how you might normally do them."

Stefano confessed, "Most Mistresses were much stricter and gave me painful consequences for any misstep, but you can get me on the path to subspace with handwashing, so what do I know?"

Riku chuckled. "You delight me."

His sub's cheeks tinted a sweet pink, making him look younger than almost thirty. "For that I'm eternally grateful."

"Brat." Riku got serious. "I'll be honest with you. I want to be careful in terms of reinforcing anything that's negative with you—"

"Goddammit! I don't need kid gloves." Stefano slapped a hand over his mouth.

"It is necessary for me. Remember, I have nonnegotiables too. I don't know enough about working with someone who has a history of abuse. You've placed your mental and physical well-being into my hands. I won't do something that has unintended consequences for you."

"But—"

"I appreciate your faith in me, but the truth is, I have to feel your faith in me is justified."

"I hate that."

"Sorry, but remember this is one of my nonnegotiables. As your Master, friend, and lover, I want to cause you no lasting harm. I wanted you to know I'm doing research and learning how I can get to that place."

"Yes, Master. I guess it's dumb to fight against what you think is best for me."

But Riku knew it wouldn't stop Stefano from doing just that if that's what he needed to do.

CHAPTER 16

"I DON'T think they're open today," Stefano said as Riku walked to the entrance of the Moroccan Palace.

Stefano wished they had met at Riku's townhouse, but Riku insisted they do something different to celebrate two months together.

Together....

Two months, that was a long time. His other relationships only lasted a few weeks or maybe a little over a month, but two.... Sixty days.... Which meant only four more months until all of this was over—

Because I'm too chickenshit to do what needs to be done.

Stefano wouldn't lose Frank or his sister over coming out, but his ma.... What if—no. He had one hundred and twenty more days with Riku, and that had to be enough to last a lifetime.

His heart clenched. Hurt sliced at him. He didn't want to give up Riku.

You always knew you weren't good enough for him. The wicked voice ripped through his hope.

Stefano swallowed hard and cleared his throat. Fuck, he wished they weren't outside so he could melt into Riku and absorb some of his strength.

"Let me text him."

"Who?"

Riku didn't look away from his phone as he danced his thumbs over the screen. "The owner."

Within a minute, the door opened. The giant man wrestled Riku into a hug. "Come in. Come in. How are you, my friend?"

"Great, Thamir, and you?" Riku clapped him on the back.

"Fine, though I've not seen you recently."

"I've been busy."

"I see that." Thamir's gaze landed on Stefano.

Did this guy know something? He looked— "Wait, I know you. I've seen you at the Edge."

The owner glanced at Riku, and once he was given the nod Thamir said, "Guilty. I've seen you around too. I'm Thamir Fadel."

"I'm Stefano."

Thamir gave Stefano a smile. "Nice to meet you. Please follow me to your table."

The bright orangey-yellow hallway was lined with arched entrances covered with red curtains. Thamir held open the privacy curtain in one of the archways and revealed low red couches that invited the diners to lounge back onto vivid blue, red, and yellow patterned pillows. The multicolored glass and brass lanterns cast shadows of color across the room. A stone fountain bubbled in the corner. The thick carpet matched the colorful design of the room.

Once they were seated on the plush couch, Riku picked up the menu from the brass table and glanced at it.

"The Sultan's feast, Riku?"

"Yes. Stefano's never had Moroccan food, so I want to give him a sampling, but I request the b'stilla with no cinnamon, chicken kebabs, and the lamb."

Thamir smiled. "With mint tea and water throughout the meal and baklava for dessert."

"Good memory," Riku praised.

"Of course. I will leave you in complete privacy without uninvited interruptions. After the sands are done and you wish for the next course, ring the bell." Thamir flipped a tiny hourglass over, set an ornate brass bell on the table, along with red bath towels, and then disappeared past the curtain.

"Did he ask your permission to speak to me?" Stefano knew it was done, but his Mistresses never maintained that expectation.

"Of course. He's a well-mannered man who would never make assumptions."

Ignoring the excitement of someone respecting his submissive status, he said, "I'm not sure I'm thrilled that he knows I'm a sub and with you."

Riku sighed. "We're just having dinner, but if you'd like, we can—"

"No. It's not a big deal?" No one was here, and—

That's why you don't deserve him. You'd deny your Master.

"It isn't. Thamir opened for us. We have complete privacy. You can be yourself." As if to prove his point, Riku leaned in and waited.

Stefano stiffened, but the temptation of Riku's lips proved too much for him to resist. He pressed his mouth to Riku's in way of apology, but as soon as their lips met, that now familiar uncontrollable need to give himself to his Master won out. He gave in to the kiss, and everything it meant.

Riku rewarded his bravery by gliding his lips over Stefano's in the softest kiss he'd ever received, and all it did was make him starved for more.

Licking his tongue out, Stefano traced Riku's lips. Parting his lips, he waited helplessly.

Riku groaned at Stefano's clear surrender, then charged in, laying claim to his mouth.

Sparks of excitement and something else Stefano didn't want to name rushed through him. His body relaxed as other things stiffened.

The kiss slowed and Riku sat back.

Stefano dropped his head onto the pillows that surrounded him. He didn't have to glance down to know his dick tried to pitch a tent in his pants.

"Your lips are swollen. I like that." Riku shifted closer and traced Stefano's mouth with an index finger.

Fuck. Such a simple thing, but the touch zapped electricity through his body and wrapped around his heart.

Stefano couldn't resist licking Riku's finger.

"I'm very lucky to have such a sweet submissive." Riku traced the wetness over Stefano's lips. Then he took one of the napkin towels, snapped out the wrinkles, and laid the red terry cloth over Stefano's lap.

"Thank you, Master." Something deep inside Stefano was satisfied by Riku's care. Maybe it would seem overbearing or pushy to some, but he felt protected and cared for in a way he'd never experienced.

He became hyperaware of how Riku's thigh rested against his. The heat of his body against Stefano's. His asscheeks clenched as he imagined what it would be like if Riku ever fucked—was inside him.

"You seem rather heated tonight." Riku's voice was low and deep.

"I am." He couldn't lie; the damned towel didn't hide the circus he could host in his pants.

Riku slipped a hand under Stefano's towel and caressed Stefano's aching erection.

"What are you doing?" He grabbed Riku's skilled hand and halfheartedly tried to stop the delicious teasing but only succeeded in thrusting for more friction.

"I'm going to give you a hand job right here in the restaurant unless you safeword." Riku unbuttoned and unzipped Stefano's jeans.

Why, oh why did he mark his "interest in public sex" on the BDSM checklist Riku gave him? What if he was caught? Why was he wiggling to help open his pants? It was dark in here and the towel blocked the view, but—oh, fuck!

His dick was out of his pants, under the towel with Riku's motherfucking fist wrapped around him. Jesus Christ, this was hotter than he'd expected. Better than at the club because it was so out-of-bounds.

Riku licked his lips and studied him. Finally, he moved his tight fist up and down. The motion was achingly slow, but the viselike grip felt perfect.

"Is my sub a harem boy trapped in a palace?" Riku's arrogant tone added to Stefano's arousal.

Harem boy? The atmosphere of the restaurant encouraged all the erotic fantasies of service to come together in his brain at once. *Oh fuck, yeah! I am your harem boy.*

Riku pursed his lips and then arched his eyebrow. "Are you so horny that your Master needs to get you off before dinner?"

"Yes, Master," Stefano whimpered. There was no other answer.

"Or maybe I should deny you. Would my submissive harem boy like to be made to wait?" Riku gave him nice firm tugs likely to bring him off in less than thirty seconds.

God, no! Yes! No!

Stefano pressed against Riku's side. He'd learned over time when his head and body were confused, he could trust Riku to give him what he needed. "Whatever you wish, Master."

"Such a good sub, I knew you'd make a fine harem boy." Riku abandoned Stefano's cock, which very much needed his attention, and picked up the bell.

Ting! Ting! Ting-a-ling!

What?

The owner appeared with a rolling cart and set glasses of ice water on the table, along with plates of food. "Please enjoy Pennsylvania's richest hummus, made from chickpeas, tahini, and garlic with a hint of lemon. And this is our baba ghanouj. It's eggplant pureed with various mild but flavorful Mediterranean spices."

When Thamir turned away, Stefano dared a look down. *Whew!* He was completely covered with the napkin towel thing. *Thank God!* He glared at Riku.

Riku sipped water like he hadn't just stopped Stefano's orgasm.

"Pita, Riku?" Thamir held out a basket the size of a clothing hamper, filled with bread.

"Yes, thank you." Riku grabbed several pockets of pita out, set them on the table in front of Stefano, and then took his own.

Thamir turned a different-size glass timer over. "Take your time," he said before disappearing again.

"We will, won't we, Stefano?" Riku gave him a smug smile.

Why, of all the— "Yes... Riku." No denial had ever been more erotic.

Riku ripped off a piece of his pita and dragged it through the hummus, or was that the eggplant thing? He held it out for Stefano to eat.

Stefano might not have been an adventurous eater, but he wouldn't hesitate to open his mouth whenever his Master indicated him to do so. Fuck, his cock throbbed.

"I think you'll like this. It's the baba ghanouj." Riku popped the piece into Stefano's mouth.

"Mmmm, good," he said around the piece.

Stefano returned the favor. Serving Riku was a pleasure in itself.

They traded pieces of pita with delicious hummus and eggplant until the first course was finished.

"And now, where were we?" Riku slid his hand back under the towel. "Ah, right there."

Stefano gasped as Riku gave his still-hard cock a slow stroke.

"You're so aroused. I could bring you right off in under a minute."

Stefano moaned, because it was true, and there was nothing he could do about it. He surrendered his body to Riku and waited to—

Ting. Ting. Ting.

That fucking bell. He was covered and so turned-on. "You really are sadistic."

"Aren't we all?"

"Yes, Master, but not everyone is so… capable." He'd had some frustratingly ruined orgasms by his Mistresses, who didn't read his body language as well as Riku. Riku kept him on a razor edge with seemingly little effort.

Riku still grinned at him when Thamir rolled the cart in and said, "Here we have three salads. Carrots marinated with garlic, vinegar, and spices, an eggplant salad, a trio of diced cucumbers, peppers, and tomatoes seasoned with parsley, vinegar, and oil."

"Looks incredible, right, Stefano?"

Putting away his disgruntled expression he said, "Yes… Master."

Riku's sharp intake of breath echoed, but Stefano didn't look at him. He fixed his eyes on Thamir, whose smile got bigger.

Once Thamir vanished, Riku said, "Thank you."

Stefano nodded at his Master. This was the first time he'd acknowledged who Riku was to him with anyone else present. It might be the only time, but in this moment, Stefano couldn't possibly deny Riku's mastery over him.

Riku leaned over him, and his hand thrust under Stefano's towel.

Their breath comingled and synced, becoming a single unit.

Stefano opened his mouth to beg to come; instead he asked for what he needed even more. "Please kiss me."

"You have my permission to come or to kiss me." Riku squeezed Stefano's cock as if to confuse the issue.

There was no confusion.

Stefano closed the distance to Riku's lips with his mouth. Happiness sparked joy and contentment as Riku took control of the kiss and Stefano surrendered to his Master's will.

The kiss gave him everything he'd been missing from his life. He felt whole, clean, and yes, maybe even a little beautiful.

After a magical eternity, Riku pulled back, breathing hard. "And now I'm going to finish you off. Come when I tell you to."

"Yes, Master." Stefano lay in the crook of Riku's arms as he was stroked to the edge of orgasm.

"I really liked that you called me Master in front of someone. I respect how hard that is for you." Riku stroked.

Acknowledging Riku as his Master shouldn't be difficult. It shamed Stefano that revealing that truth in front of others proved hard. "I'm sorry, Master" came out more of a groan.

"No need to apologize. Maybe someday it'll be easier, but for now, let's focus on this moment. Do you want to come?"

Stefano swallowed and tried to find his voice. "Yes" squeaked out.

"Good." Riku dropped the speed of his hand. "I want this memory burned into you. Me giving my harem boy a hand job in a restaurant because he can't wait. How does that make you feel?"

"Hot."

"It is hot. I adore having a horny sub willing to come when he's told. Are you ready to come?"

He nodded because he had no words other than a pathetic whimper.

"You're trembling. You're so close. Have you ever been this close to orgasming in *public*?" Riku seemed to know the exact speed and pressure to make him edge for as long as he saw fit.

In public!

He gasped, hoping Riku understood his grumbled words. "No, Master."

"Good. Come for me."

Stefano pushed his lips against Riku's mouth and let go.

Everything he had, everything he was, everything he wanted to be shot out of him because his Master told him to come.

He kissed and came in wickedly harsh waves of searing pleasure. He couldn't even count the number of pulses that rushed out of him.

Riku pulled back from the kiss and squeezed one more drop out of Stefano's cock, making him shiver with blissful completion.

He kissed his Master's cheek and curled into his shoulder.

Ting. Ting. Ting.

Stefano woke up. Had he fallen asleep? He tried to sit up and then gave in and resumed his position, tucked under Riku's arm.

"Here's a new napkin for the next course." Thamir handed an indigo napkin to Riku and gathered the red ones that Riku must have put into a cloth bag.

He glanced down, and Riku also must have tucked Stefano's junk back into his pants. Riku covered his lap again.

Stefano spent the rest of the meal lounging next to Riku, accepting bites of something with powdered sugar called b'stilla, chicken kebab, and pieces of lamb.

Afterward, Thamir brought them dessert of pieces of fruit, baklava, and more mint tea.

Stefano exclaimed, "Shit!" He sat upright.

Riku jumped. "What?"

"I should be feeding you."

Or he should have blown him; instead he selfishly basked like he was a sultan.

Caressing the back of his hand down Stefano's cheek, Riku smiled. "We can feed each other."

"Yeah, but—"

"I've had a lovely meal with my incredible harem boy."

"I acted like—"

His Master smiled like he was quite pleased. "Someone who I satisfied completely?"

Fuck. Fine. "Yes, Master. But I—"

"Let me clue you in. There's something magical about making someone lose time and space, and when I succeed in doing that with you... well, that's everything."

Stefano swallowed back his own words, emotions... though not his fear.

LATER THAT night, Riku hadn't asked and neither had Stefano about him staying the night. After they'd had another satisfying round of oral sex, and they simply crawled into Riku's bed together.

Worry slithered around Stefano's brain. He tried not to think too hard and joked, "I think we met our daily mouth goals."

Well, Riku rather bounced into bed. He kissed Stefano on each eyelid and then on his cheek. He tucked the soft, puffy duvet around them and said, "Night, harem boy."

Something had shifted between them. Riku seemed lighter, hopeful somehow. Maybe it was that Stefano was able to acknowledge Riku as his Master in front of someone else, or maybe he was still coming down from pushing Stefano's boundaries.

Whatever it was, Stefano was a bit too freaked out to sleep. Unlike Riku, who slept deeply, he kept spinning. There was a piece of him really happy to have been able to call Riku Master in front of someone else, but there was a dread creeping through him.

Was this him starting to come out? One step at a time. But he still wasn't going to therapy so... one hundred and twenty—the clock's red digital display made him change it to one hundred and nineteen days left in their six-month deal.

He strutted through the Edge, collar on. Riku held a leash connected to a ring in the leather.

Everyone stopped to stare. Some people clapped. Other people shouted, "Congratulations!"

Stefano stepped into one of the private rooms, but he wasn't in the Edge anymore.

No!

"I said stay down." Father Lucca shoved him against the desk. "Look at you, you must like it."

No! No! No! He screamed but nothing came out of his mouth, only silence.

"You're dirty and filthy. Stay there."

He couldn't move. Frozen. Stuck.

No! No! No!

Stefano scuttered off the bed and into a corner. Even though his back was pressed against the wall, he continued to shake.

Someone touched him.

"No! Don't!" His body crawled with disgust.

Riku knelt in front of him with his arms wrapped around himself. "Let me find you a therapist, Stefano. Please, you don't have to be in such pain."

"No! Goddamn you! Don't you see it? I'm broken."

"You're not—"

"Don't you see? There's no fixing this or me." Besides, therapy would take years. Riku deserved better! Stefano was going to miss the fucking deadline anyway.

I have four more months....

What difference would a few months make? Fuck this!

Riku shook his head. "Stefano, I'm not trying to fix you. You're not broken. You might need some help. We all need—"

"Fuck this!" Stefano stood and then started pulling on his jeans.

"What do you mean?" Riku jerked back as if there words punched him.

He tugged on his T-shirt so hard he almost tore it. "It could never have worked anyway."

Riku talked, but Stefano blocked out most of what he said except for "Don't do this…."

Stefano yanked at his own hair. *Fuck!* "You've given me no choice."

"That's not true. You're scared and running away. A lot happened tonight. You just—"

"I can't stay. I can't do this." Couldn't Riku see he didn't want to but he had to go?

Therapy would take too long.

"Please, Stefano. I love you." Riku's words were said almost in a whisper, destroying every part of Stefano's ripped-up mind, making everything that much worse.

Stefano screamed, "I love you too…."

"Wait, what?" Riku held up his hands, as if he could stop Stefano.

"Fuck me. Great. We love each other. It changes nothing. Where's my fucking socks?"

Riku unballed the socks and handed them to him. "No, it does. It's all the more reason why I have to reinforce the idea of therapy—"

"I can't be who you want me to be. I can't even be who I want to be. I'm locked in a box with no way out." *Over and over and I can't do anything differently.* Not even them loving each other gave Stefano any different available outcomes.

"Is coming out that difficult?"

Sure, let him think it was that. Riku had clearly been uncomfortable with being closeted again. Stefano gestured to him. "Look, I know you don't want to be my dirty little secret, so we're done."

"No, we're not." Riku shook his head, but the expression on his face said he knew the truth.

"I'm tired of living two different lives, one with you and the one with the rest of the world, so this is now over. You knew we couldn't work. But hey, I quit smoking like you wanted me to, so that's something." Nothing in Stefano's rant rang true, but Riku shouldn't have to go back into the closet for his sorry ass.

Stefano's feet moved him to the front door. He shoved his feet into his stupid boots and went out into the cold.

Riku didn't try to stop him—not that Stefano hoped for that. This was over.

No more standing on Monet's bridge of his life, wondering which way to go. There was a relief in jumping off, though. Like ripping off a Band-Aid, he hurt.

ALL DURING Sunday mass and now through his ma's dinner, his ma kept putting her wrist on his forehead. "You sure you're alright, Stefano?"

"Yeah, fine, Ma. I'm just tired." Hopefully, that would cover for his bloodshot eyes, and it was part of the truth. Between the dreams and—

Ding dong ding.

Marco grimaced and stomped to the door.

"Hey, Marco. Is Stefano here?" a familiar voice asked.

"What, you interrupting Sunday dinner 'cause you wanna play street ball, Leo? Aren't you a bit too old for that shit?"

Leo? Leo Ferraro? He had been an altar boy after—

They had gone to high school together. Stefano hadn't answered his emails, so why would he have just shown up?

Stefano jumped out of his chair. If it hadn't been so close to the wall, it would have fallen over as he rushed to the door. "Yeah, I'm here."

His mother had trailed him to the door. "Leo, would you like some—"

"No, Ma. He's fine." Stefano ushered Leo out the door and onto their small front stoop.

"No, Mrs. Rossi. I'm good." Leo easily followed Stefano's lead.

Stefano told his mother, "Don't let your food get cold, Ma. I'll only be a minute."

She narrowed her gaze on him, but she gave a nod and left.

He pulled the wooden door shut, followed by the screen. Not to be rude, Stefano asked, "How've you been, man?"

"Fine. Sorry for busting in on your family dinner, but you didn't respond to any of my emails."

No kidding. "I'm not really into emails and shit."

"Okay, yeah. Me, Anna Marie, and the boys are living in Bucks County now. Near where you and Frank live."

What did this have to do with him? "Pretty area."

Leo tried to look Stefano in the eyes, but his gaze kept slipping to the ground. "I wanted you to know there's a support group...."

"For what? I told you I don't need help with anything. Nothing happened." The lies ingrained in him fell off his tongue with ease. *Deny. Deny. Deny.* He had said it so much that the lie almost became the truth.

"Yeah, I know. You've said so, but I wanted to let you know a bunch of us meet over in the building next to the courthouse, Room 304."

"Thanks. If I know of anyone in need of help—"

"Stef, it helps to talk. I bottled that shit up for years, and, well, groups like this and my therapist have made such a difference in my life. Knowing I wasn't alone became a blessing."

Alone. Well, Leo might not be on his own—he had a wife and two boys—but Stefano was by himself and would be for life. Easier that way. "Give my best to Anna Marie and the boys."

Leo reached as if he'd pat Stefano's shoulder but dropped his hand before he made contact. "Sure, sure. But I'm gonna resend the information, just in case."

"Thanks." Stefano waved, escaped back inside, and shut the door.

He wiped his hands on his pants and tried to take a deep breath but failed. His heart raced. Confusion and anger competed for top billing. He could hear his family.

Angie stated, "Leo was hurt too."

Too. Too. Too. Who was she including with the "too"? *Catch your breath.*

His ma blew her nose. "Leo's mother told me Father Lucca was a very bad man."

Angie groaned in the way she only reserved for Marco. "Ma, he was a pedophile. He hurt children. He—"

Marco scoffed. "They must have encouraged him. He was a—"

"Priest?" Frank growled.

Ma gasped. "Let your brother go."

Stefano walked in to see Frank holding Marco by the neck of his shirt.

Frank tightened his other fist. "Marco, there's nothing else to say other than that bastard should have been sent to prison."

Marco nodded and held up his hands in surrender.

Shoving him back, Frank released Marco. Frank squeezed Stefano's shoulder as he passed him.

Marco stumbled back to his seat.

His sister added, "They sent him to another parish. I heard he died of cancer."

"Fucking good. I've got to go." Stefano kissed his ma's head and nodded to Angie. He stalked out the front door. A shiny piece of metal caught his eye, and he kicked the shiny disk, twirling it toward the gutter.

He got on his bike and rode until he accepted he'd never outrun the truth.

CHAPTER 17

STEFANO SAT down in Doc's office and wiped his palms on his jeans.

No sign of Riku anywhere, but his dumb heart kept racing at every voice in the hallway.

Doc hadn't glanced up once from his chart. Maybe the other test had been wrong and HIV showed up this testing go-round. A piece of him didn't give a flying fuck about the results.

Angie's voice echoed through his brain. *That's not healthy!*

He glanced around the room. Lots of books. He couldn't imagine anyone reading so many. Hell, he could barely pronounce the titles that seemed as long as short stories. Degrees hung on the wall, and pictures rested on one of the wooden shelves.

He swallowed hard at the picture of a younger Devon with his arm thrown over a grinning Riku's shoulders. There were some of other people, but Riku was in most of Devon's pictures: high school graduation, wearing those damned board shorts at the beach, posing with Devon in places Stefano didn't recognize, and a more recent one of them cutting the ribbon on the front door of their practice.

God, it hurt. He shouldn't still be feeling like this. Lots of Mistresses dumped him, but losing Riku had gutted him. He—

"Your tests look good. Your HDL, that's the good cholesterol, is in a very good range. Are you still exercising?"

"Yes. Every day." Just like he had when he was with—

Why did he hope Doc would tell Riku?

It didn't matter.

Doc tapped his prescription pad with his pen. "Now, where are you with insurance?"

"The garage picked me up, so I have full coverage, even dental. Janie took a copy of the card for your files." And the extra income helped.

"Good. So everything is going... well?"

What was he asking? No, nothing was going well. Anxiety was his abusive copilot, and his bad dreams had intensified. *Well* wasn't the word to describe his world. Now *terrible*, *bleak*, and *shitty* were all accurate. He was doing fucking shitty! "Great."

Doc nodded but seemed to study him closely. "How were your holidays?"

Craptastic! More dismal than usual. But he pasted a smile on his face and claimed, "Fine, yours?"

"Nice. Had dinner with Ri—friends and hung out. I didn't see you at the Edge's New Year's Eve bash. Did you ring in the New Year somewhere else?"

Yeah, on the couch with Frank. After his call to Ma at midnight, he called it quits on pretending to care about another new year. "Yeah. It was great."

Doc opened his mouth but then closed it. After a sigh, he said, "Great. Glad everything is going so well for you. Any New Year resolutions?"

"Nah, I don't believe in those." *I don't believe in anything.*

Doc nodded. "Okay. Here's a script for a three-month supply and your next round of bloodwork."

"Oh... so I don't have to come back for three months?" So long? *Doc must be trying to get rid of me.*

"Unless you have any issues before then. Or, I mean, I understand if you want to get someone else as your primary care physician."

Then there'd be no reason at all to be in this office ever again, putting the chances of running into Riku at zero. Maybe that was for the best.

Lie!

"No, that's okay. I really like this office and... um, you." His voice broke and squeaked as he pocketed the prescriptions.

TWO DAYS later, Stefano pulled into the parking lot of the place he said he'd never go to. Why was he here? He kicked off the slush from his boots before he trudged inside the building.

What room did the email—

Abuse Survivors Support Group, Room 304, this way, read the sign.

Stefano stopped at the door. The room was filled with black-and-white photos. It had a fancy conference table with about twenty chairs around it. Only about ten were filled—all men, three in business suits, four dressed in button-downs, two dressed like Stefano in jeans and a T-shirt, and one in a Phillies jersey.

The guy in the Phillies jersey looked up from his phone. It was Leo, and he stood.

The monochrome art echoed through Stefano. He no longer saw the world in color. Everything was drab shades of gray. He allowed his feet to drag him forward.

Meeting Stefano halfway into the room, Leo grabbed him into a backslapping bear hug. "Glad you came, man."

Stefano nodded. He didn't know what to say after all his denial.

Leo dragged him to the chair next to his. "Sit."

A black man in a tweed sports jacket came into the room and set down his briefcase under the table. He looked like a professor—all that was missing was a pipe.

"Welcome. This is the bimonthly Abuse Survivors Support Group. I'm Dr. Paul Benedetti. Please call me Paul or Dr. Paul."

Stefano looked around the room. They all seemed like normal guys... but they were here.

"Since we have several new people this week, I'd like to go over the rules. You don't have to say anything at all. We don't judge each other. Agreement isn't essential, but respect is. If you want to ask a question or add to what the person who's sharing is saying, please raise your hand. We listen when someone else is talking. What is said in this room stays in this room. Are we good?"

Stefano nodded along with the others.

"Is there anyone who wants to share?" Dr. Paul asked.

Over half the men raised their hands.

Why was Stefano here? It wasn't like he was going to spill out his dirty details. *To listen. Keep your mouth shut and maybe you'll learn something.*

Dr. Paul gestured to one of the guys in suits. He looked like a football player, but the fancy threads screamed accountant.

Mr. Accountant gave a small smile along with a wave. "Hi, my name is Francis. I did a big long share a few meetings ago, so this is an update. For the new people here, my biggest problem was my therapy negatively affected my relationship with Joey, my partner."

Partner? Was he gay? He didn't look—

"It was all the little things. Joey would get hurt when I'd jump a mile when he'd come up behind me and hug me. Also, sometimes during sex my mind goes to that place where it's dark and ugly. When I said it's me, not him, he didn't believe me. He thought he was doing something to cause me to feel that way. I was pretty afraid I'd lose him…."

Francis smiled. "Well, I took everyone's advice, and we've gone to counseling together. It wasn't easy doing the EMDR stuff and couple's counseling, but I made the time because it was important."

Dr. Paul raised a hand, and when Francis gave him a head nod, asked, "Could you explain what EMDR therapy is?"

"Right. Sorry. Eye Movement Desensitization and Reprocessing. It helps you reprocess traumatic memories with less stress since your mind is partially on watching the therapist waving their hand or is distracted by the buzzers you hold. That puts you in rapid eye movement so your brain can't use the usual path of processing a memory…. Anyway, the therapist helped me articulate why it really is me sometimes and gave me better ways to communicate. She gave Joey suggestions on ways to support me when I come home from EMDR therapy and can't be touched."

A guy across the table raised his hand until Francis gestured to him.

"So what was the advice, if you don't mind me asking, 'cause, you know… my wife… it's hard." He dropped his attention to the piece of patterned gold-and-white origami paper he held in his hand.

Francis nodded. "First thing was I should tell Joey when my appointments are so we can plan a down night. When I get home, we sit in front of the TV and have pizza. Usually we watch something stupid. Toward the end of the episode, I'm usually able to reach out and hold his hand. Sometimes we talk about what I discovered in therapy, sometimes not. Last night after therapy I let him hold me as I bawled like a baby."

Dr. Paul cleared his throat.

Francis shrugged. "I know, Paul. Sorry, I know crying is a step in the right direction, but I hate feeling so out of control. All my life it's been about keeping myself in check and not letting myself go down bad paths, 'cause I've been afraid I'd never come back or stop crying."

Amen! How do you get back from that? Best to simply not to go there.

"Been there." The guy nodded but didn't look up from folding his paper.

"Done that, but worth it," Leo muttered.

"Anyway, I feel like Joey and I are connecting, and for the first time in a long time, I know we can make us work again. Thank you for listening and your suggestions." Francis grabbed a bottle of water from his bag and took a big swallow.

"Thanks for sharing that with us, Francis. I'm happy that you were able to let Joey in and allowed him to comfort you. That's amazing progress. It's hard on spouses, partners, girlfriends, boyfriends, or families, because they see us say or do things, and usually they can't understand why. So it's wonderful when we're able to include them in our healing process, even if it's only letting them know it's going on in the broadest of terms."

The guy who asked the question half raised his hand until Dr. Paul motioned to him. He set the cool crane he made on the table. "Um, so could I have a recommendation of who me and my wife should see?"

"If you're not seeing someone yourself who is able to meet with you and your wife, I'll be happy to provide you a list." Dr. Paul wrote a note on his pad, then readdressed the group. "Again, you don't have to go into therapy, but talking to someone will support and give you an opportunity to get a handle on some of these traumatic events. Bringing our darkest times to light helps to reduce some of the highly charged power these memories embody. Who else would like to share?"

The origami-folder raised his hand, and once Dr. Paul pointed at the guy, he held up an origami paper bird. "I've made 999 of these. They say when you make a 1,000 you can have a wish granted."

"So what are you going to wish for?" someone asked.

He shrugged and shook his head. "I don't know. That's why I haven't made the last one. Thanks for listening."

Dr. Paul nodded. "Take your time, there's no rush. Ritualized practices like making cranes or any repetitive activity can be effective in soothing the mind. Allowing your mind to quiet can help you set a direction or a goal."

Maybe Stefano should try. He couldn't find inspiration to work on his unfinished pieces, but he missed not creating things. Maybe if the art was a matter of doing certain steps… it was worth a try.

"Who else would like to share?"

Half the guys raised their hands, clamoring to talk.

The therapist pointed right next to Stefano at Leo.

"I'm Leo, and I'm a survivor of sexual assault." His gaze skittered to Stefano. "I couldn't always say that so—yeah, um, anyway, I saw three movies."

Movies?

Leo shrugged. "Dr. Paul always says we don't know what might trigger us. Well, me and the wife streamed that old movie *Unbreakable*. It's about this guy who couldn't get hurt and another guy who kept breaking every bone in his body. Anyway, she wanted to see them in order. She likes things a certain way, so we're watching the second one, *Split*. A guy with schizophrenia who has twenty-four personalities... he kidnaps girls and kills them. Real dark shit, but there's one scene with the beast, that's what all the personalities call the killing monster, where basically he won't hurt the girl because she was abused like him. Got to say, that broke me."

Leo wiped a hand over his face and then squeezed the table. "What went through my head was, she wasn't even worthy of the beast wanting to hurt her and how maybe if she wasn't careful she'd become terrible, not like in a killing spree sort of a way, but not caring about others.

"Anyway, at the end of that movie, the abused girl is safe and in a cop car. Her abuser shows up, and the movie ends without knowing what happens. All I could think of was seeing the learned helplessness we've talked about in here. How she had been abused for so long that she no longer tried to escape even when offered the opportunity. Sort of the way I used to feel."

Me too. Stefano related. He tried to tell and had been beaten for it. Eventually it became how things were. What he learned was to section off parts of himself in order to survive.

Leo coughed. "Anyway, I felt all of her horror, and the feeling fucking ripped me apart. After I convinced the wife I had to see this horror through, we watched the third movie, *Glass*. And you know what? That girl told. She was with a happy foster family and escaped her predator. She thrived. To make a long story longer... sorry, guys, for all the spoilers. Anyway, at the end of the movie, the *Glass* character said this was an origin story. It was the beginning, not the end."

Hitting the table, Leo made the sound bounce off the wall. "I decided I'm a sexual assault survivor, but that's not all I am. I'm strong. I've got a great wife, terrific boys, and a good job. Father Lucca didn't define me. He defined himself as a monster. This is my origin story, and just because I was harmed doesn't mean that's my whole story or I'm going to turn into something horrible to survive. And I'm not going to let that fucker win. I'm going to do more than survive. I'm going to live, love, and be fucking happy in spite of that miserable prick."

Stefano wiped at the tears that streamed down his face. Hearing Leo made him shake from the inside out.

Leo put a hand on Stefano's shoulder and squeezed. "It's okay, man."

Stefano grabbed him in a hug and whispered, "I'm so sorry. I should have warned you. I'm a shit."

"Nah, man, you were a kid. Not much either of us could do. Wasn't like our parents would have let us not serve on the altar."

But guilt ate at Stefano. He could have let Leo know, so maybe he might have—

Leo slapped him on the back and released him. "Don't would have, could have, or should have on yourself. That fucker is to blame, not you."

Francis slid two unopened bottles of water down the table to them.

Stefano grabbed the bottle and nodded his thanks. Sipping the water, he tried not to puke.

By the fourth meeting, Stefano almost looked forward to being in a room with people who'd experienced the same horrors he had. The shared trauma seemed to lighten, as if each were carrying a little bit less of the weight that had always crushed him when he tried to do it alone. Not all the same guys came to each of the meetings, but there was a core group of five who were always there, like him.

Stefano set his paper out and began folding as Dr. Paul started the meeting. He wasn't the only one who made origami cranes during the sessions. There were three of them. Stefano was up to folding about twenty every day. Each one was carefully placed in a box.

"Hi, my name is Sam. I began Eye Movement Desensitization and Reprocessing therapy, you know, EMDR. The memories of when I was sexually abused were freeze-dried. I only had flashes of memories from when I was thirteen to seventeen."

Fuck, I wish. I get to relive every filthy fucking detail, feeling everything again and again. The fingerprints seemed to still mark his body no matter how much he scrubbed, except when Riku— No!

"But it seems like every session with the buzzers more memories flood—"

"Buzzers from hell," Francis said.

Sam nodded. "You got that right. I know it's part of the process, but damn, it's god-awful some days."

Stefano had done a little research on the EMDR stuff, and some people said this type of therapy worked and helped quicker. Recalling a terrible memory, then having alternating buzzers go off in your hands or watching a therapist wave a pen or fingers in slow movements put the person in rapid eye movement. The usual pathways the memory traveled were blocked by the REM, so the memory was forced to travel down different paths. Bringing up and thinking about a memory when in REM made it become less painful over the sessions. Supposedly you were able to see the traumatic event from another perspective, and it would seem different to you, based on your life experiences.

Dr. Paul cleared his throat. "Do you have more you want to share, Sam?"

"Nah, just letting you guys know I'm doing it and EMDR sucks."

The therapist nodded. "It does. Does anyone else want to share, or do we want to discuss EMDR some more?"

When no one raised their hand to share, Leo chimed in, "I've been doing EMDR for about three years on and off. Sometimes it feels like my skin is peeled off and sea salt is being rubbed on my raw parts. I hate it. I won't lie, but the thing is, it really has helped me. Sometimes the only way out of Hell is through."

"Do you want to share how, Leo?" Dr. Paul asked in his "please, I hope you share more" voice.

Leo shrugged. "What's to tell? I guess I'm able to see and accept things I couldn't before. Like I blamed myself. If I wasn't alone in the rectory, if I told someone, if, if, if... and EMDR helped me realize I couldn't have stopped that bastard. He was a predator, and I was just a kid. But that fuck didn't break me."

Riku had told Stefano that he wasn't broken. Not quite true. Not being with Riku was breaking him, but he did need help. That much was clear.

Stefano swallowed hard. He could do this. Frank always said insanity was doing the same thing and expecting a different result. He raised his hand.

Dr. Paul motioned to him.

He asked, "Could I have a list of therapists who do EMDR?"

Leo slapped him on the back. "It stinks, but it gets better."

"The more you know," Francis snarked.

Stefano smirked at living a public service announcement.

A FEW weeks later, Leo stood. "Before the meeting starts, I want to invite you all over for St. Pat's Day on Sunday. The wife and I are making corned beef hash."

"I'll bring the green beer," Francis offered.

Leo grinned. "I look forward to meeting Joey."

Most of the guys nodded or shouted out their acceptances.

Sitting, Leo smacked Stefano. "You going to be there or what?"

"What time?"

"After dinner with your mom. Come whenever, just be there."

Stefano nodded. He started folding paper to create a crane.

A few people shared. They each seemed a little lighter afterward.

Stefano knew the wish he'd make once he made the thousandth crane, but he had to do more than fold paper for it to come true. He set his folded crane upright with the others in front of him and forced himself to raise his hand.

Dr. Paul's eyes widened slightly, and then he motioned for Stefano to share.

"I'm Stefano. I'm not very good at this, but I've been coming here for about two and a half months. I've started EMDR therapy. I'm a survivor of sexual abuse and child abuse. That's only the second time I've ever said that out loud."

He gripped the table. This shit was fucking hard. "I was afraid to revisit the past, but my therapist—thanks for the list, Dr. Paul—pointed out my nightmares or *night terrors*, as she called them, force me to relive them anyway. So what did I have to lose?"

Several people nodded in encouragement.

Stefano swallowed hard and shrugged. "When I told my dad, or started to tell him about what Father Lucca had done to me, he beat me. My back's all scarred, but even worse, what he did was blame me. He said nothing happened, and if anything did, the whole thing was my fault, that I wasn't strong enough… and because I must be a fag. That I must have wanted it."

Did he go further? Could he say the words? Looking around the room, he saw no judgment, only eyes haunted by similar experiences.

"I didn't want my father to be right. So I did everything in my power to make him wrong. I mean, after that monster hurt me, how could I ever want a man? But I can finally admit, I'm bisexual. I've always been attracted to both women and men. And, well, no one knows about my orientation, but EMDR rips everything open, and I guess I have to pour some of it out of me."

His eyes got blurry, but he didn't let it stop him. He kept going. "I was with a man. A really good man who completely got me, and I pushed him away—ran away, if I'm honest."

"Can you share with us how long ago that was?" Leo asked without raising his hand, earning an arched eyebrow from Dr. Paul.

"Right before the holidays. I didn't want him to have someone so unworthy as me. Ouch!" Stefano rubbed the back of his head.

Dr. Paul growled. "Leo, should I call security?"

"No, but Stefano is worthy of any man. He's a good guy with a great big heart, and he needed a bop to the head for talking stupid."

"Leo!" Dr. Paul took off his glasses and set them on the table. He appeared to be gearing up to launch into a lecture.

Stefano waved him off and he started chuckling. He couldn't help it. One of the guys who knew him the longest whacked him, not for being bisexual, but for thinking he wasn't good enough for another guy. "It's okay, Dr. Paul. I've knocked him in the head a time or two. It's all good."

Leo crossed his arms over his chest and smiled smugly, as if he'd created a new "whack 'em on the head" therapy.

"So I want everything up until now to be my origin story." Stefano patted Leo on the shoulder.

"Aw, you big dummy, it is. Sexual assault and abuse don't define us. It only identifies us as having survived monsters."

After one other share, Dr. Paul said, "Remember as you're walking through your trauma and all the confusion, anger, and sadness that is attached to it: there is a light at the end of it."

After grunts of agreement, Dr. Paul pointed to the table. "Feel free to help yourself to coffee and doughnuts. We have the room for another half an hour."

Leo said for Stefano's ears, "And if someone's not patient enough to see the light, I'm here to smack 'em in the head."

"I'm gonna tell Dr. Paul." Stefano snorted playfully and slugged Leo's arm.

AFTER MA'S Sunday dinner, Stefano headed over to Leo's place. Leo welcomed him inside. He took Stefano's jacket and hung it for him. "We got a fire going. The food is in the dining room. Make sure you eat; otherwise you'll get my wife mad at you."

"I will. Thank you." Stefano was ashamed that he had avoided the guy for so long, but Leo easily forgave him, and their friendship seemed to pick right up where he'd abandoned it.

Stefano drank some green beer, and one of the guys who hadn't shared in the group yet approached him.

"Hey, your share last meeting meant a lot to me. Thank you."

"You're welcome." Stefano wasn't sure if he should ask for his name or—

"I'm Phillip, by the way."

Stefano shook his hand. "Nice to meet you. I'm Stefano."

"I know. I was also abused... physically, I mean. Cigar burns... anyway, you said your back was scarred. I go to a tattoo artist up in Albany."

"New York? That's like, what, four hours from here."

"About, but worth every mile. He's helped turn my pain and terrible memories into something beautiful. Weird, I never expected to find healing in ink, but whatever works. If you ever want his contact information, I'll happily give it to you."

"Thanks. I've never thought about—I try not to think about my fucked-up back."

"Just a thought." Phillip pointed at the television. "Now what is happening with the Phillies? Seriously! Take off your mittens! Catch the fricking ball!"

"Oh." Stefano grimaced as the other team scored a run.

"Glad the regular season doesn't start until next week," Phillip grumbled.

STEFANO PARKED his bike in front of the shop.

When his EMDR therapist claimed he'd been making great progress for his first few visits, she suggested, "You should do something other than make your origami cranes to mark the occasion."

Well, this was something. He had driven almost four hours, so he got his ass off his bike, stretched, took a deep breath, and then got his ass inside.

A guy with longish dark hair grinned while staring at his phone. "Okay, I've got to go. Give the sugar gliders and our man my love. Bye, sweetness."

Our man? Hmmm, poly. After researching so much on orientation, gender identity, and relationships, he didn't bat an eyelash over it. Good for them.

He glanced at Stefano. "Hi, I'm Marcus Sadir. Are you Stefano Rossi?"

"Yes."

"Right on time."

The praise, however not meant to, made Stefano smile. "Thanks so much for seeing me. You've come highly recommended."

"Thank you. So I got your email on what you were thinking about the design. May I see your back?" Marcus led him into an inner office, which seemed to resemble an edgy dentist office crossed with a sadistic punk band. A wild riot of colors appeared to have been splashed onto the walls and dripped to the polished concrete floor, and yet it somehow settled Stefano.

He took off his shirt, awaiting the typical gasp. When it didn't come, he peeked over his shoulder. "What?"

"This is an incredible road map of strength. May I?" Marcus reached out his hand. After a nod from Stefano, a warm palm ghosted over Stefano's gnarled back.

Stefano sighed. "It's a fucking mess. Is there anything you can do with it?"

"Plenty." The reverence in Marcus's voice threw Stefano.

"Um… okay?"

"Stefano, I've worked with a lot of scars. Many times, the harshest ones are the most beautiful. When a person goes through what you went through, they can either let it rot them from the inside out or they can do what you're doing, treating it like a stepping stone onto a better life."

My origin story....

Marcus stepped back in front of him and stared into his eyes. "You were forged in fire. I see someone who is incredibly strong and is morphing into who he wants to be. Um, sorry, I don't mean to get all philosophical on you."

Stefano wiped at his blurry eyes. "Nah, it's all good."

"I took your idea and expanded the design a bit. Here's a rough idea of what I was thinking." Marcus presented him with a sketch. Pointing to various sections, he listed the colors he'd use.

"Perfect." Stefano added a suggestion or two, but Marcus had this.

"What's great about this design is we can add to this as you evolve into who you are destined to become."

Stefano nodded, because that's exactly what he wanted. He lay on his stomach.

As soon as the sanitizing process was over, fire began to lick over his back. After a few minutes, he settled into the searing pain. The needle pressed him into a relaxed state. Not exactly subspace, but a place where he was calm and life seemed manageable.

"You're a sub, aren't you?"

Stefano opened his eyes to study Marcus in the mirror. "How did you—"

Marcus wiped at his back and glanced at his reflection. "The way you accept and absorb the pain. You endure, but you change the sting into something else."

"Spoken like a Dominant?" Stefano asked, but it wasn't a question. Marcus had the calm bearing of an expert in all facets of pain.

"More like a sadist with a masochist streak, but people read that as dominance, so I go with the label." He continued painting pain over parts of Stefano's back.

The loss of BDSM had been overwhelmed by losing Riku. He hadn't even acknowledged what a big hole had been left in his life.

"In between Mistresses or Masters?" No trace of judgment either way.

Stefano sighed. "Yeah."

"That was filled with longing." Marcus gave him the opening.

Should he take— "His name is Riku...." The tale of everything spun out from his lips. He ended with, "To him I'm like the scraps of metal I find. No one else can see the good in it, but to him I was everything."

Marcus worked in silence for a minute. "I think you're starting to let other people see who you are, so they can see the beauty in you as well. It also sounds like you're working your way back to him."

"I really hope I am."

CHAPTER 18

RIKU SAT in front of the painting. Staring at the blues and greens of the water... he waited. Folding his arms, he sighed and wished Monet's colors would return him to calm. Should he stop just going with the flow? Life for the past few months had been—

His cell phone vibrated his pocket. He grabbed it and saw Devon's big smile fill the screen. "Hey," he answered quietly.

"Hey yourself. You coming back into the office today?"

Riku glanced at his watch. Most of the afternoon was gone. "Wasn't planning on it."

"No worries. Dinner tomorrow night before the demo?"

"Oh, right... um...." He'd forgotten about the damned demonstration he'd committed to doing last year at the scheduling meeting.

"You forgot?" Devon's shock bounced around like a beach ball.

"Don't make it sound like a crime. People forget things." Geez, things happened.

"Riku, you don't forget things. Besides, you can't keep holing up in your house. It's been over four months," Devon reasoned with him, or tried to.

It had been one hundred and thirty days, to be exact, because Riku had indeed been counting. And actually, he could hole up in his house and did. Though waiting took more effort than he ever imagined. "How much time am I supposed to give him?"

They loved each other, but that didn't look like it mattered all that much. *Great. We love each other. It changes nothing.* But Stefano's screamed admission kept him tethered to hope.

But didn't the confession change everything? There had to be a way to make him and Stefano work. Granted there was, but Stefano had refused therapy, and without being willing to work through some of the issues affecting him, there was only so much Riku could ever do. Stefano might never be able to accept his orientation or Riku publicly. And going back into the closet was not something Riku would do, though in truth he missed Stefano enough that he'd considered the possibility of maintaining separate parts of his life—but that wasn't living.

Devon sighed. "How much time? I don't know, man, and I know waiting for someone who may never come around feels terrible. Years can pass and…."

"I'm sorry, Dev." Riku stood and paced closer to the painting. He was well aware of how skilled Devon was in the art of waiting for someone who might never come around. He had learned to live his life… mostly.

"No worries. I wish I had answers for you."

"Maybe I should reach out to him? He might not feel comfortable contacting me." That was logical. Responsible, even… no, that's what he wanted, not what Stefano needed. "You said he looked good when you saw him in January."

Devon must have been stretching his neck to the side because a decided crack was followed by a moan. "Yes, which is why I gave him the three-month prescription."

As irrational as it was, that still annoyed Riku. That quarterly prescription denied even the possibility of seeing Stefano at the office more than every three months, which was probably for the best. "Well, maybe he's so good he doesn't want me creeping after him."

"Just focus on developing yourself. I've got a couple more links for you about guiding a sub who has a history of abuse."

If he were honest, he should have been better prepared, but he would be going forward. Researching and studying was the only thing that kept Riku sane. He combed his fingers through his hair. "Thanks."

Devon groaned, probably at Riku's melancholy tone. "Jesus, get a grip. You know he has to come to terms with himself in his own way. I get it's a bitch for you, but I promise, I really believe you're helping him by giving him space."

Riku groaned, cutting off the "but what if he never comes back to me" with "I hope so too."

"So, you're going to be there tomorrow night, right?" Devon's mischievous glint could actually be heard over the phone.

"I don't know," he hedged, not wanting to commit to doing the demo.

Devon growled and probably glared at his cell phone. "Come on. You canceled on every single one of the Edge's demos you signed up to do so far this year."

Of course Devon was right, but Riku didn't want to work with another sub, even if it helped people. Wow, that was selfish on his part. "Fine, I'll do it, and yes, we'll meet before the demo."

AS THE demo drew closer, dread dragged through Riku's entire body. He felt out of it. If Devon hadn't *escorted* him to the club after dinner, he doubted he would have made it.

Riku waved Devon over. "Hey, I'm sorry, I'm not feeling well. I have to go home. I can't do this."

Devon stepped in front of him, not only preventing his escape, but manhandling Riku back toward the makeshift stage. "Bullshit."

"I can't do it, Devon." How could he? Maybe he was catching something.

"Riku, I'll do the physical part of the demo, but you do the presentation. Deal?" Devon made the whole thing sound like a decision had been reached.

He didn't like that, but…. "You'll do the aftercare?"

That was the stumbling block because he couldn't imagine bringing anyone other than Stefano back down to earth. The way he hit subspace and trusted Riku to catch him was nothing short of a miracle.

Riku couldn't handle doing that for another sub, not yet.

Devon grinned. "Of course. I've played with Amanda and David before. They're a cute couple. She's very sweet, and he's incredibly submissive."

Riku sighed. "Fine. Can you talk to them?"

He leaned back against the wall and waited, hoping they'd agree.

The two subs nodded enthusiastically, and Amanda gave Riku a thumbs-up. Devon stayed with them for a couple of minutes, probably prepping them on the demonstration's scene. When they meandered over to him, both were breathy and their eyes shone with excitement.

After confirming their readiness, Riku clapped his hands for the audience's attention. "Okay, let's get this demo underway. I'm feeling a little under the weather, so Doc will be doing the hands-on part of the demo, and I'll do the talking."

Devon stage-whispered to the crowd, "Just like always."

Several of the audience members chuckled. Riku didn't even spare a glance over his shoulder, because Devon wasn't wrong.

Riku dug deep and started the basic BDSM demo.

The couple seemed to give Devon a run for his money, each requiring something different, but he rose to the challenge.

At the end of the demonstration, Riku was exhausted. He parted ways with Devon, but instead of heading home to his empty house, he gave in to his desire to stop by the diner. He hadn't been inside since he last met Stefano there.

He swallowed hard as the waitress who used to wait on Stefano and him led him to "their" table.

This might be a bad idea, but it was as close as he'd been to Stefano in months, or at least the memory of Stefano. They had been apart for twice as long as they'd been together. Being here again made everything feel real, that it hadn't been his imagination of finding the perfect sub... and losing him.

The waitress set the menu down. With a hand on her hip, glancing over at the door, she asked, "Where's your friend?"

He didn't know what to say because he wished he knew where Stefano was and what he was doing. "Not coming tonight."

"Ah, he said the same thing when I asked where you were. Did you guys break up or something?"

"We were never together." Not really. As connected as the two of them had been, they hadn't had much of a relationship.

Yes, it was starting to develop into something, his heart whined.

She squinted her eyes at him in a clear show of disbelief and then started to move back to the kitchen.

"Wait. Stefano was here?" After she gave him a blank stare, he clarified, "My friend."

"Yeah. Tuesday night, I think." She shook her head. "And he looked as forlorn as you."

He stared after her as she continued into the kitchen.

What did that mean?

She came back to take his order.

"I'll just have water and a sugar cookie." He tried not to ask, but there was no stopping the hope reawakening in his heart. "Was that the first time you've seen him in a while?"

"Yeah, at least on my shift. The last time I saw either of you was when you both bitterly complained about pumpkin spice everything until you shared your first pumpkin spice latte. Then you both ordered one for yourselves." She grinned and hustled to the counter.

The image of Stefano's surprised and very pleased smile as he tasted the latte came to mind. *See, trying things isn't always bad.* Soon after, Stefano came to his house and tried him.

What did it mean that Stefano had returned to this diner? Had he been hoping to see Riku? Maybe he should resume coming to the diner himself....

IT WAS dumb, but Riku found himself ambling over to the diner on Tuesday night. His hands were sweaty, even though Pennsylvania's springtime warmth hadn't made an appearance in New Hope yet. He entered the diner, holding his breath as he searched the booths.

The waitress led Riku to *their* booth. He ate chicken and vegetable stir-fry.

No sign of Stefano.

Riku forced himself to go home on Wednesday night, but on Thursday he had no such self-control, and here he was again two days later hoping for a fix.

When he got to the diner, he swallowed hard on the nervous flip of his stomach. He searched the windows of the diner and jogged up the steps for a quick peek.

Again, no Stefano.

Before he could turn around and leave, the waitress ambled over to him. "Your usual booth?"

"Sure." Why not? He was already here.

"By the way, you missed your friend by thirty minutes on Tuesday." She set the menu down.

"What? I mean... oh." Stefano had come back to the diner. Excitement skittered through him.

She arched her eyebrow at him. "And I think he mentioned he'd be in tonight."

Immediately a rope seemed to tighten around Riku's heart. He clenched his jaw to keep his breathing even. "Thanks."

What should he do? Did Stefano really want him here, or was it just wishful thinking?

A motorcycle revved down the street.

Riku swallowed hard as he forced himself not to run out into the parking lot. He imagined their joyous reunion as Stefano leaping into his arms and Riku hugging him while spinning in dizzying circles. Wow, too many sappy movies set his expectations into places that were impossible to get to with a closeted man.

He rocked in the padded booth, taking deep calming breaths, trying to find his center. Minutes passed, and the only thing that happened was the waitress took his order.

Crushing disappointment almost made him call this the fool's errand it was.

A softer, slower purr made him look out the window, but he missed even catching much of a glimpse of the rider. Black helmet like Stefano's, but a lot of riders had black helmets. Maybe?

The waitress brought him the salad of the day, not that Riku could eat.

He waited and focused on his breathing. It was as if all the months, days, hours, and minutes coiled themselves, making this the longest passage of time ever.

Staring at the table, he gave up on finding his center and now just searched for a bit of balance.

Ding. Ding. Ding.

The little golden bell attached to the door gave Riku one of the sweetest sounds he'd ever heard. He couldn't keep his eyes down for another second.

There he was.

Riku's heart skipped a beat. He clutched the table and forced himself to stay seated.

Since it wasn't dusk yet, the light shone over Stefano, creating a halo of gold around him. Riku hadn't imagined it: Stefano truly was heart-stoppingly beautiful. His dark curls framed his face, and his eyes widened as his gaze tangled with Riku's.

Time ceased to exist.

Stefano face's lit with a smile. All the wants and needs he had come to Riku with were still there, yearning to be satisfied by his Master.

Their connection had definitely stayed strong.

Riku forced himself not to twine Stefano to him.

Though he couldn't suppress his lips as they turned up with the first real bit of happiness he'd felt since the last moments before everything between them went sideways.

But then Stefano suppressed his expression by pressing his lips together.

Why did he—maybe he really hadn't wanted to see me. Perhaps that wasn't longing at all but surprise, or worse, dismay.

Stefano's long, dark lashes rested on his cheeks as he focused on the floor as if he were measuring the steps to his motorcycle. He hadn't released the doorknob yet.

Some things never changed. Would he simply turn on his heel and leave?

But Riku couldn't stop smiling, though it morphed from ecstatic into more of a *please don't bolt, talk to me* smile. He tried not to move or speak. This should be however Stefano wanted this meeting to be.

Shrugging out of his leather coat, Stefano took the long way around some tables to get to Riku, as if he were dragging a weight behind him. When he reached the table, he finally looked at Riku. "Do you mind if I—"

"No, please." *Sheesh. Calm. Even. Control.*

Stefano slid into the booth across from him.

Every moment of separation between them melted. The bindings Riku hadn't known restrained him came unlatched. He sat on his hands to keep from reaching out to touch his sub.

His sub! His Stefano. Mine!

Afraid to break the spell, Riku remained silent and tried not to stare at him.

Stefano appeared to be absorbing Riku's very being, exactly the way he did when they used to accidentally-on-purpose meet here.

"How have you been?" The question was posed to Riku like he didn't want to demand exactly the same information from Stefano.

"I've been better." No pretending, no games. "It's been a difficult few months. You?"

Stefano sniffed and twisted his hands together. "Yeah, same… really hard. You canceled your demonstrations, except the last one."

"Were you there?" *How did I miss him?*

"Yeah, in the back. Devon did a good job with that couple."

"So you still go to the Edge?" Riku was annoyed at himself for the jealousy that tried to creep through him. Of course Stefano went to the club. Why wouldn't he?

"No… I only went since, *you know*—you were doing a demonstration." *You know* named the end of them, or was it only a pause for them?

Riku was too afraid to ask or hope. Hope was the enemy. In their time apart, it became evident the only thing he wanted was Stefano, and even sitting right across from him, Riku still didn't know if that was even a possibility.

"Oh…." That had to mean something… positive, right? Scrambling for something nonthreatening, Riku asked, "What have you been up to?"

"I, um, I started going to a support group."

Wow! Doing a Devon happy dance would be a bit much, so Riku controlled the urge. "How long have you been going?"

"Since January."

Riku couldn't stop his heart from singing with gratitude. His sub was trying to get help. "That's great. How are you finding it?"

Stefano squirmed in his seat, rubbing his back against the booth. "The guys are good and give lots of good suggestions. I even started working with an EMDR therapist as well."

It took everything in Riku not to leap across the table and hug him again and again. That therapy was recommended for people with Stefano's type of trauma.

The time apart seemed to have solidified in Stefano his need for some assistance. While Riku hated that distance denied him the opportunity to support and provide a safe haven for Stefano, he admired Stefano's determination. He was getting the help he needed to banish his monsters from hell, and that took an impressive amount of courage.

Keeping his voice even, Riku asked, "How are you finding EMDR? I hear it's tough but—"

"Hey. Good to see you both here at the same time." The waitress appeared at their table.

Stefano smiled and gave her a nod but focused all his attention on the menu as if the five items were in a foreign language.

"What can I get for you, hon?" The waitress grinned as she set a glass of water in front of Stefano.

"Um, I'll have the same as him." Stefano pointed to Riku's untouched salad.

"Coming right up." She gave Riku an "I told you so" smile right before she turned and vanished into the kitchen.

Riku couldn't wait another second. "You were starting to tell me about how you are finding therapy."

"You're right. EMDR is nightmarishly tough. It's the second hardest thing I've ever done in my life." Stefano traced his finger along the condensation on his water glass.

Before thinking, Riku asked, "What was harder?"

"Walking—running away from you." Stefano's casual tone almost made Riku's heart implode.

Everything in Riku stopped. He wanted Stefano back, but he....

Stefano caught his gaze. "Are you seeing anyone?"

"No. No one. I still love you. I'm hoping...." Riku couldn't finish that thought without breaking, so he pressed his lips together and willed Stefano to read everything that was in his eyes.

Well, so much for allowing Stefano to do this on own his terms without pressure.

Stay in control. Be patient.

Stefano's gaze held his. He reached across the table and grabbed Riku's hand.

Riku squeezed and instinctually wanted to tend to Stefano's hands, which he wasn't taking proper care of, but it wasn't his place... yet.

Stefano cleared his throat. "I'm working very hard. The therapist says I've made lots of progress with the EMDR therapy, and the support group has been really good for me. I can say things like 'I'm bisexual. I was sexually and physically abused.' I want to get better, or rather, handle things better."

Happiness spiked throughout Riku. If nothing else, that alone made all the pain of the last eternity apart worth it. He wasn't sure if he had any right to say it, but he couldn't stop himself. "I'm so proud of you."

"But—"

And that one word drop-kicked Riku's elation and hope to the curb. Riku's heart was stretched and bound on a St. Andrew's cross. "Ah, of course there's a *but*."

Stefano shook his head. "Not really—okay, yeah, I guess. I haven't been able to come out to my family yet, though I'm working on it."

"In therapy?" That counted. Did that mean he was really planning on coming out to them?

"Yeah."

That was still a miracle, and regardless of the reason, Riku was thrilled for him.

Stefano stood and placed a slip of paper on the table. "Riku, I have no right to ask you for anything, but would you meet me here on the first Saturday in June?"

That was a month away, and the address was in Philly. "Sure. Yes. Of course."

"Thank you. Really. I... I should go." Stefano dropped a twenty on the table and left.

Wait! Don't go yet.

But just like trying to hold water in a strainer, he couldn't keep Stefano from slipping out the door.

RIKU'S MOTHER'S teahouse didn't open for another two hours, so maybe he could talk to his parents. He tapped on the opaque glass door.

Within a minute, his mother threw open the door. "Come in, Riku. Come in."

She hugged him and ushered him through her teahouse. Since her marriage was blended, she wanted to represent more than one style of teahouse. The first section was an overly laced Victorian English tearoom. He zigzagged around wooden tables and chairs, following her through the Chinese screen doors. The Chinese tearoom was based on the hundred-year-old one in Tongli, China. Finally they passed through the ornate cherry wood to the serene Japanese tearoom in the very back.

The decor was pure simplicity, yet elegant. His father had insisted some of the tatami mats be cut out so their customers didn't have to balance on their knees the way his mother favored. He had been correct; the traditional tables were rarely booked, and usually not for a second time. People in Philly were more comfortable sitting.

His father appeared with a tray filled with two white teapots, three handleless cups, plates, and steaming baked muffins and croissants.

Riku studied them. His mother was quiet and reserved but fit his father perfectly. It was hard to believe she rebelled against her family's expectations when she not only fell in love with the Chinese boy she met at the University of Pennsylvania but married him. They'd stood together against their culture and the expectations of their families. He was the product of their rebellion.

After greeting him, his father poured the tea and his mother made sure everyone had a baked good on their plate. Then she leaned toward Riku. "I love that you surprised us, but what's on your mind?"

"That obvious?"

She smiled and pushed his long hair over his shoulder. "Only because your visits are usually planned and at night, not in the morning, and you look like you're not sleeping. It's been this way for a while. Will you talk to us about what is troubling you?"

"In October I met someone—"

"Who? When can we meet him?" His mother tapped his father on the arm.

"We can have him to dinner whenever it's convenient—" His father's offer ground to a halt. "What?"

Riku hated to disappoint them. "We aren't seeing each other... well, not yet anyway."

He unwound the entire story, leaving out the BDSM parts and focusing on them breaking up right after they said they loved each other, how difficult their time apart was, and the mysterious *meeting* Stefano requested.

Riku's mother leaned over both their teacups and grabbed his hand. "First, is he a good man, this Stefano?"

"Yes. Yes, he is. The best I've ever met." Riku couldn't stop a smile from giving away his besotted state.

"Tell us about him," his father demanded in a way that suggested the jury was still out.

"Well, he's a mechanic and really creative—an artist. Look, here's some of his pieces. He recycles scraps from his work at the garage or what he finds and makes gorgeous abstract art." Riku opened the photo albums of Stefano's art on his phone.

His mother reviewed each picture, and when she was finished scrolling through, she pulled off her glasses. "He's got a striking look and is quite talented. If you were still seeing him, I'd ask him to consider making some smaller pieces to sell in the tea shop."

Riku glanced over at his mom's new shelving unit that displayed local artists' work. "If we ever are again, I'll ask."

His father sipped some tea and then asked, "Didn't you say he asked to meet you in June?"

"Yes." Riku's heart expanded while each beat pumped hope into him.

"That's a start. I remember one young woman in college who made me wait and—"

"I wanted to tell my family face-to-face I had met you and we were serious." This was the only discussion that could make his mother lose her serenity and morph her expression into a frustrated pout.

The smirk his father wore said he enjoyed teasing her, but just like tickling a cricket, it wasn't as fun for the cricket or his mother.

"She wanted time. It was a lot I was asking of her... and you're asking a lot of Stefano. These few months, as hard as they have been, are but a drop in the bucket. Things have a way of working out—that's the scone timer." His father hustled into the kitchen to rescue the scones.

His mother patted his hand. "Have faith that love will win."

Riku nodded. "It's my faith that I'm afraid of."

CHAPTER 19

GLANCING AROUND his ma's table, everything was exactly the same as it had been almost every single Sunday of his life.

What Stefano planned to say next might change that forever.

Sweat tickled down his back, and he wiped both palms on his pants.

The therapist had told him time and time again, he didn't need to rush his decision of coming out to his family. But how much more of his life was he willing to spend not being honest about himself?

Stefano had waited long enough.

He was ready… at least he hoped.

Focusing on Frank and Angie helped. Over the years, they had made it clear how supportive they were of LGBTQIA+ people. Through therapy and leaving most of his hard denial behind, Stefano had come to realize they might have been sending him signals that they would stand by him no matter what. They were safe.

But what if he was wrong? Fuck!

Think before you speak. Figure out the consequences of everything you say. Was he supposed to continue walking on eggshells and worrying about everyone else's reactions? Putting everyone else's feelings above his own?

No, he was done with that bullshit. Maybe it was the all-or-nothing mindset he was working on in therapy, but he found he could no longer hide. He needed to break free, even if that meant breaking everything. He had to say something, and it had to be now. Right this very moment.

Clearing his throat, he said, "Um, I've got something to say."

Marco scoffed. "When don't you? You finally going to tell us you're a fag?"

Angie moved sharply toward Marco.

"Ow. Ma! Angie kicked me," Marco whined.

Ma glared at Marco, then turned her full attention to Stefano. She held her hands in her lap. "Go ahead, Stefano. We're listening."

"Well, um—" How did he put this? Fuck, now that he started, he didn't want to chicken out.

Marco growled. "For Christ's sake, spit it out."

"I'm bisexual." Stefano cast the words before he could deliberate further.

Marco grabbed Stefano's shirt, pulled him out of his chair, and got in his face. "I knew you were a fucking queer."

Ma screamed, "Stop!"

Frank peeled Stefano away from Marco. Then nonviolent Frank drew his fist back as if he was going to punch Marco in the teeth.

Angie stepped in and grabbed Frank. "Stop that, Frank."

Frank grimaced as his wild gaze darted around the room. He panted but unclenched his fist.

Angie blocked Frank with her body, did an unexpected quick turn, and kneed Marco right in the balls. When Marco doubled over, she stomped on his foot. "I'm fucking done with you. It's not okay to be a homophobic asshole! And it never was."

"Ow! Motherfucker!" Marco growled and held his crotch.

Angie winked at Stefano and then stomped on Marco's foot again. "Now sit down, you jackass."

Marco grumbled, "Bitch," and fell into his chair.

Frank patted Angie on the back. "I see you've kept up with the self-defense classes."

"Best birthday present ever. But hey, I didn't want you to hurt your hand, because you are playing volleyball on the UU team." She took her seat and gestured to Stefano. "Sorry for the interruption, Stef. You were saying?"

Stefano swallowed hard. "Um, I said I was bi."

"Goddamned queer. I knew it." Marco grimaced.

Angie talked over Marco's grumbled slur, but his words still stabbed Stefano's heart. "We love and support you, Stefano."

Frank smiled. "Thank you for trusting us. I'm sorry some of us are stupid. But you know I've always got your back."

Stefano nodded and peered over at his mother.

She stared at her clasped hands.

Oh God! This was why he hadn't said anything. He knew it. Why did he just blurt it out? She wouldn't accept him. How could she? The Church said anything other than a man and a woman was wrong, and she bought it. Hell, until therapy, parts of him believed it too.

Angie snapped, "Ma? Say something to your son."

Silence.

Ma started twisting her hands. Stefano hadn't seen her do that since his father died. She got up and hurried into her bedroom.

Her bedroom lock sliding into place echoed in the dining room, saying everything she didn't.

"Great, genius. You upset—ow! Dammit, Angie, knock it off." Marco rubbed his shin.

She pointed at Marco. "You shut the fuck up. I'm done with your stupid."

Frank cleared his throat. "Ma needs some time. You know she loves you, Stefano. We all do."

Stefano pressed his lips together. He did know, but would her love for him be unconditional? Would it be enough for her to stand against everything she'd been raised to believe?

Escape. He had to get out of here. "I'm going to go."

Marco scoffed, "Yeah, sure. You ruin everything and now— motherfucker, stop it, Angie, or I'm going to call the police."

"Oh, please do. I'm sure the boys on the force will be real sympathetic to a whiny bastard like you complaining that your little sister is kicking your ass. You want to use my phone to call them?" She put down her fork—in his hand—and held out her cell phone.

"You stabbed me with your fork."

She rolled her eyes. "I didn't break skin. Should I try again?"

Stefano had had enough of this circus. He headed to the front door.

Frank pulled him into a hug as Stefano grabbed the knob. "You good?"

"Yeah, yeah." *No. No. No.* Stefano squeezed him and stepped back. Was Frank really okay with him?

"As soon as I get things calm here, I'll head home with leftovers. We can talk, or not, but we can definitely eat in peace."

"Sounds good." At that moment, it didn't, but whatever.

"Ma needs some time. I don't even know if she really understands what bisexual is, you know?"

Stefano bobbed his head. "I'll catch you at home."

Angie flew to the door and manhandled him into a hug. "Everything is going to be fine. I'm going to see you tomorrow for lunch."

Stefano shook his head. "You don't have—"

"Oh, you're not going to deny me taking you to lunch. What you did was huge. I'll pick you up at the garage at noon." She kissed his cheek and waltzed out of the room.

Stefano hurried to his bike. He stopped short and nabbed the tiny metal cylinder lying on the street.

Frank called out, "I'll see you at home."

After putting on his helmet, Stefano pocketed his newfound treasure and waved.

Traffic, houses, and street signs bled into asphalt.

He took the backroads along the Schuylkill River to see the flowering yellow bushes on Wissahickon Avenue.

The vibrations of the bike worked to soothe his nerves over the rest of the way. Then, instead of turning into his brother's townhouse complex, he kept on going.

He turned right onto Main Street in New Hope, slowing his speed as he passed the diner. Was Riku there? Should he stop? No, he had to get through this without his Master's help.

Stefano swallowed hard. Even if they were never together again, Riku would always be his Master. His back tingled as he drove past the Edge.

Fighting the usual exodus of New Hope this time on a Sunday made him glad to pull into his usual parking spot at home.

Frank pulled up alongside him. "You just get back?"

"Yeah, I took the long way home." Via his stalking route.

Frank held up a paper bag stuffed with food. "I think Angie crammed more stuff in when I wasn't looking. We should freeze some of it."

Stefano followed Frank to their door, then unlocked it, letting Frank in.

Unpacking the containers onto the dining room table, Frank asked, "You hungry? 'Cause I'm starved."

"I could eat something."

"Want anything warmed up?"

"Nah." Stefano grabbed plates, silverware, and two bottles of beer.

"Thanks." Frank took off the lid of the last container and sat.

Frank sighed. "Ah, cold spaghetti and meatballs are a gift from God."

Grinning around his mouthful, Stefano said, "You aren't wrong."

As they were slowing down, Frank asked, "Riku?"

Stefano grabbed his beer and finished it off. He nabbed two more from the fridge and handed one to Frank. "Yeah."

"So you two broke up?"

He wasn't driving, so he opened the bottle and took a gulp. Hiding his belch, he shrugged.

"What happened?"

Apparently that was all it took for the floodgates to open, and he gushed out all the details of the past four-plus months. He even shared about his group and his therapy. "Questions?"

Frank's eyes widened, and his breath left his body in jerky puffs. He stomped to the fireplace. His hands clenched into fists as he stared at the burned log and ash. His body shook, and then he let loose a scream filled with raw pain.

The rage pierced Stefano and made tears run out of the corners of his eyes. His therapist had tried to prepare him for the possible reactions his family might have to knowing the truth about the sexual assault and abuse, but it ripped at him to see Frank so overwhelmed.

Frank's head dropped, and he gripped the mantel with two hands as if he needed the support to remain upright.

Minutes passed.

Stefano had never seen Frank upset. No matter what happened, Frank was in control; he always kept his cool. He was the polar opposite of their dad.

Maybe Stefano should—

Frank turned and came back to the table and sat. Placing his hands in prayer formation, he tapped them against his lips. His carefully crafted lawyer expression was firmly in place.

"First, I can't even begin to tell you how sorry I am I wasn't there to help you."

"Frank, don't. You were at college—"

"I knew Dad was a bastard. We all walked on eggshells, but I didn't know about Father Lucca." Frank balled his hands into fists. "I should have known."

Stefano shrugged. "How? I did my very best to hide everything. I buried that shit so deep that even I could pretend it wasn't happening. I never thought about it until he'd catch me alone. I blanked it out."

Unfortunately I couldn't block the nightmares.

"Goddammit, I'm so sorry." Frank shook his head.

Stefano held up his hands in front of him and tried to keep them from shaking. "My therapist would tell you to forgive yourself, and if you can't, she told me to give you her number."

Nodding, Frank said, "I might take you up on that. I'm still processing. I…. Look, you don't need my shit on top of yours. Just know I'm always here for you."

"I know, and I appreciate that." Stefano gave him a quick hug and then tried to end the conversation. "If you have any questions—"

"When did you know you were bisexual?" Frank's calm demeanor seemed to return as he slipped into his comfort zone.

Stefano shrugged. "I only admitted it recently, but I guess I've known since I was about eight."

Frank smiled. "So you came out today? That's incredible. How do you feel?"

Stefano took another swig of beer and tried to give words to his jumbled emotions. "I guess relieved. Win, lose, or draw, I'm finally out to the family."

"Riku?"

Pain and regret welled up from deep inside Stefano. He swallowed hard as he peeled the label off his beer. "I fucked it up."

Frank frowned. "He seemed like a nice guy."

"He was… is…." God, he was perfect for him.

"Have you come out at work?" Frank must have sensed Stefano needed a break.

Welcoming the change in topics, Stefano shook his head. "Nah, I don't know if I will, because my orientation should have nothing to do with my job, right?"

Frank bobbed his head and grimaced. "Pennsylvania was the very first state to have an executive order banning discrimination based on orientation, and they did it in 1975, but let me know if anyone gives you any issues."

"I will." His boss wasn't the most forward-thinking guy, but Stefano was pretty sure Bobby wasn't that much of an asshole.

Wanting to lighten the mood, he asked, "So what's this about volleyball?"

Frank started laughing. "*Your* sister—"

"Why is she my sister?"

"I disown her when she's being pushy."

"So you have no sister?" Stefano snorted.

Frank did his best to roll his eyes. "When Ang is annoying, you have a sister. She's determined to get me to socialize. I figure being on a volleyball team is a way to get some exercise and get her off my back."

Stefano smiled. At least some things would really be okay.

NOON ON Monday, Angie's car pulled into the parking lot of the garage.

Stefano clocked out. "Bobby, remember I'm taking a longer lunch break today."

"Yeah, yeah, go have fun. Take whatever time you need. You rarely stop more than fifteen minutes, unlike the rest of these bums." Bobby gestured to a group of mechanics clustered around the coffeepot.

Ignoring the grumbles, Stefano gave a nod.

He stepped into the sunshine and took a deep breath, but as he got closer to Angie's car, his inhale got lodged in his chest. His sister wasn't alone.

Stefano hesitated. His ma was in the car.

Angie rolled down the driver's side window and smiled her "get the fuck in and don't make a scene" smile. "Get in, Stef."

Bullied by *Frank's* sister, he slid into the back seat. "Hey."

Angie drove toward Frank's townhouse. "Hi, you and Ma have to talk, so I'm taking you to Frank's and your house. I got you takeout."

The ride to the house was filled with his sister's K-pop music, but no conversation.

When they arrived, Angie pushed the takeout bag at him and dropped them off with a simple "I've got errands. Call when you want to go back to work."

Stefano frowned but held his tongue at the ambush. "Okay."

He opened the front door and let his ma into the house.

Ma hadn't said one word as she took her seat at the dining room table.

He tossed the chicken sandwiches and fries on plates and poured ice water for both of them.

She cleared her throat. "I didn't know about Father Lucca and what he did."

Why open with that? Did Frank talk to her? Or was she trying to ignore his coming out?

Stefano shrugged, biting back *it was probably for the best*.

She continued, "I think maybe because I didn't want to know."

Swallowing the anger bubbling up from his hurt and pain, he waited.

"Stefano… were you hurt by Father Lucca?" She asked the one question she had to know the answer to, didn't she?

He could lie and spare her all the pain that came with the truth, but he no longer wanted a pretend reality. Choking a little, he admitted, "Yes."

"Oh God." She covered her mouth, and tears ran down her face. Leaning back, she shook her head like she could knock the information out of her head. She sniffed. "Why didn't you tell anyone?"

A bitter laugh came out of him. *That's right—blame the victim.* Anger twisted in his gut. "I tried to tell, and Dad beat the shit out of me for it."

"No. Your father—"

"He knocked me around all the time, and you didn't stop him."

"Your father was strict."

"Ma, what he did to me, that was abuse."

She lowered her head, slumping in the chair, no longer able to meet his gaze. "You told…."

"I wish I could forget that day. It was raining, and I missed dinner again because of Father Lucca. After I tried to tell Dad… he became furious."

"No, I—"

"You dragged Angie out of the house. She was trying to protect me, unlike you." Stefano pressed his lips together. Part of him wanted to stop, but that was the thing he found out with therapy—he didn't have much control at the moment.

His therapist promised he'd get better control, but right now all his buried hurt and rage was right at the surface, ready to be shared with anyone and everyone. He couldn't filter how it poured out of him. There seemed to be two settings: plugged or gushing. There was never a comfortable middle ground.

She covered her mouth, catching a sob. "I couldn't…."

He shook his head. No more gaslighting. "You didn't try."

"I should have left him, but the Church…."

His mind began distancing from the events, as was his defense mechanism. The therapist had explained that as he spoke about the events, sometimes they wouldn't feel quite real or as though they had happened to someone else. It was his mind's way of protecting him, but it pissed him off. "Yes, always back to the Catholic Church, right? Allow me to spell things out. I was raped by Father Lucca… repeatedly. He bent me over and hurt me. When I tried to tell Dad, he beat the shit out of me."

Tears continued to race down her face. As her sobs crested, he felt like shit making her cry.

But what about him? What about the stupid teen who didn't know what to do and reached out for help only to be punished for it?

Handing her a tissue, he said, "Ma, you let the monsters get me. You didn't protect me. I know a piece of it was you couldn't protect yourself from Dad. I get that, but… you stayed. And you didn't save me… from either of them."

He failed to keep his voice from breaking, but he got his truth out. A piece of him felt guilty because he understood how his words would embed themselves in her heart like shards of glass, but he could no longer keep silent.

"I'm so ashamed. I didn't protect my children—you—the way I should have." After a while, she wiped her eyes and continued, "Once, I even asked for help at the Church, but Father said I should submit to my husband as an obedient wife and God would protect me."

Fury whipped through Stefano. How could she listen to the Church when she had to know they were wrong? "He didn't, though, and God certainly didn't protect me."

"Did Father Lucca… what he did… is that why you're—"

"Bisexual?" Stefano didn't restrain the dark laugh that barked out. She wanted to find out what made him bisexual. "No, but what he and the Church did was make me ashamed of who I am. I didn't want to be attracted to men because after… after what he did to me, how could I want that? The Church, especially the one you attend, is very homophobic."

She didn't deny reality. "Does that mean you won't be attending mass any longer?"

Shit! He had a bunch to figure out, and he didn't even contemplate his participation in church. It never seemed to be an option, but now everything was open. "I don't think I will. I might check out Frank and Angie's church. I'm not sure."

She crossed herself. "I should have protected you."

He wasn't going to sugarcoat any of this. Having finally acknowledged his suffering and pain, he wouldn't bury it, even if his hurt came out as rage. He had a right to his feelings and to respond to the traumatic situations he'd experienced.

Stefano shrugged. "But you didn't."

She burst into tears again and pulled him into a wet hug.

His heart couldn't help but twist at causing her pain with his truth. "Ma, I love you so much, but that you couldn't stand up to him makes me—"

She petted his back. And her palm caressed over the ridges and bumps. "Oh, your poor back…. I was a different person then, too caught in how I should be."

Or rather, how the Church wanted her to be.

"I was a different person then too." He kissed her cheek, turned around, and lifted his shirt. "I had this done up in Albany."

She sniffed as her hand traced over the gnarled skin, now decorated in who he'd become.

"Even though the physical and sexual abuse affected me, I'll no longer let my past define who I am. In therapy, I'm—"

"You're in therapy?" Her shock echoed around the room.

He pulled down his shirt and faced her. "Yes, and it's helping me deal with everything. I also go to a group for survivors of sexual assault."

She grabbed the table for a moment. When she finally looked at him, she gave him a sad smile. "Good. I think that's good."

"While I wish the bad experiences hadn't happened to me, I'm learning to accept I am who am because of all my experiences."

She twisted her hands in her lap and then gestured to his back. "Well, it's beautiful ink. That's what they call it, right?"

"Yeah." Stefano sat.

His ma waved at his plate. "Eat, honey."

He ate a french fry.

She picked up her sandwich, but it never finished the journey to her mouth. "Now, Angie said bisexual means you're attracted to both men and women."

"Exactly," he confirmed after he swallowed the first bite of his sandwich.

"She said I should think of it as a scale, with straight on one side and gay on the other, and you're somewhere in the middle. Though she said you might prefer men or women a little more?"

He answered her direct question with the truth he was only beginning to discover. His preference was toward powerful men who could tame and guide him. Well, really one man. He sighed. "I lean more toward men than women, but until recently I've only dated women."

"I see." She finished her glass of water.

He got them both more water. Did that put her off?

She had ketchupped his plate like she did when he was five and the bottle was too heavy to lift. "Well, this is all new to me, but I've watched *Ellen* since it first came on. Do you know she and her partner have been married for years?"

"Wow…." Where was she going?

She pointed to his plate. "Eat. You know Carmen, two houses over, Mrs. Musto. Her grandson and his boyfriend got engaged."

Warning bells sounded. He made no sound and no sudden movements. "Oh."

"You never used to hear about these types of things. Your father would only show me outrageous pictures. Until recently, I didn't know gay people wanted to get married."

None of this was surprising, but the ignorance rubbed him the wrong way. "That's because when people are bullied and pushed around, sometimes when they come out, it's on the wild side to thumb their nose at convention. Just like there's wild straight people who feel the need to break the rules."

"You mean those *Girls Gone Wild* and spring break videos?"

Somehow he needed to clarify without getting off track. "Right. Guys do that stuff too. But there are lots of LGBTQIA people. Some want to get married, some don't, some are wild and crazy, and some are quiet and shy… like everyone else in the world."

She nodded.

He pushed himself to continue. "Being bisexual or gay or lesbian doesn't change who the person is. That's only one thing about them. It's who they are attracted to."

"There's a lot I want to learn, and you know I will. Angie has given me a bunch of books and videos I'm going to watch, because I love you and want to understand."

"Thank you, Ma. It means a lot." All he could ask was that she work to understand more.

"And did you know once Mrs. Musto's grandson gets married, he and his husband are planning to adopt, so being married to a man doesn't mean you can't have a child. There's adoption, surrogacy, and Angie said there's new technology that allows both men to be the father. It's a wonderful option." She gave Stefano the pointed Italian Mama "where's my grandchildren" stare.

"That's nice." A subject change was needed. Why was he drawing a blank when this was an all-hands-on-deck moment?

She patted the napkin over her mouth and gave him an innocent "just making conversation" smile. "Are you seeing anyone special?"

"Well, we took some time apart, but I'm hoping—"

"Good. I want to meet him. It's a him, right?"

"Yeah. Riku."

She sat back and tilted her head. "That's not an Italian name. What kind of name is that?"

"Japanese, and his last name is Tao, which is Chinese."

"Well, that's interesting." Her tone walked the line of unsure. Then something must have flicked on in her head, because she stated, "When you are back together—"

"If we get back together." Stefano was afraid to name his dearest wish.

"Please, my son is a catch. He'd be lucky to have you."

Stefano snorted.

"As I was saying, when you are back together, you'll invite him and his family over for Sunday dinner." Her tone screamed she was hanging by a thread, but she was trying.

"I'm sure Marco would love that." Stefano couldn't imagine the scene his brother would cause.

She straightened her spine. "If he doesn't, he can leave."

Giving her a noncommittal noise didn't slow her roll.

"Tell me, how long has Riku's family been in the country?"

Oh my God! "Ma, he was born here. I think his parents went to the University of Pennsylvania."

"Fancy, fancy. He's smart, then." She smiled.

"Yeah." Stefano encouraged her.

"Is he a medical doctor?"

"Close. Doctor of Chiropractic Medicine."

"Smart, rich. Is he good-looking?"

Stefano felt his face heat, but he answered, "Yeah, I guess."

"Good." Apparently, Riku checked all the boxes, because she gave Stefano a nod as if everything was decided.

LATER THAT night, Stefano pulled out his box of paper cranes. He had read several versions of the Japanese legend, but most of them stated the person who folded one thousand cranes got a wish granted by the gods. There was only one wish he had.

He only had a few more to fold by Saturday, and then he'd string them together.

Stefano was ready and worthy of Riku. Maybe he always had been, but now he believed it.

Over the last few months, he had begun to see himself as bent by life, not broken.

There was no question of what he needed to do. He selected a piece of paper and started the first folds required to make a crane.

CHAPTER 20

RIKU OPENED the door for Devon, whom he'd invited because the address Stefano gave him was along the Pride parade route in Philly. "Hey—"

"You've got a box." Devon pointed to the large box sitting on the porch.

Who would have taken the time to decorate with *washibi*? The traditional craft took patience. The box was covered in a white-and-beige patterned paper.

"Who is it from?" Riku bent at the knees and lifted.

"How should I know?"

"It's light." Riku walked back inside with the box. "You want some coffee before we go?"

Devon had already beelined to the kitchen. "You know it."

Curiosity ate at him. Who'd given him this? He set the mystery package on his island and lifted off the top.

Peering into the box, Devon scrunched his face. "Origami birds in Pride colors?"

Not just any origami birds—cranes. This was a traditional wedding gift, given to the couple to wish them a thousand years of happiness and prosperity. The red, orange, yellow, green, blue, indigo, and violet cranes were strung together and knotted on thick rainbow string.

Riku took the white envelope that rested on top and held it.

"Open it," Devon demanded.

With trembling hands, Riku slid the unsealed flap open. He pulled out the single white-patterned card.

> *Some believe the person who makes 1,000 cranes is granted a wish by the gods.*
> *I have only one wish.*
> *These past months I've worked hard on becoming a better man and the partner you deserve.*
> *My dearest wish is that you give me another chance to be yours.*

Though I'm still a work in progress.
I hope I see you today.
All my love,
Stefano

Riku read all the words again, then held the card against his chest. He wiped his eyes, because everything got blurry. Stefano wanted him enough to do everything that he needed to do to be in a relationship all the way.

Devon peered over his shoulder, grabbed the note, and slapped him on the back. "So we going to go claim your man?"

After a quick check on the time, Riku said, "Without question, but I've just got to make one stop."

A few minutes later, Devon griped, "Why are we at the office?"

Riku opened the building door and disarmed the security system, then rushed to his office. He nabbed the Daruma doll off the shelf, grabbed a marker from his pen cup, and colored in the second eye.

"What are you doing?" Devon strolled in.

He didn't spare Devon a glance, but he couldn't stop smiling. "Stefano's not the only one who had a wish."

"THIS TRAFFIC is killing me," Riku complained to Devon. He wanted to get to where Stefano wanted to meet.

"The parade route has got most of the streets blocked off. I'm pulling into the closest parking garage, and we can walk the rest of the way."

"Good plan." He clutched his wishing doll and traced a finger over the colored-in eyes.

Finally they parked, and Riku jogged through the people waving Pride flags, couples holding hands, kids dancing, parents trying to herd their children, young, old, and everyone in between, all here to celebrate. Masculine cologne, sweet perfume, buttery popcorn, cotton candy, and pheromones wove together in a unique happy scent that could only be found at a Pride fest.

Once he got to the cross streets, Riku searched the crowd until he spotted a head of dark curls blowing in the gentle breeze.

He held the Daruma doll tighter. Hard to believe his wish was coming true.

Stefano's head swiveled this way and that as he searched the crowd. Looking for Riku, perhaps?

His brother Frank stood near him, and his eyes widened in recognition as Riku got closer.

Riku returned Frank's grin.

Stefano shouted loud enough to be heard over the marching band, "Where is he? Maybe he's not coming."

Frank gestured for Stefano to turn.

He did, and as soon as Riku standing there registered for him, Stefano's eyes slid shut for a moment. Pressing his lips together, he opened his now-watery eyes. "You came."

"How could I not?"

Stefano caressed his fingers over Riku's Daruma doll. "So does this mean…?"

He handed over the proof his dreams came true to Stefano. "That you're my dearest wish… yes. The wish I made almost twenty years ago has finally come true."

As if by magnetic force, Stefano was in his arms.

Riku moaned. Nothing had felt this right before.

He barely heard Devon and Frank talking. "Hi, you must be Frank. I'm Riku's best friend, Devon Williams."

"Nice to meet you."

Riku squeezed Stefano tighter and vowed never to be separated again.

Stefano whimpered, tilted his head back, and clutched both Riku and the doll. "Riku… I'm so sorry."

"Nothing to be sorry for. You had a lot of things you needed to deal with."

Stefano frowned. "I'm still dealing with everything, so I'm still a work in progress. Will you really give me… us… another chance?"

"Without a doubt." Riku bent and pressed his mouth right on Stefano's lips.

Instead of stiffening or pushing him away, Stefano surrendered to Riku's kiss. Right there in the middle of Philadelphia they made promises with their lips, and Riku was pretty sure they were both going to fight to keep them.

Fire started to spark between them, so he slowed the kiss and pulled back. God, he'd missed Stefano's lips and the way they clung to his for every last moment of the kiss.

Riku stared down at his sub… and boyfriend. He couldn't wait to catch up with Stefano, but for right now hugging and touching him was enough.

Stefano turned to his brother, who wore a big grin. "Frank, this is Riku Tao, my boyfriend."

"Frank, tell me. After having dinner with these two, did you or did you not know they were a thing?" Devon seemed compelled to ask.

Frank held his hands out in front of him. "I plead the Fifth."

Stefano snorted and shook his head. "So I guess it wasn't on the down low."

Devon chuckled. "Stefano, you two are like emojis with heart eyes when you're near each other."

Pursing his lips, Frank added, "He's not wrong."

Riku threw an arm around Stefano and almost fist-pumped the air when Stefano reached over and entwined their fingers together.

Devon waved a hand in front of his face. "You two are too cute."

Frank nodded and held out his phone. "A picture for Angie? You know how upset she was when she got called in to work on that emergency this morning."

Stefano turned to him. "Riku? Any issues with giving my sister something to coo about?"

"Not at all. Text it to me too, Frank." Riku leaned in to rest his head on Stefano's.

"Great. Thanks."

A large man in a Phillies jersey shouted, "Stefano!"

"Leo!"

Stefano dropped Riku's hand to fist-bump with this guy. Apparently a fist bump wasn't enough, and the man yanked Stefano into a backslapping hug. "Good to see you here."

"What are you doing here?" Stefano asked.

"The wife and I bring the boys every year." Leo looked around and grinned. "It's important… you know. And hey, who doesn't love a parade."

Two boys, about six and eight years old, raced over and dragged a smiling woman with them.

The tallest one said, "Daddy, Mommy said we could get some rainbow popcorn, but she wants you to pick the size tub we get. We should get the very biggest, right?"

"Yup. But first, do you remember my friend who came over on St. Patty's Day? Your mother and I went to high school with Mr. Rossi."

"Good to see you again, and please, Stefano's fine." Stefano shook both boys' hands.

"Okay, *Mr. Rossi*." The tallest one shrugged. "But I got to listen to the boss on names, though."

The woman pulled Stefano into a hug. "Good to see you. I don't see you for twelve years, and now I see you twice in three months. I like this. More, please."

Stefano nodded and stepped back with a smile.

Leo elbowed Stefano a bit too hard for Riku's liking. "And is this your friend…?"

"Oh, yes. This is Riku Tao, my brother Frank, and Devon Williams. This is Leo, his wife, Anna Marie, and their two boys, Leonardo and Angelo."

Everyone politely shook Riku's hand.

The little one, Angelo, peered between him and Stefano and back again. "Is he your boyfriend?"

"Yes," Stefano said without hesitation, making Riku's heart fill with even more love for him.

Leo Senior smacked Stefano on the back with a big smile and a "Good for you."

The little boy nodded and said, "Oh, cool. Hey, Mr. Tao. Did you try the rainbow popcorn over there? My brother says it won't make our tongues rainbow, but I think it will. What do you think?"

Riku loved that two guys being boyfriends didn't warrant anything other than an "oh, cool" in the kid's head. This gave him an injection of optimism that the next generation would help stamp out homophobia, and hopefully, transphobia. "I'm not sure, but maybe we should all try some."

THIS HAD to be the best Pride Fest Riku had ever attended. Of course it was because Stefano was there, comfortable in his own skin. The transformation probably wasn't perfect, but it was nothing short of a miracle.

Stefano held his hand as they walked back to the parking garage Frank and Devon had parked in. Frank shook everyone's hand and hugged Stefano with a big smile. As he drove off he called out, "See you guys soon."

Devon got a text and stopped short. "Hey, I'm sure you and Stefano want to talk. Could you take my car back? I'm going to hang out with Jenna, Reese, and Pauline for a bit."

"Of course. Give my love to the Philly queens." Devon might have a crush on a couple of the drag queens, but that was to be expected. They were gorgeous, clever, and ticked all of Devon's boxes.

Devon nodded. "I'll see you two at the Edge for the Pride party?"

Stefano waved to Devon, and then asked Riku, "The Edge has a Pride party?"

"Yeah, all the allies come out to get their rainbow on and show love and support for LGBTQIA members."

Riku added, "The owners donate all the proceeds to the Trevor Project."

"Oh, the suicide-prevention program for LGBTQIA teens. That's really great. I never knew the Edge had a Pride celebration. I guess I never wanted to know." Stefano huffed out a puff of frustration.

As Riku guided him into the car, he wanted to take the frown off Stefano's face, to reassure him. This probably wouldn't be the last time Stefano voiced his regrets about how he handled things before. "The past is the past, and now you know. Do you want to go?"

Stefano hesitated but then grinned. "Yeah, but I have some *nonnegotiables.*"

He didn't enjoy having his words thrown back at him and was a tad concerned at what Stefano meant, but he nodded his agreement. Once they were on the road, he asked, "So tell me what you've been doing."

Stefano placed a hand on Riku's thigh and took his request as an order. He caught him up on everything he'd been doing during their time apart.

STANDING OUTSIDE the Edge, Riku asked, possibly for the tenth time, "Are you sure you want to go in there like this?"

Stefano's eyes sparkled. "Am I not your sub?"

Riku tugged him into a hug. "You're not only my beautiful submissive, my love, and my boyfriend, but above all my friend. I don't want you to—"

Stefano picked up the leash attached to the play collar around his neck and handed the end to Riku. "At the risk of topping too much from the bottom, I need this. I want us both to know, and everyone in there, that I'm proud to be Master Riku Tao's sub. Please."

How could he doubt the sincerity in Stefano's face? If Stefano had regrets, they would deal with them later, but he should trust that Stefano was ready and no longer required this kind of protecting.

Riku wrapped the leash around his hand, putting the slightest bit of tension on the lead.

Stefano stood taller, chin raised. He smiled as he climbed the steps to the entrance.

Holding the door for his sub, Riku gestured for Stefano to enter.

"Thank you, Master."

Riku couldn't hold back the smile at Stefano's bold declaration, loud enough for several heads to turn.

Ember's mouth dropped open, but he covered his surprise with a quick cough. "Well, look at this! Stefano R. on Master Riku's leash?"

Old worry slipped through Riku unbidden. Maybe this was too soon and too much.

Stefano straightened his spine. "That's right. I'm incredibly lucky, aren't I?"

Ember rolled his eyes and put a hand on his hip. "Luck has nothing to do with it, and you know it."

"Master, may I have a moment?" Stefano asked like they were in a strict relationship.

Next time around they should clarify their public and private interactions better. Riku made a mental note to discuss this further. "Of course, Stefano."

Riku stepped back.

Stefano cleared his throat. "Ember, I want to apologize if I was ever rude to you. I was uncomfortable because you were being exactly who you were and I was struggling to even know who I was. I'm sorry."

Ember's eyes widened comically. "Oh, well, no need to be dramatic, hon. Subs will be subs. So, tell me, how did you catch Master Riku? Many a sub has tried."

"Luck. I'm telling you, it was luck."

Riku couldn't stop his interjection. "Luck had nothing to do with it. Stefano was simply everything I've ever wanted in a life partner."

"Aww, you're going to make me puke in the nicest way. Donate, sign your name, and scoot. I should only be gagging on cock, not sweetness." Ember fluttered his hands.

Once they sat at a table in the back of the room, Riku asked, "How do you feel?"

Stefano glanced around at the tables decorated with rainbow flags. "Proud to be yours. Happy to be who I am."

Riku didn't think those words would ever not be stunning coming from Stefano. "Who is that?"

"Yours."

"I find you astounding. I couldn't be prouder of the way you've worked so hard to not only accept your orientation, but for all the work you're doing on fighting your demons. While we were separated, I used my time to get my head around dealing with my own issues about causing pain to someone who has been abused."

Stefano's eyes widened, but he only said, "Thank you, Master."

"I know you were unhappy with what you feel is lack of consequences." Before Stefano could deny it, Riku continued, "And I wanted to address it. I think we should address a lot of things, but we've got time."

Stefano shrugged like he didn't care one way or another.

"So far you haven't required any correction, but I think you need to know boundaries are in place, and what would happen if you cross them."

"Okay." His eyes were wary but trusting. He reached out a hand to Riku.

Riku clasped his hand and felt the strength of their bond. "I will never touch you out of anger, but I think you're rewarded by physical sensations, so denying you is cowardly on my part. But I still won't spank you unless you earn it."

"How?" Stefano shivered and leaned forward with eagerness.

Riku bit back a smile. "First, let's discuss negative consequences. I notice you don't like cleaning, and you said you don't like test-taking. When you've disobeyed purposely, we'll read a chapter of *The Book of Incredible Information* or *The Book of Useless Knowledge*."

"Wait, aren't those books for kids?"

"Knowledge is for everyone. After we read, you'll study, and I'll give you a test."

Stefano's grimace when he grumbled, "Fine," assured Riku he'd hit the mark. "But, um, tell me, how do I earn a spanking?"

"Meeting your goals, continuing to make good choices, and any behavior I deem rewardable. And these spankings you'll earn with good behavior, the better you are, the harder I'll give it to you."

Stefano shivered. "I must be dead, because I could only be this happy in Heaven."

CHAPTER 21

As THEY were clearing away dinner, Riku asked, "Will you stay with me tonight?"

A week had passed since Pride. Stefano had seen Riku each and every night. They had gone to dinner and the movies. Stefano still liked when they were alone the best, which wasn't because he was hiding but because he wanted to savor all of Riku.

Riku had given him several incredible scenes. Stefano had even earned impact play, which he still felt every time he sat down. They also did a whole lot of talking, but there was no mention of going beyond where they had left off a lifetime ago.

Staying was a huge question. Bigger than spending the night. Was Stefano ready?

He nodded with a smile and nabbed his phone. "Of course. Let me text Frank."

Riku put his arm around Stefano's shoulder as they moved to his bedroom. "Do you want to shower together?"

Yes! Our first shower together.... Yes! Yes! He wanted all of the little and big things a couple did together, but sometimes those things were still hard to ask for, so he nodded.

Once in the bathroom, Riku stripped and adjusted the multiple showerheads so water rained down from all sides. He stepped into the spray.

His Master… his boyfriend was hot as fuck.

This time Riku wasn't just his Master but his boyfriend. That meant something more and different, and Stefano was still figuring it out.

He shucked off his clothing as quick as he could and joined Riku.

Riku gasped when Stefano turned to pump some liquid soap into his hands. "Who did this?"

Oh shit. Yeah, the scenes this past week he'd always been half-dressed with his shirt on. How could he forget Riku hadn't seen his tattoo?

"Marcus Sadir, an artist in Albany." Didn't he like the design? Stefano glanced over his shoulder to find Riku staring at his back with his mouth open.

"How long did it take?"

"I went Upstate for several weekends, and he worked on me for a helluva lot of hours each day." The level of pain had gotten pretty intense, but it was a release of all the anguish that had been dragged to the surface by his therapy. His therapist called it a catharsis of sorts.

Riku glanced at Stefano and then traced his fingers over the ink with reverence. "It's a masterpiece. The symbolism is so rich."

All the time, energy, and money had been worth it for Stefano. Trying to lighten the mood, he said, "Glad you like the tattoo. Otherwise taking me up the ass on all fours might have been problematic… not that we've done that or I mean even that we will do that…."

Riku didn't respond to Stefano's ramble but drew lines with his fingers over the design. "This is a perfect representation of who you are. A gorgeous flowering tree with all the intricate roots and emblems embedded with meanings on the branches. The colors are vivid and alive.

"Your family name," Riku said as he traced the bold letters of Rossi at the top of his ass, made by the roots.

"The rose on the branch represents my ma. Her name is Rose, and it has the first initials of Frank, Angie, and me." Stefano left the negative parts of his family off because he no longer wanted to give energy to toxic people.

Riku traced over the ink across his back. "I love the triskele… the three-spoked wheel representing BDSM, and you did it in rainbow colors."

Stefano smiled. It combined two very essential parts of who he was. "My way of celebrating coming out."

"The wrench for your work, but why a pair of pliers?"

"The pliers represent my art. I'm a metal artist. Whether I work on the engine of a car or on an abstract piece, that's what it always comes back to." Saying he was an artist out loud felt good, and even better there was no voice criticizing him.

Cupping Stefano's cheek, Riku smiled. "I'm glad you can see how talented you are."

Stefano wouldn't go that far, but he didn't disagree. Through therapy he had started to see himself more clearly, and he was a pretty good guy.

Riku ghosted his touch over the intricate and complex designs of the heart. "I'm especially drawn to this design in the center. It's beautiful."

The deep reds and golds swirled around the heart of the tree... the truest part of himself.

"It's you... well, me with you. Us.... You allow—wrong word, you encourage me to be everything I was meant to be and help me be all the things I'm trying to be." Even now that Stefano had reclaimed his voice, he wasn't much for words. Actions and art were easier and allowed him to say everything he wanted without tripping over what he wanted to get out of his mouth.

Stefano pumped some more soap into his hands and glided the soap over Riku.

God, he loved touching Riku's body. Stefano wasn't above using washing him as an excuse to linger over the contours of his lean muscle. He might never be a clay sculptor, but he loved sliding his hands over Riku.

The purrs and groans of enjoyment Riku gave him went straight to his dick and made him feel powerful. The touch of his hands could break through Riku's cool control, and fuck if that wasn't sexy.

Taking the shower spray, Stefano rinsed him off.

"Thank you. My turn. I'm going to wash you thoroughly." Riku's deep voice soothed him. It wasn't even his Master voice but his regular one.

Riku washed every part of him with tenderness, pressing kisses everywhere. He whispered, "I love you," a million times, making Stefano's heart expand with gratefulness.

Stefano didn't hesitate to tell him back again and again how much he loved him with every touch and returned kiss. This time he would be able to appreciate the miracle of their shared love.

When Riku reached around Stefano's body and rubbed soap over his ass, Stefano felt his face heat, though it didn't stop him from leaning into Riku and pushing out his backside, offering himself.

With a gentle finger, Riku teased Stefano's opening with a tantalizing tickle that only increased his arousal—increasing the fire and making him want more.

"God," Stefano gasped. He wanted Riku in him any way he could.

Around and around, Riku taunted Stefano's hole, only hinting at but not giving Stefano what he needed.

"Please," Stefano demanded as he thrust his ass out.

Riku slid his finger inside.

Yes! Not enough! Stefano squeezed his eyes shut as he breathed through the intense want that threatened to buckle his knees.

In and out with gentle circles, Riku made him tremble.

Stefano asked with way too much hope, "Will we be together... like this... tonight?"

"I would like that. Would you?" Riku's calm control made everything that much more erotic.

Even though Stefano could see Riku's erection, so he had to be as aroused as Stefano, the fact he acted like he was simply washing Stefano's hands turned into a mind fuck of mass proportions.

Stefano squeaked out a "Yes" as Riku cleaned him thoroughly, then carefully rinsed him off with the hand sprayer, paying special attention to Stefano's ass.

Excitement slithered through Stefano. Riku was going to fuck him.

Worry started to nab at Stefano's insides. He'd never been with anyone this way who cared about him, let alone loved him.

Stefano grabbed the towel to dry Riku. He calmed himself by trying to turn the affection into service. Master-sub, he got that. This... boyfriend-boyfriend thing....

Riku shook his head and took the towel from him. He kissed the water droplets as he dried Stefano with his terry cloth caresses. "I want our first time to be about us. Not Master and submissive."

His toes curled when Riku drew him into a sweet kiss, making it impossible for Stefano to escape into the safety of submission.

Riku combed through Stefano's hair and added product.

In between kisses and licks, Stefano ran the styling stuff through Riku's hair and towel dried his long hair some more.

Riku moaned softly as their hard dicks rubbed across each other. "Come on, let's go to bed."

They stumbled out of the bathroom, Riku's mouth attached to his. Luckily, Riku protected Stefano's head as they crashed into bed a bit close to the headboard.

Riku smirked. "Careful. I guess that's why we usually play with ropes—you need to be secured."

Stefano groaned, but the noise turned into a laugh. "Maybe you should buckle me down if the ride is going to be this bumpy."

Hope at finding peace in Riku's ropes chased away some of his nerves.

Riku joined in with a chuckle but soon dragged his lips over Stefano's neck.

These gentle kisses, licks, and nibbles had no place in Stefano's world of fucking.

"I love you, Stefano."

The words were whispered, but they felt shouted. Echoes of the past tried to haunt Stefano's present.

He did as his therapist taught him. Treat the memories and persistent thoughts like a pesky kid. Ignoring them made everything worse. Pay attention to them. He identified his feelings and acknowledged them fully, and then returned to the current moment.

Yes, and Riku was in the present. Wanting to rush past the crazy in his head, Stefano crashed his mouth onto Riku's. *There. Yes, a little bit of pain.*

Within five seconds, Riku wrapped his hand in the curls at the nape of Stefano's neck. He tugged his mouth away from Stefano's needy lips.

Groaning, Stefano begged, "Please, more."

Riku tightened his grip in his hair, and fuck if that didn't feel like a stroke to Stefano's dick. Tilting his head to increase the pull made Stefano moan.

"This is not a scene. This is us. Let me show you how beautiful you are to me."

Tears sprang to Stefano's eyes. *Fucking hell!* In the past he would have shoved his emotions away, but all this therapy shit must be working. He admitted, "I don't know... if I can. I've never done it... like this."

Riku kissed his eyelids and then asked, "Can we try? Together?"

Stefano wanted to please his... Riku. Riku was more than his Master, and even more than his boyfriend. Riku was the person he wanted to spend the rest of his life with.

He tried to convince himself being with Riku in a loving way shouldn't be terrifying, but it felt overwhelming.

But he trusted Riku to do power exchanges with him…. How was this different? His voice cracked as he promised, "I'll try."

Riku studied him and waited.

Acknowledge your feelings, the therapist's voice said kindly.

I'm scared. "I'm scared that I don't deserve you, Riku. And what if…."

Riku nodded. "Just so you know, I'm terrified."

"You are?" *What? That was crazy.*

"I am. Petrified actually. What the hell do I know about having a relationship… being a boyfriend. All I've done for years is demonstrations. I haven't got a clue on how to do this."

Wanting to reassure him, Stefano kissed Riku's cheek. "You might not know it, but you're awesome at relationships. I happen to know your boyfriend personally, and he's head over heels in love with you… so you must be doing something right."

Riku grinned and shook his head. "What you're saying is, even if I screw this up, we'll get through this together."

Confidence and a certainty he'd never felt rushed through him.

"Yes. Yes, we will, because love wins. And if we need help, I know of a couple of good therapists, and we've got some good friends who'll happily whap us in the head if we need it." Stefano swallowed hard. He believed every word he said.

"I know I don't deserve you, Stefano, but I plan on making sure I do for the rest of my life."

Sometimes Riku and he weren't on the same page, but this time they were.

"Sounds like a good fucking plan. We're going to be okay." But it didn't take away all of the scary.

"What?" Riku must have seen something in his expression.

His therapist told him talking about his worries and fears drained away some if not all of their power over him. "I've had sex before but never with someone who looks at me the way you do."

Riku squeezed his eyes shut. "No looking. Is that better?"

Stefano snorted and fell into him laughing. "You're a jerk."

"Stop listening to what Devon says about me. Laughing is good. Somehow, we put a lot of pressure on ourselves. Let's just agree it's going to be terrible."

"Yup, like the worst sex ever, and then it can only get better."
Stefano grinned.

"Exactly." Riku reached over to his nightstand and pulled out some
lube and a condom.

Stefano didn't turn over onto all fours. Nope, he closed his eyes,
lay back, and parted his legs.

This position was something he had never done before. In the past,
he'd always been bent over with some spit from a bit of oral attention,
and if he was lucky he'd get enough spit so he didn't tear.

"You're trembling." Riku cupped his cheeks.

"Can't help it."

"It's okay. I've got you." Riku licked Stefano's jaw on his way to
his earlobe, followed by a tiny bite.

The sting of the nip stabilized Stefano and sparked happiness.
Another bite and he was able to focus.

Riku pressed two of his lubricated fingers inside Stefano.

Instead of pain… "Holy fuck!" It was better than in the shower.

Riku brushed near his prostate, making Stefano shift his hips and
chase his moving fingers until he gasped, "Yeah."

"Let me see your eyes." Riku's voice was husky and rough.

Stefano didn't want to, but he forced himself. He opened his eyes
and his heart tripped.

Riku was right there, staring down at him with all the love in the
world for him. He kissed the side of Stefano's knee as he kept plunging
his fingers in and out. Not once did their gazes unlock.

The connection was something beyond subspace. Instead of being
at a dreamy distance, he was synced and merged with Riku. Stefano
had no doubt: no matter what happened, they'd have each other's backs.
He was no longer alone. He was part of Riku and part of something
wondrous that they created together.

"I'm going to add a third finger."

Stefano tried to answer, he really did, but the only thing that came
out was "Ahhhh."

His cock hadn't even been touched, and it drooled a puddle of fluid
on his belly. Stefano spread his legs wider, giving Riku more access to
anything he wanted.

"You ready?"

Stefano's eyes rolled back in his head. "Yes…. Anything you want. Fuck, so good."

Riku stopped his finger slide. "No, it's supposed to be bad, remember?"

Snorting made Stefano's ass clench around Riku's fingers, making them both groan.

"Do you want me inside of you?" Riku asked like it had ever been a question.

"Now." Stefano couldn't stop wiggling his hips. He whimpered as Riku pulled out his fingers.

Riku rolled on a condom and added a ton of slippery gel to his dick.

Stefano twined his legs around Riku's waist and lined their bodies up.

Moaning "Stefano," Riku slid an inch inside.

Stefano had never wanted someone in him more than he did at this moment. His need was beyond physical. He wanted to be closer to Riku. He craved having Riku so deep inside him he wouldn't know where he ended and Riku began.

Stefano begged, "More."

On one long, wet, friction-filled slide, Riku was as deep as he could be.

"Holy fuck!" He took everything Riku had to give.

Christ! He breathed through the uncomfortable part of a cock introducing itself to his ass. This wasn't just a random cock—he got lost in Riku's kind brown eyes.

Riku didn't ask if Stefano was okay, but he paused and studied him. He leaned down and claimed his mouth.

The kiss was possession mixed with love and happiness, reminding Stefano they were in this… in everything, together.

Riku's hardness wedged inside and was exactly where he belonged. Ever so slowly, Riku dragged himself almost all the way out of Stefano's body, forcing him to wrap his legs around Riku's ass so he could use his heels to pull Riku back into him.

Riku rolled his hips, making his cock push in and out of Stefano.

Again and again, Stefano rode the movement… the connection.

The tingly feeling he usually got only after an exceptionally long denial period buzzed through his middle from his stomach to his thighs. The intense sensation spread across his entire midsection.

In and out.

Riku shifted and his stomach pressed into Stefano's dick. The quick rubs—

Not a scene; permission wasn't needed.

Stefano's cum poured out of him in a continuous orgasm. "Yes!"

His orgasms where his prostate was stimulated were always more drawn-out and intense, but this was something else.

Riku rubbed against him, giving his cock all the right friction as he still chased his own orgasm.

Although Stefano felt overstimulated and sore, his pleasure continued. Knowing this was good for Riku made an enormous difference.

Riku grunted and pulsed inside him, triggering even stronger sensations and prolonging Stefano's pleasure. His groan of pure satisfaction completed Stefano's gratification.

An eternity later, Riku tucked Stefano under his arm and combed his fingers through his damp curls. "I love you."

"I love you too. Oh, and hey, the boyfriend sex wasn't all that terrible." Stefano failed at keeping a straight face.

Riku propped himself up on his elbow. "Good to know. Your boyfriend is relieved but was totally ready to have super terrible sex with you."

"Yeah, well, maybe we should practice, because you never know...."

Riku growled. "I noticed you're not a bratty sub, but you might be a bratty boyfriend."

Feeling happy and playful wasn't something Stefano ever felt after being with anyone else, so he enjoyed the hell out of it. "Oh, no. I've never been a boyfriend, so maybe my Master can teach me a lesson."

"Shall I get the books out? We're on chapter two." Riku pretended to try to get out of bed.

Stefano tackled him into a cuddle. "I think not.... I'm very lucky. I love you as my boyfriend and as my Master. No books, but there is a paddle under the bed with my name on it."

Riku tilted his head and pressed his lips together, but it didn't stop his body from shaking from his suppressed laugh.

Shrugging, Stefano pointed out, "What? Boyfriends can spank too, you know."

"As a matter of fact, I didn't know, so I guess you'll have to teach me." Riku grinned.

"Sounds good to me." Stefano started to reach under the bed but let Riku pull him into a heavenly embrace. "Maybe later."

EPILOGUE

STEFANO COULDN'T stand still on the Taos' porch.

They had put this off for a month. If Riku hadn't been holding his hand, he surely would have considered putting this off for another month. He'd never met someone's parents before. What if they didn't like him? What if—

A smiling woman who looked nothing like his own mother opened the door, and a kind-looking gentleman holding a newspaper stood behind her.

Stefano took a deep breath.

Riku handed her the Daruma doll. "Mother, Father, this is Stefano Rossi, the reason I've finally colored in the eye."

She inspected the doll for a moment and smiled. "Stefano, I'm so glad to meet you."

He reached out a hand.

"I've been told Italian families hug." She yanked him into her arms.

True, but…. "Oh, who told you that?"

Opening the door wider, Mrs. Tao pointed to—

"Mama? What are you doing here?" Stefano thought he'd only have to worry about meeting Riku's parents, not dealing with his own mother and sister. "Angie?"

"Good to see you too, brother dearest. Mrs. Tao invited us." Angie glared at him but then gave him a warm hug.

Stefano got with the program and shook Mr. Tao's hand and passed over the box of cookies to Riku's mother. "From what Riku says, they won't compare to your husband's scones, but—"

"Thank you." She took the gift with two hands and a little bob of her head.

They entered the serene row house that reminded Stefano of Riku's townhouse, as it was decorated in a similar elegant color scheme.

"Rose, Angie, this is my son."

After pleasantries, Angie elbowed Stefano in the gut. "Well done. Mrs. Tao, I know Riku doesn't have any brothers, but how about cousins?"

Riku's parents laughed.

"What? I'm serious," Angie claimed with a smirk and a hand on her hip.

"You'll just have to come celebrate Lunar New Year with us." Mrs. Tao gave her a smile. "My husband's extended family will be visiting."

Stefano glanced over at Riku.

Riku leaned into him. "Looks like our families are making plans for next year. Are you okay with that?"

The tone of Riku's words was teasing, but there was an actual question still there.

Stefano grabbed Riku's hand and kissed the palm. "Absolutely." He might be bent, but he wasn't stupid.

Z. ALLORA never expected to share her words with anyone, but things don't always work out as planned. Growing up in Upstate NY, she was a tomboy: playing basketball in the park, twirling a rifle in color guard, but composing stories filled with angst in secret.

Z. didn't always believe in romance, although before giving up on happily ever after completely, she took out a personal ad in a college newspaper. On October 20, 1987, at 5:08 PM, she found what she didn't think existed, and married her best friend five years later.

A bit of an overachiever, Z.'s earned three bachelor's degrees (Psychology, English, and Philosophy) and a master's degree in Psychology. She loved enhancing thequality of life of people in her residential and day programs, but her love's job swept Z. overseas to Singapore, Israel, and China.

While living in China, she discovered M/M romance. The magic of the genre gave her new insights about herself and those around her. When she saw protests in Malaysia by parents who genuinely believed watching a singer could make their children gay, the ignorance was too staggering to ignore. No longer content to keep her words to herself, she published her stories hoping to add another voice to foster understanding and to promote equality.

Z. believes each of us is wonderfully unique and deserving of a happily everafter. Regardless where we are in the infinite spectrum of gender identity, orientation, or sexuality, our differences and similarities should be both respected and celebrated.

Even though Z. identifies as nonbinary of the transmasculine variety, Z. has kept her original pronouns and presents as female (according to the current gender constructs).

One of the biggest goals of her writing is to validate everyone's individual uniqueness. There's an infinite spectrum within each stripe of the rainbow and Z. wants to explore them all.

However, Z. will never apologize for having too much yaoified smexy goodness in her books. Z. teases that plot is simply the words between the sex scenes (though that's a bit of an exaggeration). Sex is one of our most important and basic forms of communication, and she feels it's a vital part of understanding her characters.

Z. Allora truly believes this rainbow romance is changing hearts and minds, and will continue to speak out for love for all of us.

Email: Z.AlloraHappyEndings@gmail.com

Facebook: Z Allora Allora and join Z.'s Yaoified Love group (for fun, character chatters,giveaways, and silliness)

Website: www.zallorabooks.com

Blog: zallora.blogspot.com

DreamspinnerPress: www.dreamspinnerpress.com/books/z-allora-637-a

THE
LONGEST
night

Z. ALLORA

The holiday season is lonely for construction worker Benjamin Morgan, a big muscular guy who just wants to submit, obey, and serve. But the men he's attracted to usually don't have a dominant bone in their bodies. He's done seeking his BDSM dreams with someone who isn't interested in putting him in his rightful place—on his knees at their feet.

When a friend sets up a meeting with Foster Ridgeway at the BDSM club, Entwined, Benjamin has his doubts. Of course he is attracted to bookish Foster, who works for the same construction company, but how will someone so small and delicate-looking master Benjamin? But when Foster—the tiny temple of dominance wielding a crop—heads toward Benjamin, he might get what he's always wanted, just in time for Solstice.

www.dreamspinnerpress.com